FINDING BEAUTY IN THE BEAST

PRAISE FOR

FINDING BEAUTY IN THE BEAST

Finding Beauty in the Beast is an enchanting, smart retelling filled with romance and transformation. Rose and Corbin will steal every reader's heart.

> —Ashtyn Newbold, author of *Mischief and Manors* and *Lies and Letters*

Jessilyn Stewart Peaslee has written yet another beautiful tale in *Finding Beauty in the Beast*. This heartwarming retelling of *Beauty and the Beast*, without the magic, creates a realistic story of kindness and love that will enchant readers of all ages. Themes of sorrow and loss and courage and loyalty are explored through the eyes of relatable characters that readers will not easily forget.

> —Melanie Bateman, author of *The Time Key*

A lovely, realistic fairy tale of redemption where the magical power of transformation is in the hero's gentle forgiveness for the heroine as she sets aside her fear and anger for love.

> —Rebecca J. Greenwood, author of *The Darkest Summer*

Jessilyn will tug at your heartstrings with riveting characters that navigate through trials and inevitable loss to bravely find the joy around them.

> —Jenni James, best-selling author of *The Jane Austen Diaries* and The Jenni James Faerie Tale Collection, and screenwriter of the soon-to-be released film *Not Cinderella's Type*

FINDING BEAUTY IN THE BEAST

JESSILYN STEWART PEASLEE

SWEETWATER
BOOKS
An imprint of Cedar Fort, Inc.
Springville, Utah

ISBN 13: 978-1-4621-2155-7

Published by Sweetwater Books, an imprint of Cedar Fort, Inc.
2373 W. 700 S., Springville, UT 84663
Distributed by Cedar Fort, Inc., www.cedarfort.com

LIBRARY OF CONGRESS CATALOGING-IN-PUBLICATION DATA

Names: Peaslee, Jessilyn Stewart, 1979- author.
Title: Finding beauty in the beast / Jessilyn Stewart Peaslee.
Description: Springville, Utah : Sweetwater Books, An imprint of Cedar Fort, Inc., [2018]
Identifiers: LCCN 2017038611 (print) | LCCN 2017042151 (ebook) | ISBN 9781462128631 (epub and Moby) | ISBN 9781462121557 ([perfect] : alk. paper)
Subjects: LCSH: Man-woman relationships--Fiction. | LCGFT: Romance fiction. | Novels.
Classification: LCC PS3616.E2665 (ebook) | LCC PS3616.E2665 F56 2018 (print) | DDC 813/.6--dc23
LC record available at https://lccn.loc.gov/2017038611

Cover design by Katie Payne
Cover design © 2018 by Cedar Fort, Inc.
Edited and typeset by Hali Bird and Erica Myers

Printed in the United States of America

10 9 8 7 6 5 4 3 2 1

Printed on acid-free paper

To Gary, for sentimental reasons

Also by
Jessilyn Stewart Peaslee

Ella
Ella's Will

"Freely we serve,
Because we freely love, as in our will
To love or not; in this we stand or fall."

—John Milton, *Paradise Lost*

PROLOGUE

ROSE

A beast. That was what they called her.

When she was in a good temper, Princess Rose's face was deceptively sweet, even beautiful. Her large, emerald eyes could appear tender, her rosebud lips touched with softness. There was a time, some would say, that her voice was warm and full of life; and though no one believed it, that she used to laugh.

But today, there was no hint of softness, no trace of tenderness. Her eyes blazed like green fire and she pursed her lips until they became indistinguishable from her pale skin. The freckles she painstakingly tried to hide glared angrily across her nose and cheeks. No tears would escape her eyes, no quivering would touch her lips. She sat—cold and aloof— her gaze fixed straight ahead, glaring at the opposite wall of the swaying carriage.

A tendril of wild, flaming red hair brushed Rose's cheek and she reached for it, stuffing it back into its rightful place in her intricate braids. As she did so, another rebellious pin came loose and more hair escaped. In a flurry of fingers, hairpins, and braids, Rose tugged at her hair until it fell around her shoulders and down her back. Her mane, as it was called, framed her face quite appropriately, and Rose felt a small sense of relief having set it free.

Maryann, her lady's maid, cowered in the opposite corner of the carriage, risking a glance or two in Rose's direction. During one of these surreptitious glances, Rose met Maryann's eyes in a cold stare, and Maryann quickly dropped her gaze to her feet. Turning away, Rose looked out the back window toward the castle shrinking behind them in the distance.

1

Immediately, she wished she hadn't. Taking a deep, silent breath, Rose closed her eyes and blinked back rebellious tears—tears that, once spilled, would only intensify her pain instead of release it.

Her hands, which clenched the ocean blue water silk folds of her dress, slowly relaxed. Soon, her eyelids drooped, the heaviness of the day finally weighing them down enough for sleep to come and provide a desperately needed escape.

The gentle rolling of the carriage became a dance as she dreamed. Behind her closed eyes, she saw Prince Kenton—the man she was supposed to marry until he decided to break off their engagement and marry a simple commoner instead.

In her dream, they were at the ball at his palace and he held her in his arms as they danced to the music—music that sounded too much like the jingling of horse reins. He begged Rose to forgive him for abandoning her, and he whispered beautiful, tender words in her ear—words she couldn't quite hear, but knew they must be beautiful. Because he was beautiful.

She looked up into his eyes, but couldn't see their blueness. She waited for her heart to pound, but it lay silent in her aching chest. In a very rude, abrupt change of scene that could only occur in a dream, she was pleading with him—pleading with him to love her, to come back to her.

"Rose, I would never be able to tame you," he said.

Then, with a violent lurch, she fell backward into nothingness. She reached for Kenton, but he simply watched, quite calmly, as she screamed without sound—only emptiness and blackness to break her endless fall.

CHAPTER 1

CORBIN

The moonlit castle loomed on the distant hill. Chirping crickets had just begun their evening song, the first of the stars twinkling in anticipation. The deep blue of night weighed down on the hazy pink of sunset and pressed it down gently into the horizon.

"It would have been a nice night for a wedding." Corbin Black winked at his fiancée on the wagon seat next to him. Her lavender silk gown ruffled in the breeze, and the moonlight bathed her honey hair, reminding Corbin of soft, moldable iron before it cooled. His free hand that wasn't holding the reins gave hers a little squeeze.

Francine pulled her gaze from the castle and met his eyes. "Darling, please don't start that again. We've been through this a hundred times."

Corbin chuckled. "I know, I know. We couldn't ask the prince to plan his ball around our wedding."

"Nor could we ask our friends to miss the ball."

"No, we couldn't." He grinned. "But it would have been a lot cheaper not to have to feed everyone." Corbin's eyes twinkled. "What we should have done is gotten married *and then* sent everyone to the ball to eat. Problem solved!"

"There was no problem. My father was paying for the food anyway." Francine lifted her chin. "But, no matter. It's going to be a glorious night. A ball at the castle, food, friends, dancing . . ." Her voice trailed off dreamily.

In front of them was a long line of grand carriages that wound all the way up to the castle. Corbin urged the horse in that direction and fell into line. With her free hand, Francine ran her gloved fingers over the splintered wood of the wagon seat.

"Couldn't you have rented a carriage?" She gazed at all the grand carriages with their polished wheels and ornamented fixtures. "We're going to a ball, not a barn raising."

"I know. I'm sorry. They were all taken by the time I thought of it." Corbin squeezed her hand again. "Don't worry. You don't need a fancy carriage like those other girls. You look absolutely beautiful without one."

Francine smiled and sighed. "Thank you, Corbin. I won't worry anymore about it. You know how my expectations always get in the way."

"Yes. Yes, I do." He chuckled at her smirk, though his eyes grew thoughtful. "And your expectation of meeting the prince?"

Francine was silent for a breath, then turned to Corbin, her eyes fervent. "I know he's going to choose his bride tonight, but I've decided. I'm engaged to you. We will be married in a week. Prince or no prince."

Corbin leaned over and kissed the top of Francine's head. It had been a difficult week. Prince Kenton had announced that he would be having a ball and that he would be choosing his bride from among his subjects. It had come as a complete shock to the entire kingdom. No prince of Claire had ever married a commoner. Besides, Prince Kenton had been betrothed to some princess from another kingdom, though apparently that was no longer true. As appealing as it was to imagine being married to a prince, Francine had promised Corbin they would be still be married . . . only a week late. The wedding between a blacksmith and a merchant's daughter could not compare with a royal ball. Francine gave Corbin's hand a little pat, then clasped her hands on her lap. After throwing him a dazzling smile, she once again turned her gaze toward the castle.

The ball was every bit as elegant as Corbin had dreaded and Francine had hoped. Glasses of punch and tiny sandwiches were carried on crystal trays by waiters with gloved hands. An orchestra played in the courtyard where people danced under the glittering, cathedral-like sky. And though he would much rather be at his own wedding, Corbin couldn't help enjoying himself. Francine seemed lit up from in the inside. She talked and giggled with her friends, occasionally reaching out to hold his hand reassuringly. How could he not enjoy himself? The early September night was clear and warm, laughter bounced off the statues and fountains . . . and the prince was nowhere to be seen.

Every now and then, a royal-looking man—a duke, Corbin guessed—would emerge from behind one of the perfectly manicured hedges of the garden, scan the crowd, then disappear. No one knew what his purpose was, but his appearances became more and more frequent. During one of these appearances, he approached a lady Corbin didn't know, spoke quietly in her ear, and he led her away from the rest of the crowd. Over the next hour or so, this occurrence increased in frequency, and soon people began to understand what was happening.

"He's taking the women to meet the prince," people began whispering behind cupped hands.

"Do you think so?"

"Yes. The prince can't very well walk through the crowds, can he? He'd be mobbed."

"He must be off where no one else can see, and that man's job is to find the most eligible maidens."

"One of the east courtyards is blocked off by guards. That's probably where he is."

Corbin and Francine couldn't help but listen to all these whisperings—Corbin with an increasingly dry throat and short breath, Francine with a tender smile while looking in his direction and increased interest while looking in others.

The duke entered the garden again, purpose in his expression and step. This time, he came to an abrupt stop when his eyes landed on Francine. His gaze traveled from her face to her hand, which was clasped in Corbin's, squinted, then he walked on. A moment later, his royal mustache twitched as he spotted two lavishly-dressed young women across the small garden and strode over to them. The crowd had hushed to silence by then, and all watched the scene with keen interest.

"Why, of course. We would be honored!" The two women's voices answered in unison to the duke's muttered words before he led them away.

Once they disappeared, the crowd began murmuring again in muted, but excited tones. Corbin released a quiet breath, though he still held Francine's hand.

"Well, that was fun. Can we go now?" Corbin laughed, though it sounded too high to be genuine.

Francine smiled and faced him. "Listen to me. You have nothing to worry about. He looked over me. I'm obviously not good enough."

Corbin was shaking his head before she finished speaking. "It's that he saw you were with me. You're more than good enough, just not eligible enough."

Francine's brow puckered, then she smiled up at him. "You need to breathe, Corbin. I've never seen you like this. You haven't told a joke in over two minutes." Corbin ducked his head and chuckled as his shoulders relaxed. "Why don't you go and get us some drinks and sandwiches. I'm famished."

"Of course." Corbin bent to kiss her, placing his fingers under her chin.

Francine pulled back slightly. "Please, darling. People are watching."

Corbin looked around and indeed saw that most in the crowd were stealing glances in their direction—people who had very recently been invited to their hastily postponed wedding. The residents of their little village of Maycott had naturally congregated in the palace courtyard and seemed particularly interested in how the night would conclude for the ill-fated couple.

Corbin nodded and kissed her hand before leaving the garden. As he walked, he heard snippets of conversation.

"What was the prince like?" a dreamy-eyed girl asked a friend.

"Too charming for words," came the wistful reply. After a heavy sigh, the girl's eyes shone brightly and her voice trembled. "I wonder what I did wrong. Why wasn't I chosen?"

"Well, he didn't choose me, either!" another voice chimed in.

"Has anyone been chosen yet?"

"I don't think so. I'm sure we'd know."

Corbin strode away from all princely conversation, and after passing through a few small crowded gardens and the large courtyard where countless people were dancing, Corbin spotted a waiter carrying a tray. A genuine smile lit Corbin's face when he recognized it was Will Hawkins, his best friend since childhood.

"Will!" Corbin called.

Will spun around, the drinks on his tray teetering dangerously. "Corbin! It's good to see a familiar face. I never knew how many people I . . . didn't know." Will laughed.

Will normally worked as a stable worker at the palace, but tonight he was playing the role of server since they needed as many helping hands as possible at the ball.

"I know what you mean." Corbin's shoulder was bumped by a man as he reached for a drink off Will's tray. "Though, there's someone I know you recognize." Corbin pointed in the direction of a young woman with golden hair and downcast eyes, her back practically glued to the wall— Ella Blakeley.

"There she is." Will grinned and began to move toward Ella, then stopped. "Wait. Where's Francine?"

"She's over in the garden. She wanted me to get her something to eat."

"Well, you came to the right place." Will held out his tray and Corbin took two drinks and two sandwiches. "Is everything . . . fine?"

Corbin grinned. "Yes. She's been reassuring me all night. She's been very sweet, actually."

"Francine? Sweet?" Will pretended to cough. "Forgive me, Corbin. I didn't mean that."

"I understand, Will." Corbin laughed, knowing Will meant exactly that. "She's just spirited, that's all."

"Spirited. That's a good word." Will winked.

Corbin sighed and looked in the direction of the garden where Francine was waiting. "I don't know. Sometimes it's hard to ask her to live in the back room of my blacksmith shop when she could live in a palace with a prince."

Will shook his head. "If she loves you, it won't matter. Besides, you're better than any old prince."

"Thanks, Will." Corbin glanced in Ella's direction. "I'll let you go now. I know you have more important people to talk to."

"You're both equally important." He smiled. "Though not equally pretty, I'm afraid."

"Thank goodness," Corbin chuckled.

With a laugh, Will strode forward, determination in his step, and a peculiar eagerness on his face. Corbin grinned when he saw Will come to a stop and smile down at Ella, who blushed deeply.

Juggling the drinks and sandwiches, Corbin suddenly felt an eagerness to return to Francine. More than once, he was bumped and the red liquid soaked the sleeve of his borrowed suit. He was smashing the sandwiches between his fingers so he wouldn't drop them and could feel the moisture from whatever was inside seeping through the bread. But he ignored it all, just as he tried to ignore the increasingly animated conversations regarding the prince and his future bride.

Finally, Corbin reached the garden, though little of the punch remained in the glasses. He scanned the crowd, but Francine wasn't where he had left her. Placing the glasses on the bench and sloshing red onto the carved gray stone, Corbin searched the crowd. As he walked, he realized he still held the ruined sandwiches, and he tossed them into the nearest bush.

Just when he was about to give up hope, he found her. She was standing in the middle of a group of giggling girls, their conversation much like the ones he had been forced to hear as he walked through the palace grounds.

Francine wasn't speaking, though she was listening with bright, wide eyes to every other woman's account of meeting the prince. Corbin stood back, content to watch from a distance and give himself time to slow his breathing. He didn't want Francine to see how worried he had been. He shook his head and chuckled to himself. Not only was there no reason to worry, but now he had to go and get more sandwiches.

As Corbin turned away from the group of girls, an infuriatingly familiar face appeared just feet from where Francine stood. Corbin yearned to cross the garden and take Francine's hand, but an inexplicable curiosity fastened his feet to the ground. Before Corbin could act, a hush fell over the crowd, followed by the sound of steady footsteps approaching the now silent girls. Corbin's heart thumped painfully and his mouth went dry. The duke met Francine's eyes and his face lit up. He stepped toward her.

"Miss, will you please come with me?" the duke whispered, though every person heard.

Francine gasped, her eyes twinkling in the moonlight, as she raised a hand to her chest. "Me? But I . . . I'm . . ." She seemed to force her mouth closed. A little pucker appeared between her eyebrows and a look of quiet resolution hardened her face just enough for Corbin to recognize it. "Yes, I would be honored."

As she took the duke's arm, she met Corbin's eyes across the small courtyard and her mouth fell open slightly. For a moment, a peculiar sheen of tears softened the blazing expression in her eyes. She seemed to be silently pleading with him to understand. Just behind Corbin, almost close enough for her to touch, was the castle—blazing and brilliant—and Corbin watched in silence as her rapt eyes took it in. Before either could act or speak, the crowd parted and the duke led Francine away.

The ground swayed beneath Corbin's feet and the sky pressed down on him. A burning pain began in his chest, as if he were standing too close to a fire and breathing in the scorching flames. But, like that pain, this pain was almost too much to comprehend, too hot to actually feel. And doubtless, it would leave a scar.

CHAPTER 2

She never looked back. Every eye was trained on Corbin, and almost every face wore the same expression of pity. Corbin weaved his way through the little group of Maycott residents, refusing to meet anyone's eyes or acknowledge the pats of sympathy he received on his arms by well-meaning friends. When he finally reached his wagon, he drove a little too swiftly away from the palace. The guards barely had enough time to open the gates to let him through, and he ignored their shouts of outrage as they closed them behind him.

Once he arrived at his blacksmith shop, he opened the doors and stood in the heavy silence for a moment. Then, he tore off the outdated suit, grateful to be free of his too-tight cravat.

Before he really thought about what he was doing, Corbin began packing. A part of him knew that this was his plan all along if things had gone the way they did. He had a desire—an almost overwhelming urge—to leave. This thought brought clarity to his mind that had recently become so dark and muddled. It was as if a bright light filled his entire being.

Unfortunately, the feeling was dampened by what he had to do now—leave the only home he had ever known. He started in his little room—the one that would be the most painful—to get that task out of the way. He had recently made a little side table and had placed it on what would have been Francine's side of the bed. It would have held her feminine things he knew little about—hairbrushes and combs, necklaces, and trinkets.

He would be leaving that here. He would also leave the little wicker basket that his mother used to keep extra scraps of fabric in, unable to imagine it anywhere else.

Corbin packed and cleaned throughout the night and most of the next day. In the late afternoon, news spread throughout the kingdom that the prince had chosen his bride . . . and it wasn't Francine. Still, Francine had never come and Corbin stopped listening for her. With his mind and body too weary, Corbin stretched out on his thin mattress, laced his hands behind his head, and fell asleep just as the sun began to fall.

Corbin shot up from bed when he heard a soft knock, then the front door creak open.

"Corbin?"

Relief brought a welcome lightness to Corbin's chest. If there was one person who could lift his spirits right now, it was Will.

Corbin emerged from his little room and saw Will standing there—one hand in his pocket, the other resting on Ella Blakeley's waist.

Ella curtsied and Corbin could see her blush even in the dim shop. "Mr. Black," she said in her quiet voice.

Will was gaping at the bare shelves, the packed bags, the swept-out corners. "You're leaving?"

Corbin nodded, feeling slightly guilty. "I think I'm going to go to Laurel."

"Laurel? Do you really have to leave the kingdom entirely?"

"Well, since I'm starting over, I figured I might as well start at the beginning. It's where I was born, and I think I'd like to see if I have any family left. Besides, a man came through town a few weeks ago and mentioned that the blacksmith in Laurel had died and they needed a new one. It just feels like it's where I should be."

Will nodded, his face uncharacteristically somber. "I hope you find what you're looking for, I truly do. I just . . . I feel like I'm losing a brother." Will laughed a little thickly. "Sorry, Corbin. This is just a little too much change for me."

Corbin stared down at the ground for a moment, then looked up and his face brightened. "Speaking of change. What's all this?" Corbin indicated to Will's arm around Ella, and they all grinned. Ella ducked her head and her blush deepened.

Will's face grew slightly troubled, and he didn't meet Corbin's eyes. "I don't know if this is the best time to tell you. I'm not sure how things are between you and Francine and I don't want to . . ."

Corbin shook his head, trying to reassure Will. "I haven't seen Francine since the ball, and I doubt I will again."

"Even if she wasn't chosen?"

"She left. She chose him, whether he chose her or not. Besides, she's probably still hoping for a miracle." Corbin surprised himself by laughing. "Please don't let my sadness affect your happiness."

Will met Corbin's eyes. "How can it not, Corbin?"

Corbin cleared his throat and looked back at the ground, touched by Will's sincerity and Ella's gentle eyes swimming with sympathy. He smiled. "What's your news? Though, I think I can guess."

Will laughed softly. "We came to invite you to our wedding, which is happening . . . well, now, actually. I wasn't able to be your best man, but . . ."

Corbin grinned and clapped a hand on Will's shoulder. "I'll gladly be yours."

CHAPTER 3

Angry wind swirled the early autumn leaves around Corbin's feet and took them swiftly toward the south. They seemed to pause before drifting out of view, almost beckoning him to follow, their crispness tapping the cobblestones like excited little feet.

The donkey that carried everything Corbin owned on its back pawed impatiently at the ground. Corbin was tightening the strap on the back of the donkey that held his bag of tools in place when the soft sound of someone clearing their throat made him turn around.

The light of morning filtered through the trees behind the blacksmith shop, illuminating the silhouette of Francine McClure. Her lips were pursed, but trembling, the tears in her eyes catching the glint of the rising sun.

Corbin turned away quickly, pretending to fasten one of the sacks closed. And though he refused to look in her direction, her presence was all he could feel.

"Corbin, please." Her whisper, choked with tears, mingled with the breeze and the leaves that danced across the ground. He dropped his hands from their feigned busyness. With a resigned sigh, he turned to her, the desire to see her just one more time weakening his pillar of resolve to nothing but a twig he could snap in two across his knee.

Being at Will and Ella's simple, quiet wedding the night before had opened Corbin's eyes. There was a depth and trust there that Corbin had never experienced with Francine. There was a willingness to sacrifice. Corbin was forced to admit that what he and Francine had was fleeting and foundationless.

Francine took a hesitant step forward. "Corbin, darling. Please don't go. I'm absolutely disconsolate."

Corbin stared at the ground. He wasn't sure what *disconsolate* meant, but he assumed it meant something along the lines of *sad*. Exasperated by his silence, Francine huffed and stomped forward, determined to make him look at her. Corbin glanced up and saw that the *disconsolate* expression that had been in her eyes had been replaced by the aggravation he had become more accustomed to in recent days. "Darling, must you leave? Won't you ever forgive me?"

When he spoke, resignation softened his voice. "What am I supposed to forgive? That you didn't love me enough to not chase after the prince? I can't forgive you for not loving me. It's just a fact I have to accept, not forgive you for."

"But you're hurting. You're not . . . yourself."

She was right, he had to admit. He had never felt such deep melancholy in his life. Perhaps he wasn't in the proper state of mind to be making dramatic life changes.

Francine took a step closer, sensing his indecision. His defenses melted away as tears shone again in her pleading, fawn-colored eyes. "You can't really be leaving. The ball's over. I'm still here. You're still here. Let's get married as we planned."

Despite her sincerity, the truth was impossible to ignore. And with that truth came a wave of pain Corbin had been trying to silence.

"If we had been married as we planned," Corbin said, "we'd be leaving on our wedding trip right now. If we had been married as we planned, we would have gone to the church instead of the palace. If we had been married as we planned, you would hate me for the rest of your life, being married to a blacksmith, knowing that you missed your chance to marry a prince."

Corbin slung a heavy leather bag over his shoulder and grabbed the rope that dangled from the donkey's neck. He tugged on the rope, but the donkey refused to budge. He yanked harder and with a defiant snort, the donkey finally lifted its obstinate hooves. Corbin couldn't get out of town fast enough, but he would have to move at a donkey's pace.

"Don't you love me anymore?" Francine whispered, her voice being carried by the wind.

Abruptly, Corbin had the same sickening feeling as the time he had been kicked in the stomach by a horse he was shoeing. The view in front of

Corbin blurred. He gripped the rope in his hands, the fibers cutting into his rough skin, and willed himself not to run to her.

Was he being as obstinate as this donkey, or was he finally making the choice that he knew he should have made a long time ago? He had decided to leave—not just to escape—but to move on from something that may not have ever been good in the first place.

But she was here now, obviously penitent. She was sad she had lost the prince, without really understanding why her sadness caused Corbin pain. She was sorry he was leaving, without really wanting him to stay.

This wasn't about how much she loved him, but about how much she needed him to love her.

Corbin stopped pulling on the rope and stood still. When he spoke, he faced the trees in front of him, his voice weak with despair.

"I will always love you, much more than you ever loved me, and that is the tragedy. Loving you will be my lifelong torment." Hesitating for a moment, the truth of his words making him breathless, he turned to face Francine. Only, she wasn't looking at him. She was looking up at the castle that would forever be in her view, the loss in her eyes bringing even more clarity to his.

Dropping the donkey's reins, and for the last time, he took Francine's face in his blackened hands and kissed her. He knew he was being foolish—that he was hurting himself more than he was hurting her. It wasn't simply a kiss of departure, or a kiss with a promise. It was a kiss that sealed the end of them.

"Goodbye, Francine," he whispered in her ear. Pulling on the reins, he left her in the road just outside his shop that was once going to be their home and heard her quiet sobs behind him.

Before he disappeared into the trees, Corbin looked back on the only home he had ever known. He expected to see Francine standing there all alone, but just behind her stood Will, his arm around Ella. Corbin didn't know how long they had been standing there, but he was grateful he got to see them one last time.

He met the eyes of the three people who watched him leave. Ella, her tender eyes shining with compassion. Will, the friend who had become like family to him. And Francine, the family Corbin had hoped to have. She had stopped crying and watched him through narrowed eyes, her hurt already turning to anger. Will's expression was not what Corbin expected at all.

It was one of hope. There was concern in his eyes for Corbin's pain, but a small smile lit his face, filling Corbin with courage.

Deep and resounding thunder rumbled through the darkening sky and Corbin's absent heart, and he smiled.

CHAPTER 4

Hunched over and exhausted, Corbin trudged up the hill that led away from the sea. Sweat trickled down his face despite the cool weather, all of his belongings either on his back or being dragged behind him—the donkey, which had utterly refused to even board the boat, was still back in Claire. The bag he dragged on the ground by a leather strap held a variety of small tools: his tongs for retrieving hot objects out of roaring fires, chisels that could slice and shape soft metal, an assortment of hammers and nails, and a holdfast that secured his work in place on the anvil as he persuaded it into compliance. Once he reached the blacksmith shop—if it was still vacant—Corbin would have to convert the abused bag into some new welding gloves; there were too many rips and tears in it now to be much use to hold anything. The bag across his back held some clean—though holey—socks, and the small anvil his father had taught him to blacksmith on.

"Mornin'!" a booming voice called out. Corbin looked up, squinting against the blinding sun. A burly man with curly, carrot-colored hair was walking toward him on the dirt road, a limp evident in his gait. "Welcome to Laurel. From out of town, are ya?"

The pleasant, lilting inflection of Laurel was heavy in the man's speech. Corbin attempted to tip his hat, but since his hands were occupied, merely nodded.

"Lose your horse, did ya?" the man asked as he voluntarily heaved the burden off Corbin's back. Though the weight was lifted off his shoulders, it took some effort to stand upright. Corbin had prided himself in being able to defeat any man in Maycott in a wrestling match—thanks to the rigors of his trade—but this burden, physical or otherwise, had nearly bested him. Corbin straightened and grimaced, the muscles in his back now preferring the stooped posture they had once rebelled against.

"Donkey, actually. And thank you," Corbin said, motioning to the sack the man had slung over his shoulder.

"'Tis nothin'. Donkey, eh? Stubborn brute, was he?" He laughed a deep, throaty laugh.

"He wouldn't even get on the boat. I've carried all of this from the harbor."

The man's bushy strawberry eyebrows shot up. "That's a full day's journey. All uphill!"

"All uphill." Corbin forced a smile for the first time in days.

"Well, ya made it. Well done!" The man grinned, revealing a partial set of teeth. "Judgin' by yer accent, I'd say ya were from the Kingdom of Claire. I'd even venture to say yer from the village of Maycott."

It was Corbin's turn to raise his eyebrows. "How did you know that?"

"I worked at the docks for most of me life. Met lots of people from many lands. Gained lots of new friends, though I did lose me leg a few years back."

The man lifted his pant leg to reveal a wooden peg where his leg would have been, a shoe glued onto the bottom.

"Oh, I'm sorry," Corbin muttered. "How did it happen?"

"Shark." The man laughed heartily when Corbin's eyes bulged. "Just pullin' yer leg. A chain holdin' a crate full of fish snapped and I got pinned underneath. Could'a been worse. Actually, I'd venture to say 'tis the best thing that's ever happened to me. I spend me days at home now with me wife, livin' the quiet life." He glanced over his shoulder at the sacks Corbin dragged behind him. "So, what's in all the sacks? For a single man, you've got a lot of baggage."

That felt especially true today. "Just my tools. Can you direct me to the blacksmith shop?"

"We don't have a blacksmith."

"I heard."

"Then why're ya askin' for him?" His eyes narrowed into slits.

"I just need to know where his shop is."

"But he's dead."

"I know."

Understanding spread across his face. "Oh. Right." He smiled. "So yer a blacksmith, eh? Folks in town'll be glad to see ya, that's for sure.

Haven't had a blacksmith in almost two months. Yer gonna be busy, I should warn ya."

"Busy sounds perfect."

"It's the first shop we reach when we get into town. It's not far now. What's yer name, anyway?"

"Corbin Black." Corbin stuck his free hand out and the man grasped it.

"Bartley Fitzjoly. Everyone calls me Bart."

"That's a relief." Corbin laughed.

Thankfully, Bart laughed too. "I had a very, shall we say, tempestuous childhood on account of me name. Made me strong, though." He sniffed, obviously proud of his bulging muscles.

"I don't doubt it." Corbin chuckled.

Corbin was grateful for Bart's jovial company, and he seemed to gain energy the longer they walked. He couldn't help noticing how the bushes on either side of the road were overgrown, sometimes completely obstructing his view ahead of him. The few houses he could see from the road were dilapidated, and even looked deserted. Soon, the dirt gave way to irregular and broken cobblestones with weeds growing between the cracks.

"Here 'tis!" Bart announced, pointing to a small building on the outskirts of town.

The back of the shop was facing them, and as they made their way up the slope, Corbin could see a small stable adjoined to the shop. Corbin's smile widened as they drew closer. The exterior boards were tight and fortified with chinking, and from what Corbin could see, there were no holes or cracks in the walls. The roof looked solid and in good repair. They reached the top of the hill and followed the road to the front of the shop. The doors were wide enough to easily allow horses to be shoed and wagons and ploughs that would need repairing.

Corbin was pleased to see that there were a few large anvils, a swage block, and a variety of files, chisels, and tongs still hanging on the wall. A small cot sat next to a fireplace in the back corner, and next to it, a small cupboard with a dusty washbasin on top.

Corbin had left his shop in Maycott absolutely sure that he would never feel at home anywhere else, especially without Francine. He forced his mind to wrap around her name, and it sent a wave of grief through him that he was positive would be a part of him until he died. But, standing in this clean, cozy shop, Corbin felt a sense of purpose and satisfaction that made his sadness fade to the back corner of his mind, if only for a moment. And in that moment, he felt like he was home.

"Nice place ya got here, lad," Bart boomed. "Mr. Marsh took great pride in it 'fore he died. I'm the baker. I work right across the way there, and me and the missus live in the back of the bakery."

"You're the baker?" Corbin chuckled. Somehow, he couldn't imagine this man wearing a white apron, making cakes.

Bart laughed. "I needed to find a job I could do with only one leg. Turns out I have a gift. I'll bring some bread over and let ya be the judge."

"I can't even tell you how good that sounds." Corbin thought of the stale bread and tough dried meat he had eaten for the past few days. "Thank you again for your help. Oh, if you don't mind my asking, how long have you lived here?"

"Laurel? Me whole life. Why, I was born in the cute little cottage we passed on the way into town."

Hope surged within Corbin. "Would you happen to know anyone with the last name of Black?"

"Black? Hmm, not that I can recall. My parents might, though."

"Can I ask them?"

"No."

"Why not?"

"They're dead."

"Oh." Corbin's face fell for a moment before he lightened. He had all the time in the world to find his family, or anyone who might have known them.

Bart pulled at his beard thoughtfully. "So, you moved to Laurel of your own free will, did ya?"

Corbin looked up, startled by the strange question. "Yes."

Bart raised his hands in a pacifying way, most likely noticing Corbin's slightly defensive expression. "I don't mean any offence. I love this place 'n all. Prettier than a fresh-baked loaf of bread, it is. We get powerful storms that roll in from the sea and rumble 'round in yer very chest. But it's, well, some say it's the worst place to live in all of creation. I would never move here if I hadn't been born here."

"Well, I was born here, if that helps. I just haven't been here since."

Bart lightened. "Oh, now that makes sense. Yer blood called ya back home. Well, just to warn ya, we're taxed up to our eyeballs here. I hope you didn't come here to get rich, 'cause . . . it's not very likely. All our money goes to *her*."

"Her who?"

"The princess, of course."

Corbin rolled his eyes. "Of course. Royals swoop in and take whatever they want."

Bart placed the sack he had been carrying on the ground at Corbin's feet and then headed toward the door, but stopped suddenly. "Speakin' of the princess. Ya might want to get settled quick. There's a . . . situation." His eyes darted to the floor, and he shifted his weight from his real foot to his wooden one.

"What situation?" Corbin said absently as he rummaged through the sack.

"Well, only that ya have to bring the princess a gift." As uncomfortable as Bart was, Corbin could tell he was fighting a smile.

"And that's 'a situation'?" Corbin laughed, feeling relieved. "Doesn't she have enough as it is? Do they make all newcomers bring your princess a gift?" He pulled some tongs out of the bag and hung them on a hook on the wall.

"No, just the ones that wanna marry her."

Corbin paused mid-step. "*Marry*! I don't want to marry any princess." His fury at the thought of marrying a royal after what he had just been through made his face burn. He turned away from Bart, sat heavily on the moth-eaten cot, and inspected a chipped nail that he had grabbed out of the bag at his feet.

"Suit yourself, but if ya don't bring her a gift, you'll be hanged. Or at least be sent to the dungeon. Depends on the princess's mood, I s'pose," Bart ended nonchalantly.

"Nice kingdom you have here."

"I told ya some say it's the worst."

Corbin couldn't help laughing a little at how much Bart loved this place so many hated, and wondered what side he would agree with. "When am I supposed to bring her a gift?"

"Tomorrow mornin'. 'Twas announced when the princess returned from Prince Kenton's ball a few days ago. 'Stead of marryin' her like they had agreed, he went off and married a commoner. But I'm sure ya know all about that. Anyway, it seems she's decided she's gonna marry a commoner like yer Prince Kenton did. Ya got here just in time." This time, Bart didn't stifle his laugh.

"Why do we have to bring a gift? Can't she just have a ball and meet people there like Prince Kenton did?"

"If I know one thing about this princess, it's that she doesn't do anything without gettin' somethin' in return."

"And a husband isn't enough?"

Bart shrugged. "Guess not. The weddin'll be held tomorrow night."

"Why so soon?"

"Pro'bly so the poor bloke can't escape." He laughed heartily.

Suddenly, Prince Kenton's silly ball idea didn't seem quite so silly. At least the women were able to choose if they wanted to go to the ball without the threat of death or imprisonment.

"So if I bring her a good enough gift, she'll choose me to marry her?"

"Right."

"Excellent. I'll bring the worst gift I can find and get it over with." The chipped nail in his hand suddenly seemed perfect.

"That's what I'd do."

Corbin looked up and met Bart's laughing eyes. "Is she really that bad?"

"They call her . . . The Beast," he said ominously, his fingers fluttering in the air, though his eyes sparkled jovially.

Corbin laughed for the first time in days. "Oh, that's right. I had forgotten that this is The Beast's kingdom. Well, I've heard enough stories to know that I want nothing to do with her."

"I hadn't realized her reputation had spread so far," Bart said, wiping his eyes, the last fits of laughter fading.

"Oh, yes. We know about her. I might know a little more than some, actually. My friend works in the palace at Claire as a groom and has had the, uh, privilege, of witnessing her charms from up close." He laughed again, remembering the stories Will had told him about her. Working at the stables, Will had had to endure Kenton and The Beast's courtship every time she came to visit their kingdom, including all the tantrums, sulking, and silent treatments. *The Beast* was an appropriate nickname, based on what Corbin had heard.

"Charms," Bart repeated with a chuckle, then he sobered slightly. "Just to warn ya, there will be some who will bring her good gifts. She is rich and royal and very pretty."

"Well, let them have her. I've had enough of women." Corbin made no attempt to veil his anger, though he hoped Bart couldn't hear the hurt behind it.

"Spoken straight from yer poor, broken heart, if I'm not mistaken." Bart smiled and Corbin scowled. "I'll be back with yer bread." Bart left without another word and closed the door behind him.

CHAPTER 5

When Corbin awoke the next morning, his black hair stood up on end and his gray eyes ached and burned after a fitful sleep. He had spent the night shivering under the few threadbare blankets he could find. The cold in Laurel felt different than in Claire. In Claire, it felt as if the trees and the lush landscape softened the cold somehow. But perhaps it was because Laurel was situated so close to the ocean, and the landscape was more stark, the cold had free reign—at least at night. It rolled off the waves and weaved its way through the holes in Corbin's socks.

But now that the sun was up, the cold cowered before its rays and retreated back into the frigid ocean waters. Corbin shook off his fatigue and got to work, and soon everything was unpacked and in its rightful place.

Corbin had been in Laurel for less than twenty-four hours and was already buried in work, which he threw himself into with a whistle on his lips. Just minutes after Bart had left, some of the townspeople began lining up outside his door. A butcher brought in four rusty, bent hinges that needed fixing, along with three dull knives that needed sharpening and shaping. A merchant brought in a wobbly wagon wheel. A horse breeder told Corbin that he would be in later that day for him to shoe five horses. Shoeing horses was essential to Corbin's livelihood—his bread and butter. It would be convenient living so close to the baker.

Most couldn't pay with money. Corbin accepted six eggs, some stale biscuits, and one shoe for payment. The people of his village in Claire weren't exactly wealthy, but Corbin had rarely seen this level of poverty.

He accepted the small payments, pity in his eyes, but only because the customers insisted.

Corbin was surprised by how at home he felt. People smiled here just as they did in Claire. The same things that broke in Claire broke here in Laurel, and he fixed them just the same. Optimism for the future, and hope for discovering his past, brought a natural smile to his face. And soon, he hoped, he wouldn't see Francine's face every time he closed his eyes.

With each new customer that entered the shop, Corbin asked if they had ever heard of or known anyone of the family Black. They each scrunched up their faces, casting their memories back, only to shrug in regret and sympathy. Corbin would answer with a word of thanks, knowing it was only a matter of time until he found someone who knew something.

Corbin was holding the last of the tailor's hinges with the tongs and placing it in the flames when a huge figure blocked the sunlight from streaming in through the open doorway.

"What're ya doin' here? Why aren't ya at the Gift Givin'?" Bart said. He had flour in his beard and was pulling gooey dough off his fingers.

Corbin shrugged. "I changed my mind. I'm new enough to town that I don't think I'll be missed. The only people who know I'm here have brought me work they need back by the end of the day. No one will care if I'm there or not. I'd rather get some work done than stand in line all day to give some beastly princess a gift, only to be sent back home." He picked up his cross peen hammer and began pounding the tailor's faulty hinge flat.

"Might be worth yer time." Bart motioned for Corbin to join him in the doorway. Still holding the hot hinge with his tongs, Corbin walked to stand next to Bart and looked out onto the road. "Guards are checkin' in on every house and shop, makin' sure every man goes."

Sure enough, a dozen guards were walking the streets, knocking on doors, making sure every single man was doing his duty. Corbin didn't know much about romance, besides what he learned from his experience with Francine, but he couldn't imagine a less romantic way of going about getting a husband than by forcing him to woo you with a compulsory gift. Still, as ridiculous as it all was, he was much too busy to be hanged.

Corbin looked up at Bart and then back to all the work he had waiting for him.

"Don't worry. I'll put the fire out," Bart said. "Follow the line of defeated men and you'll know yer in the right place." Laughter made every disheartening word he said bounce merrily.

"Thank you, Bart," Corbin said, rolling his eyes. The first twinge of regret for his hasty decision to leave Claire twisted in his stomach, but he quickly pushed it aside. There was nothing for him there anymore. He pulled his leather gloves off and placed them on the swage block. "What's her real name, anyway?"

"Rose. Princess Rose."

Corbin nodded and walked toward the doorway. Bart limped past Corbin and went straight to the fire to put it out just as a guard approached the shop.

The guard glared up at Corbin hovering in the doorway. "All single men should be lined up already!" He nudged Corbin's shoulder with the tip of his sword, then looked past Corbin to Bart who was innocently stabbing at the waning fire with a poker. "And you! Why aren't you lined up?"

"Married," Bart answered with a smile that looked both relieved and smug.

"*You're* married?" The guard's eyes darted to Bart's wooden leg that was showing under his pant leg as he knelt down, his flour-covered beard, his doughy fingers, and missing teeth. "Where's your wife?"

"At the bakery. Prettiest lass in town. She's gettin' things settled so we can go watch the Gift Givin'." Bart raised his left hand, displaying a cheap brass ring. "And let's be honest, would the princess really choose me anyway?"

The corner of the guard's mouth twitched, then he turned back to Corbin, but Corbin had swatted the sword away and had already started walking before the guard could chastise him again. The look on the guard's face told Corbin he had better hurry if he wanted to avoid any trouble. He increased his pace to a run.

Corbin had been running for a few minutes before he realized his hands were empty. He had been so preoccupied with avoiding his own hanging, he had forgotten that he needed to show up with a gift. He smirked at the thought of the damaged nail he had considered the day before. It was apparent, based on the anxiety in every guards' eyes and how the town was practically empty, that everyone was taking this ridiculous plan seriously. Now, he had to think of something real. Immediately.

As he ran, he passed by some men who were dressed in what appeared to be their Sunday best, carrying boxes and shiny things that caught the sun and blinded his eyes, and he started to panic. He still hadn't taken his leather apron off, and his hands were black with soot. The guards marched along the streets, swords swinging from their belts. There was nowhere to escape.

Corbin's desperation made him dizzy. He glanced from side to side looking for anything gift-worthy as the sweat began to form on his forehead and moisten his hair. He brushed it back from his eyes as he continued to search for something that might be acceptable to give a princess . . . just not *too* acceptable that she might actually *accept* it.

The sun beat down on his shoulders, though his head was cool from sweat and the early autumn breeze. He ran past the shops, glancing in the store windows, but there was no one there to sell him anything. Everyone had already gone to the Gift Giving. He didn't have any money anyway.

He hurried out of town, following behind a few dawdlers farther up the path, and was soon surrounded on every side by blurred green trees and brown dirt that he glanced at as he ran . . . until something red caught his eye. He came to a stop and slowly walked backward to the wild rose bush he had passed. It was on the very edge of the scant forest, surrounded by other rosebushes whose blooms had wilted and now hung dry and drooping on their stems.

Except for one.

A late-blooming bud was just beginning to unfurl its petals. A few drops of dew caught the sunlight that filtered through the trees, and they glistened like tears. The deep red of the rose stood in breathtaking contrast to the greens and browns that acted as its backdrop. It was a shame to pluck it. But it seemed to be offering itself to him—its face upturned, its petals almost reaching.

Corbin bent down to pluck the rose, wincing as a thorn pushed deep into his skin. He ignored the pain, pulled the long stem from the bush, and rushed to the ceremony.

CHAPTER 6

With the little rose in his hand and sweat trickling down his face, Corbin emerged from the forest. Looming over the top of a large, distant hill, the tips of the gray stone battlements of Laurel's castle jutted into the sky. At the bottom of the hill, a large crowd had gathered. Just as Bart had instructed, Corbin found a line of about two hundred dejected-looking men and jogged toward them.

The line curved and disappeared behind the hill to his left where Corbin was sure the princess was waiting. From what he could see, most of the men had boxes and parcels, some had animals, and others had even come in grand chariots.

When the man in front of Corbin saw that he had joined the back of the line, he insisted that Corbin go in front of him. Perplexed—but not unwilling—considering all the work he had to get back to, Corbin moved ahead in line. Once the man in front of him saw that Corbin had moved up in line, he also insisted Corbin go in front of him. Corbin moved forward until he was closer to the front of the line than the end of it, feeling very fortunate, until he took a closer look at the man nearest to him. He was doing a nervous little dance, and a drop of sweat slid down the side of his face.

The man looked down at Corbin's simple red rose with a look of utter disbelief, his eyes wide and unblinking.

"Is *that* your gift?"

"Yes," Corbin replied, a little defensively. It was a pretty flower, after all. He didn't see anything in the man's hands. "What did you bring?"

With a trembling hand, the man reached into his breast pocket, and a golden chain caught the light as he dangled it from his fingers.

"It was my mother's," he said, swallowing hard.

"That's a very nice necklace. I think you stand a good chance," Corbin said with an encouraging, relieved grin.

He didn't look back at Corbin. "I pray I don't."

Before Corbin could respond, a woman's furious voice pierced the silence. "A rock! You dare to bring your princess *a rock*!"

The men in the line all looked at each other and leaned forward to see, or at least to hear, what was going on. Corbin tried to peer around the line of men, but all he could see was the outline of a little makeshift throne with flags fluttering on top. The sun wasn't quite falling behind the hills, but the brilliance of it put everything else into shadow.

"It's h-h-her," the man with the necklace said in a shaky voice, his eyes fixed on the throne. "The Beast."

A man, who Corbin could see was standing on the top steps of the throne, addressed the princess, but spoke loudly enough for all to hear. "It *is* a very nice rock, Your Highness. When you open it up, there are little crystals inside."

Though he strained his ears, Corbin couldn't hear The Beast's muted response. But suddenly, guards surrounded the man, grabbed him by the arms, and dragged him to a horse-drawn cart with vertical rails. Corbin gulped when he saw that the man was not alone in the jail cart. It seemed that other men had brought less than desirable gifts and were going to be punished. Corbin nervously twirled his rose between his fingers and swallowed to moisten his suddenly dry throat.

As he drew closer, Corbin's thoughts turned to Francine. He wondered what she would think of him, standing in line as a potential husband to a princess Corbin had never met—especially considering the fact that he had just lost Francine to a prince *she* had never met, and yet hoped to marry. He had come to this kingdom to escape his past, and now he was reliving it in the most absurd way.

A high-pitched howl of rage snapped his head up and out of his reverie. Corbin was close enough now that he could see the entire makeshift throne, the steps that led up to where the princess sat, and the curtains that enclosed the throne. Through those curtains, Corbin could see the silhouette of the seated princess as she stomped her feet and pounded her fists angrily on her knees.

"I *hate* chocolate!" she screamed. The chocolate giver quickly stood from his humble kneeling position and ran down the steps, wildly scattering the box of chocolates across the grass, and disappeared behind the hill before any guards could reach him. He hadn't been disrespectful, just uninformed. That man had probably spent a small fortune on so rare a confection. Corbin had simply plucked his gift out of the ground on his way here. He wondered how cold the dungeon would be in the winter.

Corbin looked around again at the gifts that were held in shaking hands. Some men had family heirlooms, brooches, hair pins, and even birds in a birdcage.

"Birds. That's a nice gift," he whispered to the bird giver.

The man holding the birdcage seemed oddly confident in this line of fearful suitors. "Yes, it is. They're Aritanga birds. Closely related to Love Birds. I think she'll see it as a *very* romantic gesture." He looked around and then spoke conspiratorially out of the side of his mouth. "They look pretty, but they bite *hard* and their song sounds like a dog being beaten." He chuckled.

"Aren't you worried?" Corbin nodded in the direction of the men in the prison cart. It was getting very full.

"No. If she chooses me, I'll be rich and married to a beautiful woman. Besides, they're only loud early in the morning or if they're frightened. And with the wedding taking place tonight, she won't even know about it until after we're married, and by then . . ." he smirked, "too late."

Corbin was close enough now he could see the The Beast's illuminated figure fading with the sunlight. There were no more reprimands or fits of displeasure. Bored, she was now simply waving off unwanted gifts without really looking at them. The bird-giver approached the throne, ascended the steps, and grandly held out the birdcage.

"My beautiful, regal, and, dare I say, well-groomed Princess Rose, these are Aritanga birds—the birds of love and, ahem, fertility. Their heavenly song is said to wake a sleeping Aphrodite to bless a newly married couple with bliss and joy, and even happiness, forever and ever . . . and ever."

He swooped into a grand bow, and Corbin stifled a laugh. Corbin still couldn't see The Beast's face, but her hands were in her lap and her feet were still. No tantrum. That was a good sign.

Suddenly, a dog in the crowd barked and everyone jumped. The birds fluttered erratically around inside their cage and punctured the tense air with their hideous squawks and shrieks. Some people in the crowd held their hands to their ears, and the little children cried. One of the guards rushed to the cage and quickly draped a cloak over it while two other guards grabbed the bird giver and threw him into the jail cart with the other undesirable suitors.

The squawking continued despite the heavy cloak covering the cage, the horrible sounds grating on every raw nerve. The guard with the cage went out behind the throne and another followed him with a quiver of arrows on his back and a bow clutched in his hand. Moments later, there were two swift bursts of air, followed by welcome silence.

A few nervous sniggers lightened the mood as hands were pulled away from ears. The cries of frightened children dwindled to whimpers as the silence pressed down again.

Suddenly, a low rumbling carried over from behind the line of men and everyone turned to see a man in a chariot racing up the slope.

Corbin sighed in relief when he saw that this man was no commoner, but a prince. He wore a crown with multi-colored jewels and a crimson cape that fluttered in the wind.

"Princess Rose!" he called as he approached, the line of men scattering to let him through. "It is I, Prince Felix of Hollow Mountain!" The looks on the faces of the men were almost silly with relief. The necklace man looked like he would faint with joy.

Prince Felix hopped down from the gold chariot, his horse sweating and foaming with thirst. Underneath his crown, a mass of golden hair was windswept across his high forehead, and he walked with purpose on spindly legs. He passed by Corbin and the other waiting men and climbed the five steps up to the princess, his brilliant teeth catching the sun as he grinned. With one hand, the prince flung his cape back over his shoulder jauntily, and in the other, he held a jewel-encrusted gold box. He bowed so deeply that his cape flung over his head, dangling on the ground between him and the princess. Standing quickly, he frantically smoothed it down.

"My Princess. In this box lies the crown worn by my great-great-grandmother, Queen Helga of Hollow Mountain, when she signed the treaty that ended the Tri-Kingdom War." He lifted the lid of the box, eager to see her reaction at his grand gift.

The entire kingdom held their breath, waiting for Princess Rose's response. Surely this was the most priceless gift offered her that day. Certainly it was good enough for her.

Corbin watched as the silhouetted princess placed her hands on either side of her chair and pushed herself up. Slowly, she reached into the golden box, lifted out the crown and bent her head over it, her fingers tracing its shape and caressing the jewels. Corbin pursed his lips and tapped anxiously against the stem of the rose.

She took a step forward, though she was still concealed by the curtain. When she spoke, her voice was hushed with unconcealed malice. "You may recall, Prince Felix, that you proposed to me two years ago, and I refused you."

Prince Felix squared his shoulders and tossed his head, clearing his vision of his floppy hair. "Yes, my dear, but you weren't as desperate as you are now, were you?"

After an uneasy moment, Princess Rose suddenly flung her arm out, and the crown flew from her fingers. There was a collective gasp as everyone watched the crown fly through the air and land in the tall grass.

Prince Felix shrieked, stumbled down the stairs, stopped, then returned to The Beast and grabbed the golden box out of her hands. Once he plucked the crown from out of the grass, he stomped off and called for his horse. His horse, who had been grazing nearby, walked off in the opposite direction, pulling the chariot behind him. Prince Felix ran after it, his wavy hair bouncing in the sunlight.

The line of men was no longer a line. It was a mass of panicked, frightened men who felt like lambs going to slaughter, the anxiety in their faces no longer concealed. She had rejected a prince . . . with a crown! Necklace man had indeed fainted and was very nearly trampled by all the nervous feet. None of the men knew their place in line anymore. Guards argued, children cried, and the princess shouted about shutting everyone in prison.

Corbin looked out over the crowd and felt the despair in each unfamiliar face. No one would notice if he slipped away now. He looked behind him and indeed saw a dozen or so men defect from the line and tear down the hill like rabbits before an arrow. As much as he understood their desire to escape, he was filled with irritation at their cowardice.

He knew he wouldn't escape as those men had. The only other option in his mind now was to do what he had come to do.

Before he let himself consider the implications of his decision, Corbin swallowed against the dryness of his throat and moved forward. He risked a glance at the crowd, and towering taller than anyone else stood Bart, an unmistakable look of pity and dread in his eyes. Next to him was a plump, freckled woman with flour sprinkled all over her patched blue apron. She grasped Bart's hand in both of hers. Bart looked down at Corbin's rose, blinked slowly, and shook his head back and forth as if in grief.

With each step he took toward the throne, the crowd grew quieter. It had become so silent that Corbin could hear the gentle tap as his shoes hit the first step of the throne. He counted the steps as he ascended. One. Two. Three. Four. Five. Until he reached the top. Without looking up, he knelt down on one knee, his head bowed. The tips of The Beast's slippered feet peeked out from under her thick skirts. He willed his eyes upward, and he looked at the princess for the first time.

The sun shone hazily from the west, lighting half of her face through the thin silk curtains. Her hair was secured tightly underneath a shawl, giving her a rather stark appearance, emphasizing the paleness of her skin and the wideness of her eyes. It was in those eyes that Corbin could identify an anxious and penetrating expression. He noticed that she was absently wringing her hands.

In the dim, soft light and with the world spinning slightly around him, Corbin couldn't tell if she were beautiful or not, or if she were short or tall. He couldn't perceive the exact color of her eyes or of her dress. He couldn't, at that moment, even see why she was called The Beast.

Somewhere between the moment when he realized he had to step forward, and now as he knelt before her, Corbin had unconsciously hidden the rose behind his back, almost in shame. Remembering the fate of the man who had brought her a rock, and with his gaze fixed on the wood planks he knelt on, he slowly moved the rose out from behind him to hold it in front of her. He couldn't speak. He simply kept his eyes down and waited.

At any moment, Corbin expected her fury, her screams of outrage, the guards' rough hands on his arms pulling him to the prison cart. But all was still.

As the silence wore on, curiosity forced Corbin's eyes up again. He began at the hem of her dress—which he now saw was a deep blue. His gaze moved upward, and he saw that The Beast hadn't moved—besides her hands, which were now calm at her sides. Finally, their eyes met, and Corbin now perceived something else besides impatience and scrutiny. Her face had softened and all hints of her anger and disappointment were replaced with an expression Corbin couldn't name.

The Beast blinked slowly, and Corbin heard her exhale. A sheen had come to her eyes. He could see now that they were the most brilliant green he had ever seen. Fierce and lovely. He looked closer at her face and saw that underneath her head scarf, a tendril of flaming red hair fell across her forehead.

He put a name to the expression he saw in this stranger's eyes then. Hope. Pure, quiet hope. He couldn't understand it and it made no sense, but it was there just the same.

Corbin felt a cold touch on his fingers, and he looked down. Princess Rose's hand was outstretched and she had placed her ghostly white fingers over his. Underneath hers, Corbin's hands were utterly filthy, covered in grime and dried blood from the thorns.

Slowly, she withdrew the rose from out of Corbin's hand before he even knew what had happened.

"Behold!" a man's voice boomed over the delicate silence. "Your future king!"

CHAPTER 7

Not since Prince Kenton had announced his ridiculous ball back home had Corbin experienced such unleashed madness. The crowd screamed and cheered, mostly, he suspected, in liberation that the princess had finally accepted a gift and they were all free to return to their own lives. He just couldn't grasp that his simple rose was the gift she had chosen.

Corbin was still kneeling on the wood planks of the throne when two guards walked up and pulled him to his feet, then turned him around to face the crowd. One of the guards grabbed Corbin's arm and flung it up in the air for him. With Corbin's hand held limply in the air, the cheers grew louder. His gaze ran over the unfamiliar faces until he saw Bart standing near the front of the crowd, clapping slowly, a look of utter disbelief on his red face.

An official-looking man barked a brusque command, and the guards pulled Corbin down the stairs. Corbin was too numb to fight and didn't even struggle.

As they approached one of two very ostentatious carriages, Corbin felt his body tense, and he tried to pull his arms out of the guards' grips. Their hands tightened painfully, pinching the nerves under his arms. The other carriage was farther up the hill and as Corbin was being pulled across the grass, he saw a flash of deep blue skirts as The Beast climbed into it.

Another guard was waiting at the door of the carriage, and he held it open while the other two pushed Corbin inside. They followed in after him and one sat next to him while the other sat on the opposite seat.

Corbin looked out the window and saw that all the townspeople were hastily returning to the village and their normal lives. "Can I please go and check on my shop?" Corbin said, facing the guards. "I just have to finish up a few things."

The guard opposite Corbin sat stony-faced and silent, ignoring Corbin's pleas. The other guard scoffed.

"Sure, and while you're finishing up a few things, you'll disappear to another kingdom."

Corbin shook his head, too astounded to speak. He looked out the window once more. Why had The Beast chosen him? And what was it about a rose that had brought that strange, soft gleam into her eyes?

He thought of Francine and what she would think of all this. Would she think this was his way of getting revenge? His way of hurting her for hurting him? Surely she knew him better than that. Corbin shook his head. It didn't matter now.

Someone outside shouted an order, and the carriage lurched forward. Dozens of horses' hooves pounded the ground. Corbin looked out the window, but the guard next to him reached over and snapped the curtains shut.

The desire to escape was so powerful, Corbin had to grip the seat cushion. But he knew he wouldn't run. He thought back to those poor, frightened men who had deserted the Gift Giving and fled down the hill. He wasn't like those men. He had been chosen . . . because he had decided to step forward. His grip loosened on the cushion, and he took a steadying breath.

The guards seemed relaxed enough now that Corbin casually pulled the window curtain back, revealing endless green rolling hills. Occasionally, farms with their neat little squares carved through the landscape, and they soon gave way to long, lush grasses and random, sparse forests. After a while, the dilapidated dirt road became gravel, and Corbin looked up in time to see a forbidding stone wall thirty feet high. An enormous door was pushed open by three guards, the hinges moaning from neglect.

As soon as the carriage passed through the opening, the door was pushed closed, sealing the wall.

After a ride that felt excruciatingly long, but nowhere near long enough, the carriage came to a stop. The door swung open and the guards' hands encircled Corbin's arms.

Shouts and cries came from behind his carriage, and Corbin twisted his neck far enough to see that the jail cart had followed them up to the castle. Men's arms reached through the rails, demanding justice, pleading for mercy.

"What will happen to them?" Corbin asked one of the guards.

"It's off to the dungeons for them, at least for the time being. They humiliated the princess. They're lucky they're still alive."

Corbin allowed himself to be pulled toward the castle. As they drew closer, he looked up and couldn't tell where the walls met the roof and where the roof met the sky. He couldn't even grasp how immense the castle was, how towering the walls and formidable the battlements. Though he did notice, vaguely, the irregular stones and how they had been placed in no particular order, but that they had somehow formed a smooth and solid wall.

The guards led Corbin into the Grand Foyer, dropped their hands, and stepped back a few paces, allowing him space to breathe. To his right, he saw that The Beast had already entered the castle and was rounding a corner, followed by half a dozen maids. She yanked the shawl off her head, revealing a mass of brilliant red hair, before disappearing out of view. Against the backdrop of hard gray stones, it was the only thing that looked alive in this cold, stark place.

Corbin craned his neck to take in the enormity of the room that seemed ready to swallow him whole. The walls were all made of stone, with corridors leading off in every direction. He had entered the palace at Claire only once, but he couldn't help comparing it to this castle. The palace at Claire was built with perfectly cut, neatly stacked stones. The walls were paneled in dark, polished wood, and tapestries draped the walls and brought them to life. And though it could have just been because Corbin had been at that palace for a ball, the palace at Claire had felt light and warm, filled with a tangible energy.

An eerie emptiness enveloped this castle. Corbin had assumed, after what Bart had said about being overtaxed, that this castle would be ornate and gaudy. But it wasn't. If anything, it felt even more neglected than the roads that led to it.

A chill reached Corbin's neck and he shivered. The heavy doors closed behind him and the sound seemed to echo for miles through the corridors. Corbin exhaled sharply, feeling like a part of his soul had been sucked out by the sound. The air grew thick and oppressive, and though they were towering and vast, the walls felt as if they were falling in all around him.

He had only been inside for a few seconds, but he got the impression that time moved more slowly here. The ancient air seemed to reach out and tug on whatever it could grasp, slowing everything down so that it could keep up.

Light footsteps broke the silence and Corbin stood straighter, realizing he had been hunching under the imaginary weight of the walls. A few maids congregated to stand in front of him. They all wore the same pale gray, ankle-length dresses with spotless white aprons, and though they seemed to be trying to behave professionally, a few of them giggled at each other, pink rising to their cheeks.

Corbin nodded and tried to smile, feeling painfully self-conscious at the attention. A serious yet kind-looking woman strode forward and clapped her hands. The girls stopped giggling and stood at attention.

"Decorum, ladies. Please." Despite her youthful appearance, her voice rang with authority. As she walked closer to him, Corbin could now see the indication of lines around her eyes and the shimmering of gray in her chestnut hair. Her dark, wise eyes took him in from head to toe, including his filthy apron and blackened hands. When she met his eyes, hers widened slightly and her complexion paled at least two shades of color.

"What is your name?"

"Corbin."

"Corbin?" she repeated softly. Corbin ducked his head and stared at the stones at his feet. He hadn't said, "His Royal Highness, Prince Corbin of Claire," or anything even close to it. He was simply Corbin. That was all he had ever been. And the way that her face had become impossibly more pale emphasized just how absurd this situation was. Her astonishment was obvious, but whether it was directed at the princess for actually following through with her plan to marry a commoner, or at Corbin who was the most common of them all, Corbin couldn't be sure.

"You know where to take him," the woman whispered to the nearest maid before she spun away and swiftly exited the foyer. The girls looked at each other and shrugged their shoulders. Finally, the oldest-looking one stepped forward.

"I told you this was ridiculous," she said out of the corner of her mouth to the girl standing closest to her. She spoke louder, addressing Corbin now, and began walking toward a wide marble staircase. "Follow me. We'll take you to the washing room to prepare for the wedding."

The wedding. *His* wedding. The reality of the situation sunk deeper into his stomach. With one last look at the heavily guarded front doors,

Corbin followed the women through corridors, down some stairs, up some different stairs, and past huge, stained-glass windows. The maid in front of the line named the rooms nonchalantly as they passed by: the Throne Room, the Great Hall, the Banquet Hall, the Armory, the Treasury . . . Corbin eventually stopped listening. He couldn't appreciate the grandeur, but he could appreciate that he could easily get lost in a place like this.

Finally, they reached an open door. The women all stopped outside the door, and the maid in charge motioned for Corbin to go inside. He walked past them and into a steam-filled room.

"We'll just wait out here," the girl said, closing the door behind her, but not before Corbin heard a burst of giggles bounce off the corridor walls.

He walked forward and saw a large tub filled with water in the middle of the room. A fire had been lit, and he crossed the room to stand near the flames and let the heat envelop him, warming his fingers and toes. He tried to take a deep breath, but steam and perfumes filled his lungs and he coughed instead.

As he stood, he surveyed the tub and realized he was supposed to wash his clothes before the wedding. Knowing it would take all day for his clothes to dry and seeing that the sun was about to set, Corbin thought this a very impractical plan. He walked over to the door, opened it, and stuck his head out.

"I don't think my clothes will be dry in time for the wedding if I wash them now," he said. The girls looked at each other incredulously and then back at him, a few bursting into yet another round of laughter. One of the girls shook her head, then pointed at Corbin with raised eyebrows. "Oh, me?" he whispered. "That's for me?"

That would explain the whispers and sniggers, which had now become uncontrollable. Corbin's face burned. Quickly, he ducked back inside and latched the door. Turning back around to face the big tub full of water, he thought of his little basin of water he washed in back at home. In the winter, he would have to break the layer of ice on top so he could dip his hands in, but only when it was absolutely necessary.

He immersed his fingers in the water, but pulled them out quickly with a wince. Potatoes could have been boiled in that water. Braving the water again, he ignored the searing heat on his fingertips and lowered his hands in deeper. Every burn scar he had acquired in his trade screamed as if it had become fresh again. Eventually, the pain subsided and the heat became soothing and pleasant. With one more wary glance at the door, Corbin quickly removed his apron and clothes and for the first time in his life, immersed himself in a tub of hot water. As good as it felt, he couldn't help feeling more like a dirty pair of socks sitting in this water than a human being.

After scrubbing at the blackness on his hands and fingernails and making little progress, Corbin was resigned to the fact that they were probably stained for life. Near the tub sat a table with different soaps on top of it, and he chose the least offensive smelling one. After he got out and dried off, he found another little table holding a neatly folded towel and a sharp, pearl-handled blade. He picked it up, unwittingly impressed by the craftsmanship of the blade, then scraped the rough stubble on his jaw and trimmed his neglected hair.

Once he was clean, shaven, and trimmed, Corbin looked around for something to put on, assuming he couldn't wear his old clothes. Thankfully, in the corner of the room, he spotted a suit laid out in pieces along a linen-covered table.

There were more layers of clothing than Corbin had ever worn in his life, and he had to assume he was putting them all on correctly and in the right order. First, the beige breeches, followed by the starched white shirt that tied at the neck. He rolled his eyes as he pulled on the flowery silk waistcoat and then the black frockcoat with its intricately embroidered cuffs and painted buttons. He heard a rip when he pulled it over his shoulders, winced, then decided to ignore it.

He got everything on, including the too-small white gloves, but left the cravat hanging loosely around his neck. A lump unexpectedly came to his throat as he remembered Francine tying his cravat for him when he arrived at her house to take her to Prince Kenton's ball. He tried to forget how her fingers had gently grazed his neck and how her hands had brushed across his shoulders to smooth out his coat. Only now did he realize how impassive her eyes had been and how she kept glancing up at the palace.

Corbin shook his head. He was about to be married, as preposterous as that seemed. He was here to forget the past, to move on, and to leave his memories where they couldn't hurt anymore.

He just didn't know where that was.

CHAPTER 8

When Corbin entered the corridor, the maids had all left, and the only person standing there was the woman in charge who had left so abruptly earlier. All traces of her previous disappointment had fled from her face, but her eyes were oddly swollen.

"I'm sorry I'm not a prince," Corbin finally said, his eyes staring at his shiny, pinching shoes.

"Nonsense. Please forgive me for my rude introduction. It has been a trying day . . . a trying week. And please allow me to welcome you as I should have. I am Mrs. Whiting. Welcome home, my dear." Her tender yet tactful voice contradicted the gravity in her expression.

Home. Corbin couldn't reply a thank you. This was not a home.

"So, Corbin, I'm curious. Where does such a name come from?"

Corbin cleared his throat uncomfortably, remembering how she paled at his laughably less-than-royal name. "I was told that it means 'raven.' I was born with black hair, which I never really lost, I suppose." He smiled, his eyes glancing up to his hair that fell across his forehead.

"Hmm, raven? Well, it *seems* appropriate," she said, her brows knitting together. Corbin shifted his weight, and Mrs. Whiting's eyes softened slightly as she took a small step toward him. "I know this all seems very strange to you, and believe me, none of us have tread these waters before either, so you're in good company. We'll just all learn together, shall we?" Corbin nodded again and she smiled in response.

"I don't know how to tie this," he said, flipping the cravat with his hand. "I've never been much of a cravat-wearer."

"Come here, my dear," she said, chuckling. With her displeasure at the marriage either vanished or concealed, Mrs. Whiting was now practical and professional. Her hands expertly tied the cravat as Corbin stood helpless and glanced out the window. Through the thick, warped glass, Corbin could see the roof of a stable and other buildings within the castle walls.

After a few moments, Mrs. Whiting stood back to survey her work, a pleased smile on her face. "You'll have your own servant after the wedding, but for now, you'll have to bear with this old woman."

"It's much better than I could do. Thank you." Corbin laughed nervously. "Do I look as ridiculous as I feel?"

Instead of laughing along with him, Mrs. Whiting's eyes became gentle. "You do not look at all ridiculous. You look like a gentleman who is about to marry a princess." That touch of disbelief from earlier returned, only this time it brought a sheen to her eyes. "Forgive me, my dear. I've known the princess her entire life and this is quite a momentous day. I can't believe she chose you."

"Me neither." Corbin wasn't even offended. No one was more astonished than he.

She smiled and shook her head. "Forgive me. I didn't mean it that way. I was skeptical at first, but . . . I think everything will work out just fine."

Without another word, Mrs. Whiting turned away and motioned for Corbin to follow her, but his feet remained planted.

"Please, Mrs. Whiting. I don't ask for much, but can you please tell me a little of what I'm getting into?"

Mrs. Whiting pursed her lips. "Of course, my dear. I'll tell you what I can." She walked to the window. "I'm not sure how much you know, but Princess Rose is the only child of the late King Ross and Queen Marion of Laurel. They were a good king and queen, but they caught a fever while they were away in another kingdom. They died suddenly ten years ago on the same day—she in the morning, and he was gone by sunset. The princess was here, waiting for them to return. She was only thirteen years old, and has never been the same."

Remembrance dawned on Corbin. When he was about fifteen years old working in the blacksmith shop, a herald came running through the middle of town announcing the tragic and untimely deaths of the King and Queen of Laurel. It was sad news, but not news that had affected Corbin in any way. He couldn't remember ever thinking on it again.

"Do you see those planters bordering the gardens?" she said.

Corbin stepped closer to the window and could just make out the overgrown hedges and bushes, and finally the planters Mrs. Whiting referred to. "The weed-covered ones?"

"Yes. When Princess Rose was born, the queen had rose bushes planted around every garden. Every spring her father would . . ." Mrs. Whiting's voice became misty once more. "Well, I'll just say that when Rose learned of her parents' deaths, she ordered that the rose bushes be ripped out of the ground and burned. And that was just the beginning. Everything changed that day. I suppose everything and everyone died a little when the king and queen died, but no one more than Princess Rose."

The sound of instruments tuning floated up to them. "Goodness! We must hurry." She paused to look at Corbin, a mixture of compassion and conviction on her face. "I don't want you to worry. I'm not saying that it won't be difficult at times, but if there's one thing I've learned in my life, it's that things have a way of working themselves out. Have courage! Come along, dear."

Corbin followed her through the corridors, passing rows of empty suits of armor that made the back of Corbin's head tingle, their hollow eyes following him as he passed.

The tuning instruments, mingled with the low hum of voices, greeted Corbin as he rounded what he hoped would be the last corner. As soon as they passed through the Great Hall and entered what Corbin remembered was the Throne Room, voices hushed and the instruments quieted. After a few coughs and throat clearing in the heavy silence, the musicians began playing a somewhat somber tune at a regular rhythm. Corbin was relieved, though surprised, that there was only a handful of people gathered. A few royal-looking people stood close together, but most of the crowd consisted of maids, a few guards, and a heavy, white-aproned man with a ladle sticking out of his pocket.

The sparse crowd parted to reveal a single throne sitting at the opposite end of the vast room. Corbin gulped, his legs suddenly as heavy as anvils. With a little pat on his back, Mrs. Whiting propelled him forward, and he shuffled his feet in the direction of the lonely throne.

Every eye was locked on him. Their scrutinizing, baffled expressions had a strange effect on Corbin. He knew just as well—if not better than everyone else—how preposterous this situation was. Standing straight, Corbin walked up the newly formed aisle, feeling like he was in a dream, or at least hoping he was. Corbin glanced at the empty spot where his best man would have stood. He grinned incredulously in spite of himself, wondering what Will Hawkins would think of this unimaginable turn of events.

He remembered Will's expression of hope he had worn as Corbin trudged out of town. As peculiar as Will's expression had been at the time, and as strange as it was that Corbin would remember it now, it brought him a feeling of peace as he felt so very far from home.

Corbin knew he was trying to think of any friend, any familiar face that could help him make it to the end of the aisle. Because at the moment, Corbin could see no friendly, familiar face, nothing he recognized that would make what was happening feel real. All he could grasp was that a week earlier he was engaged and today he was marrying someone else he had never spoken to.

And that she was called The Beast.

Corbin reached the steps at the foot of the throne and stopped. With nowhere else to go, he turned to face the crowd of staring strangers. Almost all wore the same expression of quiet disapproval.

The few royal women's dresses looked like ornate, upside-down tea-cups that a grandmother would keep on a dusty shelf. The crimson of their pouting lips seemed too brilliant to be real, their skin too colorless to be worn by someone still living. The men looked especially thin next to the women's poufy dresses, but no less decorative—their shoulders narrow, their faces pale and fragile-looking.

The loud knocking of a staff against the stones brought Corbin's head around sharply. "Let the coronation of the king begin!" a man bellowed from the back of the room.

"Coronation?" Corbin whispered to no one.

A man wearing a tall, pointed hat and gold-embroidered robes emerged from behind the crowd and walked until he stood in front of the throne. A young boy appeared at the priest's elbow, holding an elaborate, bejeweled crown on a purple pillow.

Corbin glanced around the room, looking for support, then back at the priest. "I'm sorry, but I didn't know about this part. I don't know if I can handle becoming a husband *and* a king in one day."

"Handle?" The priest said quietly, an eyebrow raised. "This is not something one *handles*. This is a great honor. Besides, the princess cannot marry a commoner."

"Please. I am not fit to be a king. There are laws, rules, diplomacy, royal . . . things . . . I have absolutely no . . ."

The crowd's dissatisfaction suddenly took on new meaning. They weren't just irritated that this commoner was marrying the princess, they were outraged he would soon rule over them.

The tension was suddenly eased by a voice coming from behind Corbin. "Father Goode, if I may." Footsteps approached from the direction of the voice, and Corbin turned to face the man who had been giving orders at the Gift Giving.

"I think we need to consider what is being asked of this man. I am *certain* he appreciates the great honor it is to be married to the princess and to rule by her side, and I think we should be grateful that the princess, in her great wisdom and foresight, has chosen such a man. Think of it! A man who doesn't *want* to be king! Why, it's extraordinary! I propose that we give him some time. Perhaps just crown him, say, prince today, and then king when he's ready. A prince is just a king in training, after all. I can certainly see the wisdom in this. Can't you?"

After a moment of inaudible mumbling to himself, his face troubled and thoughtful, Father Goode answered. "Very well."

The man clapped Corbin on the shoulder before Corbin could look away from the priest and his grave expression. "Prince Corbin it is!"

Corbin was grateful for this turn of events. The priest smiled reluctantly and turned to the boy. "The smaller crown, if you please."

The boy reappeared a moment later with a smaller, though still ornamented and elaborate crown and the coronation began. The priest spoke entirely in some unknown language, but Corbin didn't mind at all. He didn't want to know the words. He felt like a fool—an imposter—kneeling on the stone floor, his black-stained, white-gloved hands fiddling with the hem of his coat.

The strange, foreign droning ended and the priest turned, lifted the crown off the pillow, and placed it on Corbin's head. The weight of it seemed to lower him several inches into the stones.

"Behold! His Royal Highness, Prince Corbin of Laurel!"

CHAPTER 9

A few people clapped, but most just stood in disbelieving silence. "Prince Corbin," Father Goode said in a low, urgent voice to Corbin who still knelt on the floor, "take your position seriously. Learn all you can. Grow into this responsibility. This kingdom needs a ruler."

Before Corbin could respond, the guard in the back of the room knocked his staff against the stones once more. Father Goode tugged on Corbin's sleeve, pulling him to his feet.

The room became impossibly still for a moment, until, emerging from behind the crowd, a bouquet of roses held in her slender fingers, stood Princess Rose. A few breathless maids held the train of her ivory gown, and as Rose began her walk down the aisle, they let go of the hem, letting it fall gracefully behind her to the floor. The musicians began playing a new melody as she moved forward—more grand and majestic than Corbin's subdued tune.

Unable to meet her eyes, Corbin instead watched the tips of her shoes take turns peeking out from under her hem. She walked briskly, and the small orchestra increased their tempo to try to match her pace.

Too soon and rather abruptly, she came to a stop—at least two arm lengths away from Corbin. He knew she was called a beast, but as he worked on gathering his courage to look into the face of the woman he was about to marry, all he could see in his mind was the beautiful, hopeful expression she wore when he gave her the rose. He had seen no beast when he looked into her eyes. And whatever she had seen in him had made her accept his gift. He prayed that whatever he had felt and seen in those few seconds would be what he felt and saw when he looked at her now.

Swallowing hard, he forced his eyes away from her now hidden toes to the billowing ivory skirts and to the bouquet she held in her hands. He felt his eyebrows furrow when he looked at it more closely. Her bouquet was comprised of thirteen dried, shriveled roses with one brilliant red rose in the center. It was an ugly display of decay, except for the new rose, and an uneasy knot settled in the pit of Corbin's stomach at the sight.

His eyes traveled away from the dusty bunch of withered roses to the neckline of her dress adorned with pearls, to the tight line of her mouth, and finally to her scrutinizing eyes. The soft, almost yearning expression from when she had taken the rose was nowhere to be seen. Corbin had hoped to see that expression, hoped that it would remind him of how he felt when he had first seen her. Unfortunately, The Beast standing before him tainted the memory.

Corbin could see her red hair through the intricate lace of her veil. The pink in her cheeks would have been lovely if it wasn't a flame of what looked like loathing that caused them to burn. As he looked more closely at her face, Corbin could now see a particular sadness behind the scrutiny in her fiercely green eyes. Was she as bewildered as he was by this absurd situation she had created, that it had gone this far? Did her stubbornness, pride, and thirst for revenge—notorious throughout at least three king-doms—prevent her from calling it all off?

Father Goode opened his enormous bible and began speaking in the same, droning language he had during the coronation. The white cravat at Corbin's throat suddenly felt like it was choking him, his shoes felt like they were pinching his feet, and he didn't know what to do with his hands.

Rose sighed every now and then, her gaze wandering around the room almost as if she were counting the stones. After an agonizingly long time, the stones failed to hold her vague attention, and she met Corbin's eyes. Finally, she spoke, but not to him.

"That's enough," she said, looking toward Father Goode. "You're speaking in Latin. *He*," she gestured to Corbin with the roses she held in her hand, "doesn't even know what language you're speaking, and I don't care what you're saying anyway. Get on with it."

Corbin's wide eyes glanced from Rose to the priest and to the few guests he could see off to his side. He was stunned, but it seemed he was the only one. All the guests had shrunk closer to each other and to the walls, but that was the only difference in the room.

"Yes, Your Highness," the priest said. Father Goode turned to Corbin, his hand that clutched the Bible trembling slightly. "Do you, Prince Corbin, take Princess Rose . . ."

As soon as he spoke Corbin's name, Princess Rose rolled her eyes. Corbin knew what she was thinking. For the past year, she had been engaged to Prince Kenton—a real prince of a royal bloodline—and now she was marrying a blacksmith who happened to be wearing a crown. Well, she wanted a commoner and she got one.

Corbin didn't realize Father Goode had finished his question until the room fell completely silent, every disbelieving ear waiting for his answer.

"I do," Corbin whispered. As he said the words, Rose met his eyes and some of her irritation seemed to dissipate. Her eyes narrowed slightly, but a softness touched the corners of her mouth.

Princess Rose said her slightly defeated "I do" when it was her turn, her listless eyes on the priest.

Finally, they were declared man and wife. No applause disturbed the silence for a long moment, and when it eventually broke out, it was hesitant and awkward. No smiles warmed anyone's face. Everyone wore a not-so-subtle hint of uncertainty on their faces. Except for three.

The man who had helped Corbin out of being crowned king stood clapping and smiling in approval. He bowed when Corbin met his eye.

Mrs. Whiting beamed, a tender sheen of tears in her eyes. Her gaze went from the princess to Corbin and back again with an expression of deep satisfaction, her hands clasped underneath her chin.

The last face Corbin looked at was the princess's. There was a gleam in her eyes too, though it wasn't accompanied by the joy that had been in Mrs. Whiting's eyes. On the contrary, the princess wore an expression of such deep despair, such profound distress that Corbin felt the breath whoosh out of his lungs.

She was an enigma, to say the least. She wanted to marry a commoner and she had. And she had chosen the most common one of all. If he had been her choice, why did she stand off to the side, her misty eyes staring at nothing?

"Princess Rose and Prince Corbin!" The royal man shouted just as the applause was beginning to die down. Like a wagon wheel struggling to roll again from a stop, the cheering recommenced and Corbin sighed. Would this day ever end? The man with the apron was clapping his ladle on his opposite hand and glancing in the direction that Corbin assumed were the kitchens. A maid yawned, daintily covering her mouth with the backs of her fingers.

Corbin couldn't take any more if this. He attempted a smile, failed, and began walking toward the back of the room. Then, he stopped. As perplexing and ludicrous as it was, he was now a married man, and a prince. He didn't know anything about the duties, responsibilities, and the expectations that were now heaped upon him. He didn't know this woman who was now his wife, but he did know that he shouldn't leave her standing there, unescorted, as he walked back down the aisle.

He stepped closer to her and offered her his arm. She looked at him, her eyes mocking and so full of disdain that the last remnants of Corbin's patience burned away. He dropped his arm back to his side as the clapping died and the room hushed to silence.

Princess Rose faced the crowd, her chin lifted in defiance. She wrenched the veil off her head and stomped down the aisle, pulling off bracelets and earrings, leaving a glittering, fluffy trail of white behind her. She never dropped the roses.

She turned around the corner and was gone, and with her, the hostility that had permeated the room throughout the entire ceremony. A weighty fatigue hovered over Corbin. Just being in her presence was exhausting. And when she left, the energy didn't return. She had taken it all.

Corbin stood alone, wishing for nothing more than sleep. Even more than escape, even more than answers, he wanted sleep. A clap on his back tensed his already strained muscles, and Corbin turned to face the man who had come to his aid moments earlier.

"Congratulations, Prince Corbin. This is a historic day." The man's slicked back brown hair and matching goatee stood out against the regal whiteness of his skin. His pale blue eyes smiled merrily.

Corbin forced a small smile onto his face. "I suppose *historic* is as good a word as any. Though *disastrous* might be more appropriate."

"On the contrary. I think this day has marked a turning point in the somewhat sad history of the last, oh, ten years for our kingdom."

Grateful he had taken the time to ask Mrs. Whiting for a little information about his bride, Corbin knew that the man was referring to when the king and queen died. Perhaps that would explain at least some of Rose's displeasure with this day—her parents weren't there to witness it. But based on how she felt about marrying Corbin, he would think that their absence would be more of a relief.

The man nodded gravely, giving Corbin time to let everything sink in. "We haven't had any true rulers in Laurel since that dreadful day. Rose was still a child when they died and never tried to fill their shoes. I've helped where I can, but I was still a young man myself and . . . well, let's not dwell on that. This is a celebration! There is a feast prepared. There hasn't been one in this castle for ages! I don't know if you're feeling up to it. It looks like the princess has retired, but if you want to mingle with some fellow royals, this is your chance. They probably won't be back any time soon. They're mostly here just for appearances and loyalty to the late king and queen, anyway . . ."

"I don't think so." Corbin felt the blood drain from his face as he imagined sitting in a room with these royal people who, besides this man, all seemed to hate him.

"Understandable. Get some rest. Oh, and my name is Lord Stanford, Chief Governor. I live in the Governor's House at the opposite end of the castle grounds. I don't venture into the castle much . . ." he spoke out of the corner of his mouth. "It's just a little too beastly in here, if you know what I mean." He returned to a regular volume. "But I'll be near if you need anything." He began to walk away and then turned back, a sympathetic smile on his face. "And don't worry about your blushing bride. No one has ever been able to tame her."

Corbin wasn't sure if that comment was supposed to comfort or challenge him, but he was too tired to care. A touch on his arm turned him away from Lord Stanford and to Mrs. Whiting.

"We can send you up some food if you'd rather not eat with everyone else."

"I'm not really hungry, thank you." Corbin's stomach grumbled.

She nodded and smiled. "Let's show you to your room then, shall we?" Some maids appeared at her side, and Mrs. Whiting whispered some orders before they disappeared. She looked up at Corbin. "Your room is almost ready. I just need to check on how dinner is going and I'll be right back. You wait here."

Everyone had already filed out of the Throne Room—the maids, guards, and royals. Corbin stood alone in the cavernous Great Hall—a married man, a prince. The crown poked his head through his hair.

An unexpected, disbelieving smile crept across his face. Rose had acted exactly the way he had wanted to, though he would never allow himself. He imagined stomping out of the room, a trail of buttons, embroidery, and silk behind him.

But just as quickly as it had come, the smile died on his lips. That was his wife. The woman he was doomed to spend the rest of his life with. She had stomped down the aisle, leaving her new husband alone in this strange castle in a room full of unfamiliar faces. She had no compassion, no benevolence.

She truly was a beast.

CHAPTER 10

Corbin strode out of the room, certain he could find his bedchamber without Mrs. Whiting's help. He opened door after door, but was met with only empty, dusty rooms, and his searching soon became wandering. The unfriendly, vast corridors seemed to stretch for miles. There were countless stairways—some so narrow it felt as if the breath was being squeezed out of his lungs, and others so wide he could have placed his entire blacksmith shop on top of them.

Hundreds of windows lined the walls, some tall and ornate and embellished with stained glass that colored the moonlight and bathed the stones. Others were plain and drafty, letting the biting night air seep in and roam the corridors and seek out Corbin's bare neck.

The entire castle seemed void of life and comfort. The stones were unyielding and cold, the few paintings on the wall depicting people who looked down on him with severe, dissatisfied eyes.

Finally, after what seemed like hours, Corbin found a stone window seat and sat down. He bent over and removed one of his shoes from his aching feet, and when he looked around, realized he hadn't been in this part of the castle yet.

A swift click-clacking of heels on the stones announced someone's arrival—a woman by the sound of it. Corbin quickly replaced his shoe and stood, dreading to meet the eyes of The Beast who would very soon be rounding the corner.

Corbin couldn't contain the sigh of relief when Mrs. Whiting appeared before him.

"Prince Corbin! There you are! You poor thing. Were you lost?"

Corbin smiled down at her slanting, kind eyes. Her tone made him feel like a helpless child, but also strangely comforted.

"Please, call me Corbin, Mrs. Whiting. And yes . . . I was lost." Corbin stood and stifled a yawn.

"Come along with me, *Prince* Corbin." She grinned back at him with a mischievous smile. "Miraculously, you showed up right where you were supposed to be." She walked only a few feet and stopped abruptly in front of a door, pushing it open. "Here is your bedchamber."

Corbin's eyes widened as he took in the grandeur of the room. A fireplace took up half of the wall to his left, and an enormous bed took up the opposite wall to his right. A huge, brown bearskin rug filled the area in between, with the head—and teeth—still attached. A dozen windows lined the wall across from him, and two grand wardrobes fit snugly in the far corners. Three large candelabras with candles already lit brightened the room. A tray of food sat on a table next to the fireplace. Just looking at this room made Corbin sleepy, and he didn't stifle the next yawn that overtook him.

"This has been the bedchamber of princes and kings for hundreds of years," Mrs. Whiting said. Corbin was grateful that she hadn't mentioned princesses and queens. It appeared that the Laurel monarchs had their own bedchambers.

This was a ridiculous room for a blacksmith, which he would always consider himself, even with that absurd crown on his head. If he had been less tired, he might have put up a fight, demanding a smaller room, but the bed looked more inviting than anything he had ever seen, and his aching body and drooping eyes decided to save that fight for another day. If at all. The cold that had seeped through the corridors on his meandering search melted off of his fingers, ears, and neck and was replaced with a warm weariness.

Footsteps approached from behind, and Mrs. Whiting and Corbin turned to see an old man enter the room, carrying some more firewood. "Pardon me, Your Highness. I'll just feed the fire a bit before bed."

Mrs. Whiting smiled in satisfaction. "Right, then. It looks like you're all taken care of, my little prince. Arthur, here, will get you settled. If you need anything, just ring." She gestured to the tasseled bell pull by the bed, curtsied, and ducked out of the room.

"Almost done, Your Highness, then you can get some rest." Arthur knelt down in front of the fireplace.

"Please, call me Corbin." *Your Highness* had never sounded more laughable on Corbin's ears. How was he any higher than this man?

"I cannot, Your Highness," Arthur replied as he began placing the wood on the dying flames.

"Here, let me do that," Corbin said, reaching his hands toward the pile of logs.

"I have been instructed to not allow you to help me."

Corbin thought for a second, a scheming grin on his face. "Aren't princes allowed to do anything they want?"

"I was told that when you said that I was supposed to say *no.*" He turned away from Corbin and finished feeding the fire.

"Who has been telling you all of this?"

Arthur only smirked and nodded toward the open door where Mrs. Whiting had just exited. Resigned, Corbin huffed out an exasperated breath, removed the crown from his aching head, and gently tossed it on the bed. He began trying to loosen his cravat, but it seemed to only get tighter. He had never felt more useless. Actually, he had never felt useless in his life at all. He had always been needed for something—in his shop, around town, helping his parents and friends. And now, not only was he not allowed to start his own fire, a task he had performed more than anyone in this entire castle, he couldn't even untie his cravat. How had Mrs. Whiting tied this? Was it just a million knots on top of each other? Corbin had tied and loosened knots his whole life, and now this ridiculous, royal knot was trying to strangle him. When Francine had tied his cravat, he was able to loosen it with one swift, angry motion the moment he had left the ball in Claire.

"Allow me, Your Highness. We can't have you strangling yourself on your wedding night, now can we? Most improper." Arthur stood, brushed off his hands, and walked over to where Corbin stood.

He let his arms fall to his sides, knowing he wouldn't win and knowing he needed help anyway, unless he was going to die in this suit. While Arthur worked on loosening the cravat, Corbin got to work on trying to pry the cufflinks off with his teeth.

Arthur clicked his tongue in mild rebuke. "Please, Your Highness. I'll get to those in a moment. Those cufflinks have been worn by three generations of Laurel kings."

Just then, Corbin heard the squeak of rusty hinges as a door was pushed open. He turned to face his chamber door, only it hadn't moved. He spun to look behind him and saw that a conjoining door was slowly opening—a door he hadn't noticed because it had been obscured by bed curtains when he had surveyed the room. Corbin turned back around quickly when the firelight caught the flaming hair that was emerging from behind the door. Immediately, Arthur ceased his work and rushed to the door that led to the corridor.

"Royalty . . . commoners . . . strange . . ." Arthur mumbled to himself before closing the door behind him. Corbin hoped Arthur would return to help with the infernal cufflinks, or at least be understanding when he found teeth marks on them.

Placing his hands in his pockets, Corbin turned to face The Beast. She stood in the doorway that joined their two rooms, wearing a nightgown and wrapper, her hair in a braid that draped over one shoulder.

"In case you get any . . . *indecorous* notions, I should tell you that I will be locking my door."

"Very well. I don't know what *indecorous* means, so I don't think you need to worry." Corbin tried to smile through his confusion and fatigue.

The stranger that Corbin was supposed to be married to glared at him through the emerald slits that were her eyes. He had heard her speak only a handful of words, each one more perplexing than the last. These eyes that glared at him now had looked on him with softness only a few hours before. Her hands that had gently taken the rose out of his hand were now in white-knuckled fists on her hips.

What had he done to displease her? He had gone to the Gift Giving, given her the rose that she had chosen, and then married her. Yes, it was to avoid his own hanging, and he never imagined she would accept his rose, but he hadn't escaped like the others. He hadn't been disrespectful or even afraid. Had he been too numbed by the pain of losing Francine to feel any of those things? Should he have run when he had the chance?

He thought back to the gentleness that had been in her eyes when she saw the rose, the expression that made the world go quiet and still his racing thoughts. Had he imagined it? Was it his own hope that he saw reflected in this stranger's eyes, and not hers?

A million more questions filled his mind, but as she reached behind her for the latch, he asked the most vital one.

"Why did you choose me?" Corbin held his breath, not wanting to disturb the silence as he waited.

Her gaze faltered for a moment, and her haughtiness faded just long enough for Corbin to see it. But when she met his eyes again, it was with a look of bored indifference.

"Because."

The corner of her mouth twitched in defiance and the breath whooshed out of his lungs. He opened his mouth to demand a real answer, but she simply lifted the corner of her nightgown, curtsied, and closed the door behind her. Corbin heard the timber bar being dropped heavily onto the bar hole.

Arthur never returned, but Corbin managed to get the rest of his ridiculous suit off, even figuring out how to remove the cufflinks without using his teeth. He was sure that three generations of Laurel kings looked down on him in gratitude. Corbin tried to sleep in the bed, but the mattress was too soft, and he found himself longing for his thin, lumpy cot back at home. Finally, he pulled the blankets off the bed and dragged them in front of the fire. Lying down on the bearskin rug, Corbin slept soundly, having nothing to dream of.

CHAPTER 11

E very morning before this one, it had been the coldness of dawn that had woken Corbin. The fact that he was still warm in the morning reminded him that he was very far from home. The thick, wool blanket that was wrapped around him and the bear head he used as a pillow were also fairly obvious clues. Corbin rolled from his side onto his back. The candles in the candelabras above him had been snuffed out sometime in the night. The fireplace still had hints of heat that trickled out into the room and made his eyes feel sleepy and his body heavy.

Soon, though, curiosity forced Corbin to face the day. He stood, dropped the blanket on the bed as he passed, and saw that the crown had been placed on a dignified pedestal between the two wardrobes. Since the rising sun was on the opposite side of the castle, he couldn't tell how high it was, but judging by the hazy lavender of the sky, he knew it must still be early.

Crossing the icy stones, Corbin opened one of the wardrobes, and to his dismay—but not surprise—saw that it was filled with clothes that were stiff, royal, and ridiculous. He opened the doors of the other wardrobe, which contained dozens of starched cravats, handkerchiefs, and polished shoes ornamented with jeweled buckles. Though, he did smile when he saw a box filled with thick, wool socks on a low shelf in the wardrobe and pulled a pair onto his now-frozen feet.

With warm toes, Corbin felt a peculiar optimism for this new day and new life. Any place that could provide thick, wool socks couldn't be so bad. He hoped.

He turned in the direction of the conjoining door and remembered the thud of the beam locking the door on The Beast's side. Corbin wondered if she were sleeping, but he couldn't imagine it. It seemed too tranquil an activity for someone so full of fury. But his curiosity got the better of him and he found himself tiptoeing to the conjoining door, grateful the floors were stone and didn't creak. There were no sounds coming from her side, and Corbin backed away quickly and silently.

Smoothing out the fur of the bear skin rug with his foot, he resigned himself to the fact that he couldn't walk around the palace in his breaches all day. He scrunched up his face as he imagined putting on any of the clothes in the wardrobe, especially tying one of those infuriating cravats. His old clothes must be somewhere, unless someone had them burned, which wouldn't surprise him. Still, it was worth investigating . . . if no one really was awake yet.

Corbin felt slightly foolish, though a bit rebellious, as he opened the door and peeked his head out. He was bare above the waist—his burn scars on his torso and arms glaring in the filtered sunlight. He risked a step into the corridor and looked in both directions. Seeing no one, he risked another step and then another. And then stopped.

Sitting on a window seat directly across from The Beast's room was a woman—a young, plain woman in a maid's dress. Her eyes were closed, and a tiny trickle of drool by her mouth shone in the morning sun. Corbin thought it a strange place to take a nap, especially at this odd hour, but he thought nothing more of it. He had to find some clothes before anyone awoke.

Tiptoeing unnecessarily across the stones, Corbin sneaked past the sleeping woman. As he inched down the corridor, the unmistakable and familiar scent of lye wafted through a crack in one of the doors.

Corbin opened the door, wincing at the low groaning that penetrated the silence. He didn't close the door behind him, not wanting to risk any more noise. The smell of lye grew stronger and with it, Corbin's hope for regular clothes. The only thing behind the door was a narrow stairway, and Corbin descended it quickly.

A wall greeted him at the bottom of the stairs, and Corbin saw that to his left was what must be the linen washing room. A large bin filled the middle of the room, surrounded by smaller buckets, with steam billowing out of each one. Heat poured into the room from a fire roaring in the fireplace, a large black kettle splattering boiling water on the rush-strewn floor. Water filled his eyes as he entered the room. He blinked and once his vision cleared, he saw a sight that he never would have imagined would bring him such overwhelming joy and relief. His clothes.

They were cleaned and pressed and hanging on a line across the room. Corbin hurried over to them, yanked them off the line, and put them on. The stains from his former life still claimed them, the burn hole on the sleeve unrepaired. On the floor next to the wall sat his boots. He pulled them on, the leather supple and comforting. For the first time since the morning before, he felt more like his normal, common self.

Laughter and the cheerful sound of young women's voices entered the room through the open windows. Still standing far away from the window, Corbin craned his neck to glance outside. Trudging up the hill, buckets of water being carried on poles across their shoulders, was a line of maids. Corbin ducked out of the room and flew up the stairs to the corridor.

The sun was slightly higher now, and the sleeping girl at the window had disappeared. Corbin sat on the seat and looked out over the palace grounds as well as he could through the stained glass. He thought about what Mrs. Whiting had said—that a little Princess Rose had ordered that all the rose bushes be ripped out of the ground. He decided to ask Mrs. Whiting what she had been about to say about Rose's father. He hoped he could try to piece together the puzzle that was his new wife.

Corbin pulled his gaze away from the window and looked down each end of the vacant corridor. There were no sounds, no voices. He thought of his friends back home. He tried to picture the shock on Will Hawkins's face when he found out Corbin was married, and to The Beast, no less. He tried to imagine the expression that would be on Francine's face. Would she be shocked? Hurt? Relieved? Jealous?

A fresh pang of agony ripped through Corbin's chest as he pictured Francine's face, the way she used to gaze up at him. He had always felt like a prince in her presence . . . until an actual prince came along.

Across the corridor, behind a heavy oak door, slept the woman he had married yesterday. Corbin rested an arm on the windowsill and his chin on his hand. Married. What had he been thinking?

He ran his fingers through his hair. A terrible, heavy feeling overwhelmed him as he imagined waking up in the silent, empty castle every day for the rest of his life, sleeping next door to a beast.

He stood. He needed to move. After walking down the corridor, and another, and another, he found the grand staircase. At the bottom of the steps, past the Great Hall and the Grand Foyer, were the doors that led to the outside world. Either all the guards from the day before were still sleeping, or they weren't needed anymore now that the coronation and wedding were over. Whatever the reason, there was no one there to prevent Corbin from leaving.

He ran down the steps, crossed the ancient stones, and as he passed by the Throne Room, saw that there were now two thrones at the other end of the room. Eager to leave that room behind, he continued running until he came to a stop in front of two great mahogany doors. His fingers wrapped around one of the handles, the shape of it making him pause.

The graceful curve of it, the sturdiness and practicality—it looked exactly like a holdfast. He thought of the one he had just made and had been forced to leave at his new shop only the day before. He had used holdfasts every day before this one as he worked at the anvil to hold his work in place, and now this handle seemed to serve the same purpose. It anchored him. His choice had been made and he would not go back on it now. He smiled at the strange irony—that he could find anything here that reminded him of home—and that it could somehow convince him to stay.

He pulled the thick, heavy handle of the door and closed it with an ominous thud. Heading east to the other side of the castle, he finally reached another set of heavy doors and pushed them open.

Pulling his collar up higher on his neck, Corbin stepped out into the morning. The air was cool and invigorating, the dew dripping from the grass and catching the sun. The sun's rays warmed everything they touched, unlike inside the castle where the walls absorbed the very hope of heat.

Corbin crossed the gardens, which were overrun with wild grasses, the hedges overgrown. The brownness of dying trees and bushes spotted the landscape with ugliness and decay. Corbin bent down, close to one of the now-empty planters where the roses had once blossomed. Stepping closer, he found a littering of dried thorns in the soil.

Brushing off his knees, Corbin stood and made his way over to the stable and peered inside. The familiar scents of hay and leather filled the air, but that was it. No whinnying horses. No lazy flies. The stable stood empty and lonely. Horses had pulled the carriages the day before. Where were they now?

His face falling slightly, Corbin continued on to the other buildings behind the stables. The first one he came to appeared to be where the hunters would bring animals to be skinned and the leather to be treated.

There were long, dull blades and dozens of hooks hanging from the wall. The next shop held all kinds of dilapidated wood-working tools. Half-finished chairs sat in a corner, and a few rusty tools lay scattered on work benches. The shavings on the ground were covered in dust, their fresh, woody smell absent. Corbin entered the third building that must have once been an armory. Pegs and shelves lined the walls, and a broken, tarnished sword leaned against a corner.

The last building was the farthest one away from the castle. A thick lock prevented Corbin's entrance, and the windows were too thick and dusty to see into the darkness inside, though he was certain it was another shop like the others. There was another building, bigger and in better repair than these shops, at the other end of the grounds. The Chief Governor's house.

What had happened? Where was everyone? The stables sat empty, work left unfinished, buildings locked up. Except for the dozen or so maids, the necessary guards, cooks, and housekeepers, this castle screamed neglect and abandonment.

Corbin's stomach grumbled. Being out in the sunshine had made him almost forget the helplessness he felt in this new situation. His spirits had lifted as he breathed in the fresh air. But the thought of returning to the confining stones of the palace walls reawakened his feelings of despair.

But he would have to eat sometime. After finding a sad little broom and using a moth-eaten piece of cloth for a rag, Corbin cleaned up the three open shops as a way of delaying the inevitable. He promised himself that he would break the lock of the last shop whenever he returned and plodded back to the castle. He looked up at the towering walls as he approached and had to admit it was quite impressive, at least from the outside. The brilliant sun illuminated and enlivened the colors of the stained glass windows. Majestic towers stood as sentries at every corner, and evenly spaced flank towers dotted the tops of every immense wall. Battlements lined the north and south, while a covered parapet walk lined the east and west, secured by an iron rail and stone pillars.

As Corbin took in the majesty of his new residence, a flash of red hair stood out against the monotony of the stones. The Beast's gaze pierced him even from four stories up, her hands gripping the rail in front of her, her body leaning forward in what looked like longing. She stood motionless until their eyes met. At that moment, she spun away quickly, rounded the corner, and disappeared down the open parapet.

Shrugging, Corbin continued walking until he passed a well pump at the edge of the garden. He stopped to pump some water onto his hands, and ended up sticking his entire head and neck in the flow of water. After raking his fingers through his hair, ridding it of most of the excess water, he continued toward the palace.

A guard stood waiting at the door, and he opened it when Corbin approached.

"I promise I can open the door on my own," Corbin said with a sigh and a roll of his eyes. The guard responded by looking straight ahead.

The water dripped off Corbin's hair and soaked the shoulders of his tattered shirt. He stopped as soon as he entered the castle, realizing he had no idea where he could find some food. He was just about to ask the nearest guard when Mrs. Whiting appeared from around a corner. If she felt any dissatisfaction in Corbin's appearance, she didn't mention it. She did, however, cross her arms in gentle rebuke.

"We've been looking everywhere for you, you know."

"Oh, I'm sorry. Everyone was still asleep when I got up, so I went to explore a bit."

"Yes, we know that now." She smiled. "So, you're an early riser, are you? Well, that makes two of us. I'm sorry I missed you when you awoke. I was down in the kitchens. I thought you'd have liked to sleep late after your long day yesterday, but we'll be prepared from now on. Please forgive us." She began walking and waved a hand, motioning for Corbin to follow her. "I wish I could say that Princess Rose is an early riser, but I haven't seen her before noon in ages. Now that she has someone else to occupy her days with, I hope she'll wake earlier."

Corbin couldn't share her hope. He wasn't exactly enthusiastic about the prospect of occupying The Beast's days. A wave of gloom overcame him as he imagined spending the rest of his life being married to a woman he only saw at dinner, sleeping in a separate bedroom, walking alone, talking to guards and servants who weren't allowed to answer back. Suddenly, he understood why Rose slept until noon every day. What was the point of waking up?

"Mrs. Whiting, where is everyone? I mean, why have all the shops been closed up and the gardens neglected? Where are all the horses that pulled the carriages yesterday?"

Mrs. Whiting nodded, seeming to expect his questions. "The carriages are stored away and the horses were borrowed from town. The unnecessary guards were sent home, only being summoned as needed.

Yes, this castle used to be full of life and industry. We do the best we can, of course, but things aren't the same. We don't have nearly as many servants here as before the king and queen died. They simply aren't needed. Most of the rooms are locked up; no one visits. I'm afraid the work that used to be done in those shops just isn't important anymore. The gardens used to be Princess Rose's favorite place to play. She used to ride the horses with her parents. But now . . ." Mrs. Whiting let the unspoken words dangle in the heavy, ancient air.

"Can you tell me now what you were going to say yesterday about the king? What he would do every spring?"

Mrs. Whiting opened her mouth and then closed it, a thoughtful expression softening her eyes. "I would love to tell you, my dear. But I think that's something Princess Rose should tell you."

Corbin frowned. He couldn't imagine having an actual conversation with that woman, especially not about her late father. She had ordered a whole garden of roses to be ripped out and burned when her parents died. Would she rip Corbin's head off if he had the audacity to ask her anything about them?

Mrs. Whiting led Corbin to a dining hall where a plate of food sat waiting on a polished walnut table. With a nod, she left Corbin to devour his lunch—roast beef and onions and three fist-sized rolls. He ate in silence, trying to shake the feeling that he was being watched. His neck tingled, but he resisted the urge to turn around. He felt like the very walls watched him, the windows listened, and that the stones whispered as he walked by.

Once he was so full he was sure he wouldn't have to be bothered with eating ever again, Corbin wandered around the castle, trying to orient himself. Unfortunately, after a few turns, Corbin was lost once again. Though, he did find some treasures in his wanderings. He discovered the Armory that the maid had pointed out on his hasty tour of the castle. It was filled with fascinating weapons—crossbows, maces, and swords. This armory was grander than the little shop outside. The shop stored common weapons—ones that were used to hunt small animals—or once had. This was where weapons of war were kept, or displayed might be more appropriate. Corbin lightly ran his fingers along the dull edges of the blades, the blunt tips of the arrows, and wished he could spend just one day in his shop repairing the neglected weapons.

A few floors up in the opposite wing, Corbin found another interesting room filled with what appeared to be statues of oddly-shaped ghosts.

As he got closer, Corbin could see that they were musical instruments covered in white sheets. He carefully lifted the dusty sheets and found two pianofortes, a pipe organ, a harpsichord, lutes, violins . . . Every instrument Corbin had ever seen, and many he hadn't.

After he covered each instrument back up, he quietly exited the room. He was just closing the door when the familiar sensation of being watched sent a chill down his neck. He turned toward the feeling, and at the end of the corridor stood The Beast. Her face was accusatory, her lips a tight line, and her eyes blazing. Corbin's face burned and he dropped his gaze to the floor.

Her anger heated the cold corridor as she marched toward him.

"Do not ever enter this room." She didn't speak in words, but more like a hiss of sounds. "No one ever enters this room. This room was my moth—" She closed her mouth, her lips white.

Reaching around Corbin, she yanked the door closed, and as she did so, the handle pulled right out of the rotting wood. She stared at the handle, her eyes and mouth wide, then looked all around her for somewhere to put it. There was no place for her to deposit the handle, and her face colored all the way to her hairline—the different hues of red creating an unexpectedly comical contrast.

Corbin held out his hand, his lips twitching, though Rose didn't meet his eyes. She dropped the handle in his hand, spun around, and stomped off in the opposite direction.

"Are there any other rooms you don't want me to enter?" Amusement lightened Corbin's voice. She made no reply, but steadily moved as far away from him as possible. "I'll just look for doors without handles and let that be my answer, then."

Corbin laughed softly to himself, but as she disappeared out of sight, he instantly sobered. It wasn't really all that funny.

CHAPTER 12

Mrs. Whiting found Corbin just in time to change for dinner, despite his best efforts. No matter how lost he tried to be, he kept being found.

"Mrs. Whiting," Corbin said, trying not to plead as she led him to his chamber, "I eat just fine in my normal clothes."

"My dear little prince, I don't doubt it, but a little decorum never hurt anyone."

"Not yet," Corbin mumbled, and he saw Mrs. Whiting's cheek lift in a small smile.

Arthur stood waiting outside Corbin's chamber, and Mrs. Whiting left Corbin in his care. As Arthur tied the cravat around Corbin's neck, Corbin couldn't help sticking a finger in the knot to loosen it a bit.

"Please, Your Highness. There is nothing worse than a limp cravat. Nothing."

Corbin was about to laugh when he saw the gravity in Arthur's eyes, and coughed instead. "All right, then. Since I'm doomed to wear cravats, can you show me how to tie my own?"

"No, Your Highness. That is what I'm here for."

"Yes, I understand that. But it would feel much better to me if I at least knew how to tie it myself, and that I was simply *allowing* you to help me, instead of *needing* you to help me."

Arthur chuckled, deep wrinkles creasing his eyes. "Very good, Your Highness." He lowered his voice as if to talk to himself, though he was only inches away from Corbin. "*Allowing* me to help . . . I'll just let him think that . . ." He then proceeded to demonstrate how to tie a cravat knot.

After a few tries, Corbin had his cravat tied to Arthur's high standards.

"Excellent, Your Majesty. Perfection!" Arthur didn't attempt to hide his surprise as he turned away to hang up the rest of the unused cravats once Corbin had his tied.

Corbin grinned. "Thank you."

Arthur spun around in surprise as Corbin spoke, but smiled warmly. "Not at all, Your Majesty." He walked over to the pedestal where the crown sat. "And now for your crown."

"No, thank you. I'm going to save that for . . . special occasions." Which meant *no* occasions.

Arthur shot Corbin a disapproving look, but thankfully didn't argue. As Arthur gathered up clothing and socks, Corbin heard his quiet mutterings. ". . . wants to tie his own cravat . . . says *thank you* . . . won't wear his crown . . . strange . . ." With one last slow shake of his wispy white head, Arthur exited the room.

As soon as Arthur left, the sudden sound of an angry Princess Rose reverberated through their shared wall. Corbin couldn't hear every word, but it was apparent that The Beast wasn't quite pleased with something, to say the least.

Corbin couldn't help remembering that when Francine was displeased, she would sulk in silence for as long as she deemed appropriate for the situation. He had to admit he hadn't always cared for Francine's mood swings and occasional brooding resentment, but now, as he stood listening to the woman he was now married to, silent sulking seemed quite preferable.

The Beast's voice rose in volume and Corbin had no problem hearing every word.

"I told you I'm wearing the blue dress!"

"But my princess, this is your first meal with the new prince and you look so beautiful in the green dress." The maid's voice quivered, but there was a note of quiet determination.

"Do you think I want to look beautiful for a *blacksmith* who hates me?" The Beast's rage practically vibrated the door.

Corbin took the opportunity to escape to the dining room while The Beast was preoccupied. He slipped out to the corridor, rushed past the room next to his, took a few wrong turns, and finally found the grand staircase.

A few meandering minutes later, Corbin found the dining room where he had devoured his lonely lunch. But before he could enter, the guard at the door shook his head and motioned to another door. Apparently, every meal was to be eaten in a different room here. Corbin sighed and continued on to the next door where another guard stood waiting.

This door was already opened, and the light streamed out onto the Grand Foyer. As soon as Corbin entered the formal dining room, he was overpowered by a smell that was too much like an algae-covered pond to be even close to appetizing. A table that could have fit fifty people filled the immense room, though only two place settings were on the table—one at the head of the table and the other diagonally across from it to the right. To Corbin's dismay, he saw that The Beast was somehow already seated at the head of the table. He must have taken longer than he thought to find the right room. Looking away from her glaring eyes, Corbin glanced down at the table and cringed at the array of forks and knives and other instruments he had never seen before.

"Forgive me for being late. I got lost . . . and I didn't know about all the different eating rooms."

"*Dining* rooms," Rose said, rolling her eyes and huffing out an exasperated breath. "We don't eat. We dine." She grabbed her napkin from off the table, flicked it with a severe motion of her wrist, and smoothed it onto her lap.

"*You* dine. *I* eat," Corbin mumbled, his mood souring as the pond smell intensified as he sat down.

"We could have *dined* a long time ago if you hadn't taken a leisurely stroll on your way to dinner."

Corbin's face flushed and his eyes narrowed. He fought back the urge to explain again that he had gotten lost, knowing it was no use. "You look lovely tonight. Though, I think *green* would suit you better." Rose's cheeks paled and her eyes widened, and Corbin realized it might have been wise to remain silent. He had never spoken unkindly to a woman before and what little sense of chivalry he possessed prevented him from saying anything further. He had been given glimpses into Rose's beastliness, but that didn't mean he had to become a beast himself.

Corbin looked down at his plate and couldn't help screwing his face up at the bizarre, pinkish, multi-legged creature on his plate. It looked like it was about to get up and run off the table.

"That is called crab." Rose addressed Corbin as if she were speaking to a toddler.

"I know what it is. I've just never had it before," he said, his nose wrinkling at the stale fish smell that hovered around the room.

There was a loud cracking sound, and he looked up to see that a servant was prying open the claws and skinny legs of the crab on Rose's plate with some sort of tool that looked a lot like Corbin's farrier tongs.

Without thinking it through, Corbin addressed Rose as she watched the servant crack open the crab legs. "May I ask you something, Rose? . . . May I call you Rose?"

"Is that your question?" she said, her eyes meeting his for a moment.

Corbin grinned. "No, it's not, actually. But may I?"

Rose shrugged, her gaze back on her plate.

Corbin waited, then realized that was probably as much of an answer as he was going to get. "Rose, if you chose me, I would assume it's because you wanted me here. If I'm wrong, please correct me."

Rose remained still, her unblinking eyes still downcast.

"And if I'm correct in assuming that, my question is why are you treating me like I barged in here and demanded a room next to yours and a place at your table? I think you're forgetting that we were . . . *compelled* into bringing you a gift. I gave you one and you chose it, but it certainly doesn't feel that way. I don't mean to complain; I'm simply curious."

Awkward silence filled the room. Servants shifted on their feet while Corbin looked at Rose, waiting for an answer.

Corbin laced his fingers on the table in front of him. "If you're not ready to answer me yet, that's fine. Just as long as you know that I have these questions and would like them answered at some point is good enough for me. For now."

If Corbin silently hoped that his civility might coerce an answer out of Rose, he was disappointed. When she didn't meet his eyes, Corbin looked up and saw that the servants were all looking at him with wide eyes, their mouths slightly gaping. He faced Rose again.

"All right. Well, may I at least ask what my role is here—what's expected of me?"

Finally, Rose looked up. "Expected of you?"

"Yes. A reason to get up in the morning."

The way Rose stared back vacantly at him made Corbin realize he had asked this of the wrong person. She didn't even know the answer for herself.

Unable to stand the discomfort any longer and resigning himself to the fact that Rose had no intention of answering him, Corbin focused on his food. He picked up the utensils next to his plate.

"No, thank you. I can do this," he said when the servant nearest him offered his help. Corbin wanted to tackle this challenge, especially if it meant he got to use a tool to crack open his food in order to eat it.

Unfortunately, after five minutes of crushing and squeezing the claws and legs with his tongs, Corbin was only able to get a small amount of meat, and what little meat he could salvage was littered with shards of shell. Despite the putrid odor, his mouth watered and his stomach grumbled. He glanced over at Rose and watched, his lips taught with envy, as she lifted a finger-sized piece of meat to her mouth. Determined, Corbin got back to work on his crab and was able to pull a pea-sized amount out of one of the skinny legs. Abandoning his fork, he used his fingers to place the meat on his tongue.

His eyes widened. It tasted like the sweetest, saltiest chicken he had ever eaten, and it absolutely melted in his mouth. He looked up, wanting to share the goodness he had discovered with someone. But Rose was studiously ignoring him and the servants were all watching her, waiting to know what they were needed for next. Corbin, feeling abruptly lonely, resumed prying open the shell with a little more enthusiasm now that he had tasted the goodness inside.

"Butter."

Corbin looked up. Rose had spoken it. Before Corbin even knew what was happening, the servant to her left stepped forward and lifted up a miniature pitcher. The pitcher had been well within Rose's reach, but she hadn't simply reached out and grabbed it. The servant lightly drizzled her plate with melted butter, placed it back on its saucer, and then stepped back.

Corbin puzzled over this as he put the precious now-pebble-sized bits of crab meat into his mouth. He knew Rose slept until noon and was prone to laziness, but this seemed to be something else in addition to laziness.

"Salt," Rose spoke again, only this time, she was looking directly at Corbin, then to a salt shaker right in front of him. Corbin glanced at it and realized she wanted him to give her the salt, or maybe even sprinkle it on her food for her. She wouldn't answer his simple question, and now she was demanding something of him. It was silly and childish, but unexpected anger boiled up inside of Corbin. He was still hungry, though he had been trying to eat for the better part of an hour. No one would look at him, and now this beast was demanding the salt in the most infuriating way.

"Yes, it is salt," Corbin answered, keeping his eyes on his mangled mess of a dinner.

"*Give* me the salt."

Corbin put a bit of crab in his mouth and pretended he hadn't also put a little piece of shell in with it that shattered unpleasantly between his teeth. He forced himself to swallow. "I would love to, if you ask nicely for it."

Rose gasped and the servants all looked at each other with even wider eyes than before as Corbin went back to wrestling his crab. Out of the corner of his eye, he could see that Rose's mouth was gaping, one hand poised as if she were about to place a forkful of food in her mouth, but was now frozen with shock.

"Princesses don't beg. Princesses don't grovel," she sputtered. "And, I might remind you that you are now a prince and a husband and I don't appreciate your tone."

"Well, unfortunately, this prince and this husband doesn't cater to demanding beasts who don't know how to say *please*."

Rose took in a sharp breath through her nose. "Salt," she said through clenched teeth.

The same servant from before stepped forward and gave her the salt shaker. Rose's face softened and she smiled contentedly as she sprinkled salt over her vegetables.

"Don't you need someone to do that for you?" Corbin asked sarcastically, gesturing to her salt-shaking arm.

She stopped, then quickly placed the salt shaker on the table. "Matthew!" Rose snapped, looking at the servant, her eyes wicked in their fury.

The servant named Matthew stepped forward and shook one final sprinkle of salt over Rose's plate and returned to his spot at her elbow, throwing Corbin a tiny glare before composing his face. Guilt swept over Corbin. He had only been trying to stand his ground, not make everyone else more miserable. Apparently, they didn't seem to mind or question that Rose could behave as horribly as she wished.

The tension in the room grew thick and unbearable. Rose ate delicately, an infuriatingly satisfied smile on her lips. Looking at her lips curved up as they were, and even in the midst of this exasperating situation, Corbin wondered what Rose would look like if she *really* smiled. She was undeniably beautiful—at least on the outside. But, angry as he was, Corbin promised himself in that moment that he would never tell her.

The servants stood stiff, their eyes accusatory. Finally, Corbin pushed his chair back from the table and rose, ignoring his napkin that fell to the floor. He strode toward the door, but before he reached it, gnawing emptiness twisted in his stomach. The tiny morsels of meat he had managed to wrestle out of the crab had done nothing to ease his hunger. Abandoning his pride, he strode back to the table and picked up his plate.

"This doesn't mean that I like the food!" Corbin shouted as he marched back toward the door. The servant opened and closed it for him, not even giving Corbin the satisfaction of slamming it himself.

CHAPTER 13

The fire was already roaring in Corbin's room. He tore off his suit coat and threw it over the back of a chair and kicked off his shoes, one of them hitting the poor dead bear right in the head. After a few minutes of struggling with his cravat, he gave up on it. Grabbing his plate that he had placed on the bed, he sat cross-legged in front of the fire, not realizing he was shivering until he got close to the heat and it warmed his tense muscles. He tried to finish the rest of his crab, or at least all he could persuade out of the stubborn—and now cold—shell.

Satisfied, but not quite full, Corbin was ready for sleep . . . and to end this endless day. One sock was removed and his shirt was halfway untucked when he heard the conjoining door open. Corbin rolled his eyes, sensing a tiresome tradition in the making.

He turned toward the door. Rose stood there, her eyes narrowed, her hands clenched on her hips just as the night before.

"Good evening, Rose. How was the rest of your dinner?" Corbin asked, turning away from her to get started on his waistcoat buttons.

"How dare you treat me this way!" He heard her take a step forward.

"Are you asking me *how* I dare, or simply making a statement?" Corbin said to his buttons. He turned back to her and flashed her one of his most charming smiles.

She blinked slowly, and then stepped forward, farther into his room. And though it was only his second night there, it felt like she was encroaching on his space, and his defenses went up. Her breaths came in short puffs out of her nose, and her lips were pressed together so tightly they disappeared.

71

"I think you have an anger problem," he mused, grinning more widely, trying to hide his own.

"No one has ever treated me with such contempt!"

"Well, not to your face, anyway."

The tenseness of her features relaxed in what looked like disbelief for a moment. She blinked and recovered. "I am a princess!"

"Yes, I know. I am a prince *because* you are a princess. I would just be a regular husband if I had married a regular woman. I might even be a good one. But mixing prince and husband has been a bit of a challenge for me."

"You ungrateful, filthy brute! I can't believe your audacity. I rescued you from poverty. I saved you from a life of misery and filth!"

Corbin's hands shook too badly for him to undo even one button, and he dropped his arms to his sides. He walked closer to her then, his own anger propelling him forward.

"No, you took me away from a life where I was useful, where I had a purpose. You took me away from a new life I was just starting to build. You even took me away from my *old* life. And even though I was trying to leave that old life behind, at least I knew who I was in it. Here, I have no idea who I am. I have no idea what to do. You not only took away my past, you took away my future. Please don't act like you've done me any favors."

As soon as he finished, Corbin's face burned with shame. He sounded like a whining child, instead of a man who had willingly stepped forward and done what had needed to be done.

Rose's face became scrutinizing, like she was trying to figure out how much a blacksmith was supposed to pay in taxes, and she stepped closer to him, so close he could have touched her. She studied him a moment longer, saying nothing.

"Why did you choose me?" he asked, as he had the night before.

Like a chink in her armor, her face became vulnerable for one tiny instant. Pain. Longing. Hope. Corbin could see it, he was sure. He didn't know if he would ever expose the meaning of that expression, but for a moment she looked human. She looked beautiful.

Thankfully, he had promised himself he would never tell her if he thought she was beautiful. But as he looked at her soft, unguarded eyes and smooth mouth, he wondered if he would ever be able to keep that promise. Too quickly, her face returned to stone. Corbin felt distinct disappointment . . . and relief.

They looked at each other, the warmth from the fire heating the room uncomfortably. He turned away from her and got back to work on his buttons.

"Good night, Rose."

After a moment, Corbin heard her soft, retreating footsteps, and the adjoining door closed just as Arthur entered the other door. Now Corbin could see why royal people needed help undressing. They were too preoccupied with how infuriated they all were with their royal dramas that they couldn't concentrate on something as simple as unbuttoning a blasted button.

Corbin lay awake on the bearskin rug long after the fire had died out. The heat that had raged in the room earlier crept out of the cracks in the windows, and a chill trickled into the room. With his toes and heart too cold for sleep, he stood, put his boots and old clothes back on, and stepped out into the corridor.

The blue moonlight filtering in through the windows made the cold feel even colder. Winter had decided to come early, in the course of one day, it seemed, and it felt quite appropriate. Ice and frost seem to accompany isolation.

His thoughts turned to home as he paced the corridor, and he wondered if winter had arrived in Maycott as well. He wondered if a new blacksmith had moved into his old shop yet and if new chinking had been placed between the cracks in the walls before the cold came. The cracks hadn't bothered Corbin during the warm months, but he had planned to fix them once he and Francine had arrived home from their wedding trip.

He wondered about Will and Ella. As he had countless times in his life, Corbin wished he had learned to read and write so that he could write to Will and ask how everything had worked out so well for them. How had they overcome their obstacles and found each other at last? Corbin tried to brush off the twinge of jealousy he felt when he imagined them happily married, or at least not filled with loathing toward each other.

And though he fought against it, his mind wandered to Francine and what she might be doing. Most likely, she was asleep in her house, her mother in the next room, breathing what Corbin could imagine to be a millionth sigh of relief that her daughter hadn't married the town blacksmith.

Corbin jumped and turned when he heard a door open behind him. Rose's half-exposed face was bathed in moonlight, and she resembled a hard, unfeeling statue. Her red hair framed her face wildly, and her weary eyes glowed in the pale light. Her hand clutched her nightgown tightly around her neck.

"Good evening, Rose. Sleeping well?" Corbin said, bowing. It surprised him how quickly she could bring out the acrimony in him.

She closed her eyes and sighed wearily. "What hath night to do with sleep?"

Corbin stepped closer, his eyebrows furrowed in confusion. "What was that?"

Rose opened her eyes, ignoring his question. "Well, it seems I'm not accustomed to common, angry men stomping around the corridors in the middle of the night."

"Is that a *yes*?"

"I don't appreciate your facetiousness."

"I'm not sure what that means, but I will work on correcting it." Corbin stepped closer to her, not wanting to wake anyone else up. "So, what bothers you the most? That I'm common and angry, or that I'm stomping?"

Rose's body tensed and her eyes widened as Corbin drew closer. He wasn't sure if it was the reflection of the stained glass on her face, but her cheeks grew pink. She wrapped her arms more tightly around herself as she composed her expression.

"Your being common and angry doesn't wake me, but your stomping does."

"So . . . the stomping bothers you." He nodded, feigning contemplation. "Apparently, my stomping is the low-class type of stomping. If you teach me how the royals stomp, maybe you'll get a better night's sleep. I've noticed that you're quite an expert."

"Are you planning on making a habit out of this?"

He wanted to tell her that as long as she continued to behave the way she did, then yes, stomping late at night would most likely become his new habit. But, he didn't even open his mouth to answer. Thinking about home and the person he had been reminded Corbin that he wasn't really an ungrateful, grumbling, solemn person. That reminder prevented him from answering her sarcastically, as had become his habit with her in so short a time.

Bending over, Corbin removed his boots and placed them on the stone floor. "I can't sleep, and so I will most likely be walking for a little while longer, but I will try my best not to stomp."

His feet now bare and especially freezing against the cold stones of the floor, even through his socks, he turned away from her. Without another word, she closed the door.

As soon as she was gone, his eyes began to droop. He didn't know if his energy had once again been drained from being in her presence, or if he felt an exhausting shame for his behavior.

He walked along the corridors for only a few more minutes, but the fatigue became too much. He returned to his corridor and saw, once more, that a servant lay asleep on the window seat across from Rose's chamber. Were they watching him, making sure he didn't escape? Making sure he stayed away from The Beast? Why didn't they simply lock his door from the outside, then? Corbin shrugged and tiptoed past the drooling, sleeping servant. He scooped up his boots and closed the door noiselessly behind him just as the first raindrops began to tap against the window.

CHAPTER 14

Sometime in the deep darkness of night, Corbin was awoken by a mysterious wailing. He jumped up off the bearskin rug and ran to the window, expecting to see wolves or some other animal out on the fields surrounding the castle. But the sound had been too close, so close he could almost feel it. Rain drizzled against the glass and dripped down in sheets. A blinding streak of lighting was followed by a boom of thunder that resounded off the castle walls. Corbin realized that the wind must have been howling and awoken him, and he left the window to lie back down on the rug. He wrapped the blanket tightly around his shoulders, a violent shiver overtaking him, his gaze still on the flashing window.

Corbin sat up and threw the blanket off him when yet another cry like a wounded animal echoed through the corridor. He ran to the door and pulled it open. The corridor was empty, the maid no longer sleeping on the window seat. The wailing and crying had ceased, and with it, the violence of the storm.

Arthur was whistling a high-pitched tune when he entered Corbin's room the next morning and tossed a pile of logs into the fire. Corbin groaned and rolled over on the rug, feeling like he had finally been able to fall asleep when Arthur came in.

Arthur gasped and spun around. "Forgive me, Your Highness! I was told you like to rise early and didn't think you would still be asleep at this hour."

Corbin glanced at the window. Brilliant sunshine flooded the room, the sky a piercing blue, washed clean by the storm.

Arthur hurried toward the door, but Corbin sat up and rubbed his eyes. "No, Arthur. Don't go. I can't believe I slept so late. That was quite a storm last night, wasn't it?"

"Oh, yes. But the rainy season *is* nigh upon us, Your Highness. That was just a taste of things to come."

Corbin groaned again. "Back home we had a rainy season too. But it was nothing like the storm last night. It would drizzle for a couple of weeks and eventually turn to snow that would stay on the ground until spring."

"Snow? You'll see no snow here, I'm afraid. Just rain. Months and months of it. I haven't seen snow since I was a child."

"But it feels cold enough for snow."

"Yes, but it just never quite does. We do get hail on occasion that feels like it will shatter the windows, but no snow."

Corbin nodded. Even the weather was fierce here. "Oh, Arthur, do you know why a maid sleeps out in the corridor? I think she was crying or something. Doesn't she have a bed?"

Arthur stood up from the fire that was now crackling in the fireplace. His eyes were wary, but he casually brushed the soot off his knees.

"Princess Rose requires it."

"Princess Rose requires that a servant wail through the corridors in the middle of the night?" Before Corbin could ask any more questions, there was a soft knock at the door.

"Good almost afternoon, my little prince," Mrs. Whiting's voice called from the open doorway. "I daresay the storm kept you up all night?" Arthur crossed the room and took a tray out of Mrs. Whiting's hands and set it on the corner of Corbin's bed.

"Yes, and someone crying."

"Oh dear. I'm sorry. I'll look into it." She puckered her brow, but didn't seem quite as concerned as Corbin would think. She brightened. "Well, we saved some breakfast for you. Eat up!" Mrs. Whiting disappeared and Arthur left Corbin to eat his breakfast.

Just then, Rose's disgruntled voice carried over from the adjoining room. Corbin couldn't make out any words, but he could distinguish Rose's voice from the maid he now knew was Maryann. With their mingling voices as the backdrop, he tried to make sense of this peculiar practice of someone always sleeping in the corridor. Corbin could understand if it was for her own protection—Corbin was a stranger, and a common one at that—but why send a maid and not one of the guards?

Corbin ate his breakfast, put on his old clothes, and decided to try a new way out to the grounds. As he passed by new windows, he seemed to be moving farther and farther away from the outdoors and deeper into the castle. He went down every set of stairs he found, hoping one of them would lead him outside, chastising himself for not just sticking with what little he knew.

The deeper into the castle he went, the narrower the steps and the danker the air became. Rats scurried away as he approached, and decaying odors saturated the air and damp walls. The few torches that had been lit provided little light, and no warmth—their flames unable to penetrate the coldness.

Corbin knew he had now gone underground by this time, but his curiosity drove him still downward. When Corbin reached the bottom of the stairs, a low mumbling of voices filled the gloom. He followed the sound until he came to a wall of rusty, iron bars.

"If she would have just looked closer, she'd have seen the crystals inside the rock."

"Those crystals are worthless. I don't think they can even be called crystals."

"I know, but it don't mean they ain't pretty all the same."

A moment of silence, and then a forlorn, defeated voice spoke. "The birds were probably a mistake."

"Oh, you see that now, do you?"

"Watch it, Lloyd! I actually *wanted* to marry her."

"No, you didn't want to marry *her*, you wanted to marry her money."

"And her face," a new voice answered. "Wouldn't mind looking at that for the rest of my life."

"But look at who she chose! That man, what was he? A blacksmith? And he gave her a rose! How is that better than birds?"

"Because it was silent."

A few chuckles followed this remark, and Corbin felt the corners of his mouth lift. These men were not criminals. They may have been overzealous, or slightly brazen, but not criminal.

"Good afternoon," Corbin said.

"Oh, afternoon is it? Couldn't tell by the slant of the sun," came the sarcastic reply in the windowless darkness.

Corbin moved closer until he could finally make out the dim faces of the fifteen or so men who had been crammed into a single jail cell.

"Oh! It's the new prince!" one of them announced and they all stood quickly.

Corbin lifted his hands and gestured for the men to sit. "I'm sorry for interrupting."

"He's just a regular bloke. What did she see in him that she didn't see in me?" Corbin heard one of them whisper, the sound bouncing off the stones and having nowhere to go but into every ear.

Corbin laughed softly. "Trust me, I'm still trying to figure that out." The men chuckled hesitantly.

As the laughter quieted, Corbin glanced around, not quite knowing what he was supposed to do next, or what he *could* do. He left the cell of men and approached the next one over. Squinting in the darkness, he saw that it was occupied by the portly chef who had attended the wedding. He had his white apron still tied around his waist, and as Corbin's eyes adjusted, he saw that the man looked rather bored.

"Why are you down here?" Corbin whispered, though everyone heard.

"Oh, The Bea . . . the princess's breakfast was cold yesterday morning. Doesn't eat until noon, that one. How am I supposed to keep it warm all day long? I was told that she might be up earlier, now that you're here. Not so, I suppose."

"No, I'm afraid she might stay in her room even longer now."

One of the gift givers laughed.

The chef shrugged. "No matter. I'm down here weekly, so this is nothing new. Just ask *her*." He jabbed a thumb in the direction of the next cell.

Corbin approached the cell and heard a small sniffle. Maryann, who he had just heard in The Beast's conjoining room, sat in a corner. He crouched down so he could see her better.

"Why are you here?" he asked quietly.

There was a soft sob in the darkness before she answered. "I-I poked Princess Rose in the head with a pin."

Corbin heard the chef stifle a laugh.

"Oh. That doesn't sound too terrible. How long do you think you'll have to stay down here?"

"Last time, it was only two days. But the longest was two weeks."

"For poking her head?"

"No. That time, I burned her dress with the hot iron."

79

"Well, it happens, I'm sure."

"She was still wearing it!" Maryann wailed, burying her face in her hands.

Terribly uncomfortable, Corbin stood and inched back over to the chef and looked at him questioningly. The chef approached him and spoke low enough so he couldn't be heard over Maryann's cries.

"The Beast can't dismiss Maryann, you see. There's practically a whole town of former lady's maids. No one else will come. She has to make do with this one. So, she sends her to the dungeon instead of sending her away." The chef looked over at Maryann. "Poor thing. She has to deal with The Beast more than anyone else does."

Maryann's sniffles had quieted, and a sense of anticipation filled the silence. She and the other prisoners were now looking expectantly at Corbin. He hadn't been told what his duties might be, but he thought that freeing prisoners, especially those who had been imprisoned for such trivial matters, must be under his realm of influence.

"Well, I see no reason why any of you should be here. Well, except for Maryann." Fresh tears filled her eyes in the dim candlelight, but he winked and smiled before she could cry any more. She blinked slowly and the corners of her mouth lifted in timid relief. "I'm going to see about setting you free."

"And what about you?" The voice came from the group of huddled men. "You, Prince Blacksmith, are as much imprisoned as we are." The remark was followed by a grunt of pain, but the man continued. "She's a beast! Look what she's done to us! What's she going to do to you?"

There was a low rumbling of agreement. One of the men stepped forward, and Corbin recognized him as the man who gave the princess the squawking birds. His once-stiff cravat hung loosely around his neck. "If I were you, I'd come with us."

For just a moment, Corbin could imagine himself disguised as one of these prisoners and being set free. But immediately, he saw in his mind the handle on the door that looked like a holdfast—the anchor that held him here, held him to his fate, and to his word.

"You will all be freed within the hour."

Leaving them in stunned silence, Corbin quickly climbed the stairs, breathing in the ancient air of the upper floors with new appreciation. He passed by the door he knew was the armory and stopped for a moment. The handle had been wrenched out of the decaying wood, and he knew that Rose had taken him up on his challenge. She did not want him in this room. The handle lay on the ground, and Corbin picked it up and placed it in his pocket. An unwitting smile stole across his face.

He knew where he needed to go, he just needed to figure out how to get there. Winding through the corridors, he reached the doors that led to the outside. He threw the doors open and made his way through the gardens, past the abandoned shops, and to the Chief Governor's House.

He knocked on the door, perhaps a little too boldly in his agitation. There was a shuffling of papers and then footsteps approaching the door.

Lord Stanford opened the door, blinking against the late afternoon sun.

"Why, Prince Corbin! What a wonderful surp . . . What's the matter?"

"Do I have the authority to free prisoners?"

"Of course," Lord Stanford smiled. "You're the prince."

"Do you know where the key is kept?"

"Why, I happen to have it right here." Lord Stanford disappeared, then reappeared a moment later holding a ring of keys. He picked out the right one for Corbin and handed it to him. "Glad to see you embracing your new role, Prince Corbin."

"Oh, I don't know about that. Just saw something that needed to be done."

"And you're doing it. That is the very definition of embracing it, Your Majesty. Well done."

Corbin nodded, not knowing how to respond, and spun away in the direction of the castle. He congratulated himself for finding it much more quickly this time, though returning to the stench was nothing to celebrate. As the men heard the jingling of the keys, they all stood and cheered and pounded each other on the back.

"He did it! He came back for us!"

"The kingdom is finally in good hands!"

"The princess would have left us in here to rot."

Corbin was just about to turn the key in the lock when their comments made him pause. What would these men say about the princess now? That her new husband had gone behind her back and freed them while she truly would have left them to rot, as they said? The rift between the princess and her people was painfully obvious, but Corbin didn't want to be responsible for widening it.

Still, these men did not deserve imprisonment because she had been in a beastly mood. The dungeon had grown silent as Corbin deliberated. He could not take credit for freeing them when their level of respect for the princess was understandably low, or even nonexistent. As a commoner, he could see that. And as a prince, he could fix it. When he spoke, he chose his words carefully, his voice grave.

"I want you all to know that it is the princess's wish that you are set free."

"Oh, sure it is," came a sarcastic reply.

"What's this all about?"

"You expect us to believe that?"

Corbin raised a hand. "No, wait. I will not turn this key until you understand that this is the princess's wish." He couldn't embellish it. He couldn't say that he had just spoken to her and she had gleefully given her permission. They would see right through him. "Do you understand?"

"Yes."

"We understand."

"Bless you and the princess."

Whether they believed him or not, he couldn't say, but it would have to be enough. He turned the key.

CHAPTER 15

O nce he was free, the chef returned to the upper floors, throwing Corbin a grateful glance. Maryann seemed frozen for a moment, too afraid to leave her cell.

Corbin reached out a hand and led her toward the stairs. "You may want to stay out of Princess Rose's sight for now until I can figure this out."

She nodded, looking at Corbin with worried eyes, before running in the direction of the servants' quarters. Corbin quietly ushered the men to the first door he could find that led to the outside, hurried out to the front of the castle, and pulled open the heavy gate, grateful that all unnecessary guards were sent home after the Gift Giving. The men ran through it, some of them shaking his hand, others running past before he could change his mind. As Corbin pushed the door closed, he smiled at the whoops and hollers of the freed men until they disappeared down the hill. He closed the gate with a heavy thud and he stood there for a while, staring at it, praying he had done the right thing.

Corbin walked up the front steps of the castle, not even allowing himself to look back, closing his ears to the joyous cries of liberation.

He opened the front door and closed it behind him, gripping the handle, blinking in the sudden darkness. Being out in the fresh air had reminded Corbin that he still hadn't opened the locked door of the last shop. Eager to discover what that last shop was, he weaved his way toward the back of the castle, when the scent of food wafted to him. He stopped, realizing there was one more job left to do.

Corbin followed the scent of food cooking until he found the kitchens. He stood in the doorway, not wanting to enter, but knowing he needed to if anything was going to change. Before he entered, he heard people speaking.

"Back so soon?" someone was saying, a chuckle in their voice.

The chef answered. "Yes, well. Funny story. You see, I was down there and the new prince . . ."

Before he could continue, Corbin entered the room.

All cooks, maids, and waiters stopped what they were doing and turned to face Corbin, their eyes wide. "Your Majesty!" they said in unison.

Corbin gaped back at them, suddenly unsure of what to say. Swallowing hard, he met the eyes of Matthew, the servant who had been forced to salt Princess Rose's food for her because of Corbin's refusal to comply.

"I wanted to come and apologize for making dinner difficult last night. I have no idea what I'm doing and . . ."

"Please, Your Majesty, do not apologize," Matthew answered, his face uncomfortable.

"I want you to consider me a friend. I don't feel any different or . . . higher than any of you. I'm just a blacksmith, and as I said, I don't know what I'm doing, but . . ." Corbin's words faded as he looked into the faces of the cooks, maids, and servants. They only saw him as a prince, had only ever known him as a prince. An unexpected weight settled on his shoulders and he felt even lonelier than he had before. He had hoped to find camaraderie with these people who were closer to his station than the princess was, but he was wrong.

Matthew met Corbin's eyes, seeming to sense his despair. He stepped closer and spoke quietly. "Thank you for coming down here to speak with us, Your Highness. Please forgive me for offering a bit of advice, but . . . never admit you don't know what you're doing. For us to follow, you must lead. And we will follow you, willingly. Just give us direction." Matthew stepped back and cleared his throat as if the conversation had never happened.

Corbin looked around the kitchen and saw that the discomfort had mostly fled from the servants' faces and was replaced with quiet encouragement.

"I'm not used to how things have always been done here, but maybe that's a good thing." Corbin's voice was stronger now, realizing the truth of his words. "Some things might have to change. It may be uncomfortable, but I believe it will be worth it. Please know that when I do things differently, it is not to cause anyone grief—including The Bea . . . the princess." Some awkwardness returned to the room as Corbin again felt the strange gravity of his situation. "Please, consider me your friend. Please call me Corbin."

The chef stepped forward then, maneuvering his round belly from behind the wooden counter. "We will call you Prince Corbin. We will revere and honor you as such." He grinned, his mustache twitching. "*And* . . . we will consider you our friend."

Corbin didn't have time to escape to the grounds before dinner, nor did he have time to wash or change into his fancy royal clothes. This didn't bother him at all until Rose entered the room.

Her hair was left down tonight, a halo of red curls catching the candle-light and cascading down her back. Corbin figured she had left it undone because Maryann was supposedly in the dungeon, though he knew she was free and was keeping her distance as instructed. As he caught his breath, he wondered if he should have left Maryann there a little longer, then chastised himself for the thought.

Rose's neck was white and graceful and adorned with a necklace bear-ing one amber-colored stone, which exactly matched her gown. As she walked to her chair, she didn't meet his eyes, though his rebellious eyes refused to look away.

For dinner, there were tiny, red potato-type vegetables that Corbin had never seen before, and the main course was a kind of bird. It was so small, the entire bird fit on his plate, head and all. The only sound during the meal was the irritating clinking of forks and knives against their plates. Until she spoke.

"Salt."

Keeping his eyes on the half-eaten, tiny bird on his plate, Corbin sighed, sensing a battle. Just behind Rose, Matthew hesitated and then stepped forward, his eyes darting to Corbin.

"Have I ever told you about the time my friend Will and I went hunting for ducks?" Corbin laughed, remembering the story, and also laughing because there was no way Rose could know the story. Matthew stopped mid-step. "Anyway, we were out in this field with our bows. I had never been taught to shoot, but Will was teaching me with an extra set he had . . ."

"Salt," Rose said, louder.

Without interrupting his story, Corbin placed a hand over the salt shaker and Matthew's eyes widened. Corbin smiled, and Matthew relaxed a bit.

"Well, I pulled back on the string, but the arrow kept falling off to the side. You know how they do that. Anyway, Will showed me how to keep it on the bow, and as soon as it was steady . . ."

"*Salt*," Rose hissed. Corbin clenched the shaker tighter. He could almost feel the heat radiating off Rose's face, but he continued his story, laughing all by himself. "I pulled back hard, but just before I let go, the arrow fell off to the side again, and went straight into Will's boot."

Rose stood so quickly her chair scraped loudly against the floor and then toppled over.

"Salt!" she screamed.

"I had to carry Will on my back all the way to Dr. Clayton's house, two miles away. Quite a trek for a twelve-year-old boy, let me tell you." Corbin sat back in his chair and laughed, his hand still on the shaker.

"Salt." Rose's green eyes were blazing and furious, her flaming hair quivering.

"Oh, I'm sorry. What about the salt?" Corbin asked.

Rose gaped for a moment and then very royally stomped out of the room. Corbin didn't know if it was because she was a woman, or that she was a princess, but he noticed that her stomp was indeed much quieter than his.

The guard, who Corbin had learned was named Baines, slammed the door for Rose. Corbin looked at him, mouth open in surprise. Baines smiled and bowed slightly, as if that had been his plan all along.

"May I ask that when the situation is right, I might have my own door slamming?" Corbin's eyes twinkled.

"Of course, Prince Corbin." Baines's mustache failed to conceal his grin.

Matthew cleared his throat. "What happened to Will's foot?" he whispered.

Corbin laughed. "The arrow went clean through the leather. He almost lost a toe and he limped for months. Still has an ugly scar. He usually tells people who ask about it that he jumped in front of an arrow that a bandit shot at us and saved my life." Corbin laughed and then sighed, a pang of homesickness washing over him. He smiled at everyone, then left the dining room.

Corbin entered the Grand Foyer and headed to the stairs. As he rounded the corner, he ran right into a small, angry, red-headed person wearing an amber gown. Rose gasped and Corbin almost reached out to hold onto her arms to keep her from falling over, but thought better of it. She teetered on her feet, but steadied herself.

"Why do you have to be so difficult?" she asked, though her voice was softer now that she wasn't demanding something as important as a salt shaker.

"Once again, I am astounded by your hypocrisy. But, to answer your question, I have to be so difficult because I refuse to be ordered around by someone who is supposed to be my . . ."

He couldn't say it. She was not his wife. This was not his life.

"Wife," Rose finished for him. "I am your wife. You are my . . . you are my . . ."

Corbin waited for a moment and then chuckled. "Exactly." The tiniest hint of a smile touched the corner of Rose's mouth, and it softened her expression into something maddeningly lovely. But before Corbin could believe it was really there, Rose spun away from him and marched up the stairs that led to her bedchamber.

Corbin knew that sleep would evade him once more and that he would wander the corridors again. Only this time, he would leave his clomping boots in his room. A maid, a different one this time, slept on the window seat. Corbin thought about waking her and asking why she was there, but knew he'd get the same answers as he had that morning.

Would things ever change? And if they did, how would that even begin to happen? Did it bother Rose—the thought of living with a common stranger for the rest of her life? The man who slept next door who refused to give her the salt?

CHAPTER 16

That night, Corbin didn't wake up anyone on his little exploration of the palace. And when the morning came, he woke at his regular pre-palace-life time. He quickly dressed in his old clothes, found some food in the kitchens, and after he laughed and talked with the cooks and servants for a while, went out to the grounds. Spotting some weeds in the gardens, he pulled them up and tossed them onto a pile he knew he would be adding to in the days to come. He straightened up the wood-shop, sweeping out the old wood shavings. Under a decaying mound of sawdust, Corbin found an old, dull axe. Once those other shops were cleaned out, Corbin's curiosity brought him to stand in front of the last shop, the axe in his hand.

The lock on the shop door was sturdy but rusted. It only took three solid whacks before the lock fell open and landed on the ground with a heavy thud. The wood planks of the door were warped. The bottoms curled up and cracks ran all the way up the lengths. When Corbin pushed the door open, the hinges protested so loudly it sounded like he had awoken a possessed witch from the dead. Even through the thick dust and cobwebs, Corbin immediately knew what this building was. A blacksmith shop.

A sense of coming home enveloped him as he walked in, carefully avoiding the rats that scurried away as he approached. He ran his hand over the solid, sturdy equipment—the anvils, swage blocks, chisels, hammers, and tongs. The fireplace bricks were crumbling and spiders crawled out of the gaping holes. But Corbin smiled. If there was ever a place that had—and could create—so much potential, it was this place.

He didn't stop to eat or drink. Corbin worked through the entire day and into the evening—dusting, polishing, sharpening. He would have to save the fixing of the crumbling fireplace for when he had stones and mortar, but by the time the sun touched the distant hills, the workbenches were sanded, the leather for the bellows was stitched and oiled, and the rust on the tools polished away.

Corbin was just hanging up the last chisel when he heard footsteps approaching. Turning warily to face the door, Corbin's face broke into a smile when he saw Mrs. Whiting.

"You found it!" Mrs. Whiting's voice called happily. "This shop has been locked up for years. I'm glad you brought it out of its hibernation."

"Oh? That's good. I was worried I would be forbidden to come here."

"No, my dear. I'm sure you're welcome here any time you'd like. Except, that is, when it's far past dinnertime. Aren't you hungry?"

"No. When I get working, I don't feel anything—fatigue, hunger, thirst—I just want to get the job done."

"Well, that makes two of us. But, just as people do for me, I'm going to let you know that it's probably time for a rest. Just think of how disappointed you'll be if you're too weak and sick to come out here because you've missed meals and sleep."

Corbin smiled and looked out into the fading sunlight. "You're right. It has gotten late. Let me just put a few things away and I'll be right in. And, thank you. It's nice to have someone looking out for me."

"I'm not the only one who looks out for you, my little prince."

As soon as she spoke, Corbin felt the familiar pricking feeling he had ever since he walked inside the castle.

"Maybe not, but it's not the same thing."

"She hasn't eaten yet, my dear. I think she's waiting for you."

"Yes, so she can have someone to torment."

Mrs. Whiting smiled sympathetically, though with a touch of reproach, and Corbin regretted his tone.

"I'll be in soon. I promise."

Mrs. Whiting ducked out into the night, her ever-present grin wide and wise. Corbin closed the warped door behind him, his mind filled with ideas and plans for putting the shop to good use. As he approached the castle, his eyes were drawn up to a familiar flash of red on the parapet. He stared into Rose's face, but he couldn't read her eyes—the distance and the darkness making it impossible. She didn't disappear immediately as she had the other times he'd caught her watching him. Maybe it was because the smoky light of dusk seemed to dull the awkwardness between them, as opposed to daylight, which emphasized it. Instead of running away, Rose stepped forward, her hands grasping the railing and Corbin stopped, looking back at her, searching for answers in her expressionless face.

Why had she chosen him? What had he seen on her face in that one moment that had obliterated all traces of her beastliness?

He would receive no answers standing in the darkness, and he was tired of asking them, if only to himself. With a sigh, he turned away and quickly washed his hands at the well and hurried to the formal dining room. Rose was already seated, slightly out of breath, her cheeks rosy. She didn't meet Corbin's eyes when he entered. Now that they were in the same room, the lack of awkwardness only a few minutes ago was replaced with uncomfortable silence.

Corbin took a breath and forced himself to speak. "Good evening, Rose. I'm sorry I stayed out so long."

Rose answered by methodically flicking her napkin onto her lap, though her face wasn't as harsh as he expected. They began eating, the usual tension filling the air.

"Rose," Corbin said when he could bear the silence no longer, "I have no problem giving you the salt, or the butter, or anything you want . . . gladly. I just think a little civility between us couldn't hurt."

Rose made no answer. Corbin was about to speak again when Baines entered the room.

"Letter for you, my Princess."

"For me?" she said in an unusually high voice, then cleared her throat. Rose looked pleasantly expectant, her eyes touched with rare tenderness, as she took the letter from Baines's hand. But her face fell when she looked at the splotched black writing on the parchment.

She tore open the seal, and Corbin watched as her pale face became pink and then slowly burned crimson.

"What is the meaning of this?" she said through clenched teeth.

"What is it?" Corbin asked, pausing before popping a potato into his mouth. He prayed she wouldn't ask him to read the letter. He wondered what she would say when she learned that he couldn't.

Rose cleared her throat. "'To our benevolent, well-groomed Princess. We express our deepest and most heartfelt gratitude to you for freeing us from your nasty, rat-infested dungeon. Though the food was actually quite good.'" Corbin suppressed a grin as Rose continued. "'While we all wish you would have chosen us to be your husband, we all feel that you have chosen a good enough bloke.'" She rolled her eyes. "'We will all be praying for your happiness forever, and ever, and ever . . . and ever.'" Corbin knew at those last words that the bird giver had been the scribe, and he couldn't help smiling.

"You freed those men, and made it look like it was *my* idea?"

Corbin's smile died on his lips as he met her blazing emerald eyes evenly. "Yes. And while we're on the subject, I should tell you that I also freed the chef and Maryann."

Rose began stuttering, the freckles on her face standing out against the redness.

"And before you send me or anyone else to the dungeon, you should know that I have the keys," Corbin said calmly, and Rose's breath came out in a whoosh. "You shouldn't be so upset. I did you a favor."

"Really? How so?"

"Your beastliness—you know, the way you treat me and everyone else around you—has created a rift between you and your subjects. It's well-known even throughout my kingdom. My . . . former kingdom. Your subjects don't respect you. What looks like respect is really just fear. What I did for you is make you look benevolent. You see that they wrote to *you*, not to me."

"They're laughing at me."

"They're thanking you."

"You went behind my back."

"To save your face."

Rose placed her elbows on the table, clasped her fingers, and rested her chin on her hands. "You had no right to do that. You are still a blacksmith in understanding and wisdom, or lack thereof. Those men needed to be taught a lesson. They needed to serve as a warning against anyone else who dares insult me." Rose shook her head. "You don't even know what I'm talking about. You'd rather spend all day out in some dirty shop than inside the castle."

"I'm more comfortable out there."

"Exactly. Now, in the future, you will leave the royal duties to me."

"What future? *Our* future? We don't even have a past, we barely have a present! How can there be a future?" He leaned back heavily in his chair and took a breath. When he spoke again, his voice was even. "I'm sorry I intruded. Well, kind of sorry. I know I don't know anything about royal matters, but at least I was doing *something*." He leaned forward and looked into her eyes. "What did your father do every spring? Why can't I go into the music room? The armory? Why does someone sleep in the corridor every night? Why did you choose me? I have more questions, but if you have any of your own you'd like to ask me, I'll be happy to oblige."

"I know all I need to know about you." Rose stood and dropped her napkin on the table, though her eyes didn't glare and her voice didn't snap. She seemed weary, weighed down by some burden Corbin couldn't understand.

Because she wouldn't tell him.

CHAPTER 17

Before the sun rose the next morning, Corbin grabbed the broken handles off his bedside table and stuffed them into his pockets. After he ate a quick breakfast in the kitchens, he raced out to his sanctuary. He spent all day straightening the nails that had been angrily ripped out of the doors and polishing the handles until he could see his reflection. Once they were finished, Corbin returned to the castle, replaced them on their respective doors, and searched for other broken things to mend.

He filled a sack with chipped tin cups, a pitched whoop handle that had snapped off a pitcher, more broken door handles, and squeaky hinges. Once those were all fixed and replaced after days of incessant work, he even went into the forbidden armory, gathered all the weapons, and sharpened, polished, and repaired each one. He patched and fixed the fireplace in the shop, every stone now secure.

Day after endless day, he worked from the darkness of morning to the darkness of night, waiting for a sense of accomplishment. When sleep finally came, Corbin was often awoken by strange and tragic cries, which gripped his chest with a cold and aching tightness. But always, by the time he was fully awake, the cries were gone.

A deep and rare melancholy settled over Corbin. He did exactly two things every day—eat, and work in the blacksmith shop. It was all he had ever done before coming here, besides occasionally mingling with friends, and spending his evenings with Francine. But now, it just wasn't enough.

He found that when he was out in the blacksmith shop, he tried to become more of the person he used to know, but there were some problems that came along with that. The person he used to know had been in love with Francine. The person he used to know could do whatever and go wherever he wanted. Here, if he was out too late, Mrs. Whiting came out to fetch him. And always, when he returned, Rose stood on the parapet, watching—and what felt like waiting—for him to return. But waiting for what? He contributed nothing inside the castle, except to anger her.

His skin grew darker, his beard now thick and heavy. His gray eyes seemed dull and lifeless, even as he worked. There was nothing left to fix. The handles were polished, the nails smooth and straight. The hinges on all the doors were rust free and opened and closed noiselessly—except for one. He had left the hinges that joined his and Rose's rooms alone. He wanted to be warned when she opened the door, though she hadn't since those first days.

A particularly frigid storm forced Corbin inside one day. Corbin skipped his usual handwashing at the well, the icy rain providing enough cleanliness and too much cold for him to consider it. Water dripped from his beard and onto his now threadbare shirt from his former life. He always folded up the sleeves now, no matter how cold it was, because the cuffs were so ripped and tattered they often dangled too close to the fire. There was a burn hole just above his waistline, revealing some skin, which he didn't concern himself much about. His pants had holes in both knees, and the hems were so ragged, they dragged underneath his worn boots.

He had hoped to find himself in that blacksmith shop, but all he had accomplished was losing what little he had known. True, he had fixed everything he could find in the castle, but he felt more broken than ever.

Now forced inside and with nothing left to fix, he found himself wandering the corridors again and soon found himself in a part of the castle he had not yet discovered. It seemed newer, the stones cleaner and cut more precisely. It was also warmer here, possibly because the wind couldn't seep through the tight cracks as easily. He approached two polished walnut doors and his eyes widened as he pushed them open.

Hundreds . . . thousands of books lined the walls on countless shelves. The room was circular, and Corbin realized it must be part of the large, northeast tower. Inviting settees, sofas, tables, and over-sized chairs were situated throughout the library. One enormous fireplace took up an entire wall, and the fire roaring inside of it instantly warmed Corbin to the point of sleepiness. He wanted nothing more than to collapse in one of the soft chairs, close his eyes, and close out the world.

But that was impossible, for sitting in one of the overstuffed chairs, talking to Baines, was Lord Stanford. Baines was speaking in low tones and Lord Stanford listened, the fingers of one hand stroking his goatee, his other hand holding a book.

"I see. Thank you for the report, Baines."

"Not at all, my lord." Baines made his way to the door and spotted Corbin just as he was turning away. "Good evening, Prince Corbin!"

Corbin sighed. He had hoped to sneak away unnoticed. He wasn't in the mood to talk.

"Ah, Prince Corbin!" Lord Stanford called as Baines exited the library. With one swift motion, he snapped the book shut and rose from his seat. He crossed the room in a few quick steps and stuck out his hand. Corbin grasped his and noticed that his own blackened, sun-browned hand almost enveloped the soft, lily white hand of Lord Stanford.

"Come, let's walk. If I have to sit in this room for one more minute, I'll lose my mind. I simply can't make myself read another word. Do you know the feeling?"

Corbin made no answer, but smiled in what he hoped looked like sympathy. He couldn't imagine what Lord Stanford would say if he knew how little Corbin understood such a problem.

"I normally avoid the castle, for obvious . . . beastly reasons." He chuckled. "But heavens, I do get bored in that little house all alone. Besides, the fireplace in here is worth the risk. Best in the castle. And the books here! My personal library just doesn't compare. I've become something of an expert in laws and legal issues in my years of handling matters for the princess. Setting the tax rate, for example. Making sure we get what we deserve for our exports, making sure we don't pay too much for our imports, that sort of thing. Lately, though, I've been reexamining our domestic relations. Forgive me. This must all seem very boring to you. So, married to a princess. How has that been?"

Lord Stanford spoke so quickly and changed subjects without a breath of warning that Corbin felt like he was spinning. He was tempted to say that he didn't know, but thought better of it.

"Interesting," was the best word Corbin could think to say. "I'm still trying to figure out why I'm here. Why she didn't marry, well . . . *you*, for example. She actually knew you, and you are much more comfortable here than I am."

"That's kind of you and I can't say that I haven't wondered myself. Forgive my frankness, but I don't have the stomach for marriage, especially to . . . *her*." He elbowed Corbin in the ribs to indicate he was only in jest, but Corbin couldn't quite manage a smile. "But of course, you know that she was engaged to Prince Kenton and that he broke it off to marry a commoner, right?"

"Yes."

"Well, she got her own commoner, and any lingering questions about her and me were put to rest. Besides, I never was able to compete with a prince, or multiple princes, whether I was interested in her or not. Well, no matter. She found you and all of that can be left in the past. It is nice to see you inside the castle, I must say. I wish I could understand the lure of dirty old shops."

Corbin shrugged. "I suppose I'm looking for a purpose. I can't find my place inside these walls." Corbin placed his hands in his pockets, his finger finding a new hole inside.

"Nonsense. You freed those men; you've befriended the staff. They don't have a negative word to say about you."

There was a soft knock at the library door. Baines had returned, poking his head in the library. "Dinner is served." He grinned at Corbin, bowed to Lord Stanford, and disappeared.

"You don't mind if I stay, do you?" Lord Stanford asked Corbin. "I'm just fine eating at my house. I used to dine here more, but I didn't want to bother you two newlyweds so I've kept my distance, but . . ."

"You're welcome to stay," Corbin said, grateful to have a buffer between him and Rose for a meal. They left the library, and the coolness of the corridor was an unexpected relief.

"Are you going to change your clothes? I can meet you in the foyer," Lord Stanford asked as he straightened his already impeccable cravat.

"Change? No. I haven't done that in a long time."

Lord Stanford nodded, taking in Corbin's scruffy beard and tattered appearance, and smiled sympathetically.

"This has been a rough transition. But truly, you have already breathed new life into this stuffy old castle."

"But not into the princess."

"Yes, cold as ever. I can't argue with that. Once a beast, always a beast."

"Talking about me?" Rose's voice said from behind them.

CHAPTER 18

Corbin and Lord Stanford froze. Corbin's stomach turned to ice, his ears burning as Rose walked past without waiting for an answer. Once she passed, Corbin met Lord Stanford's eyes and was surprised to see that he grinned back unapologetically, rolling his eyes.

In the dining hall, a servant pulled a chair out for Rose, and Corbin saw that Lord Stanford waited for Rose to be seated before he sat down himself. Corbin had already been seated and he stood up quickly, only to sit immediately back down.

Once everyone was settled and eating, Lord Stanford began telling a story about the time he forgot to bow to a king and was threatened with spending the night in the dungeon, but won the king over with a song he played on the lute.

"But then, a string broke on the lute. I froze, too shocked to continue, when . . ."

"Gravy," Rose said.

Lord Stanford didn't even pause in his story as he reached out and handed the gravy boat to Rose. Rose reached for it and glanced over at Corbin, the corners of her mouth lifting condescendingly.

It couldn't even be called a smile, but Corbin's breath caught inexplicably in his throat. Once again, he couldn't help imagining, at least for a moment, how beautiful she would be if she really did smile—the softness that would come to her face, how her green eyes would sparkle. However, Corbin didn't have enough time to dwell on the thought for long because she looked away, haughtily tossing her head. He sat silently, incensed by her arrogance.

"Salt," Rose said a moment later. Corbin was really beginning to hate that word. Lord Stanford casually handed the shaker to Rose as he continued talking. Corbin refused to look at Rose this time, dreading to see her angelic, infuriating nonsmile.

Rose finished eating, stood, and headed toward the doors without another word. This time, Corbin remembered to stand when she stood.

Lord Stanford raised a finger. "Wait, Princess Rose. I have some documents I need you to sign."

Sighing, Rose walked over to Lord Stanford who pulled some folded papers out of his breast pocket. Matthew disappeared for a moment and then returned with a quill. Rose scratched her signature at the bottom of each page, not bothering to read any of them, and left the room.

Lord Stanford chuckled as he placed the documents back in his pocket. "And that, Prince Corbin, is why I stay as far away as possible. How about joining me for a pipe?"

Corbin nodded, though he had never had a pipe in his life. He breathed in enough smoke in his shop all day long to ever feel the need. He followed Lord Stanford to a small drawing room he had never entered before, situated across from the dining rooms on the opposite side of the foyer.

They entered the drawing room, but the fire was so large—too large for such a small room—and they scooted their chairs back five feet.

"So, tell me about Corbin Black," Lord Stanford said, leaning back and loosening his cravat with infuriating ease.

Corbin shrugged. "I was a blacksmith before I came here."

"Yes, I know that." Lord Stanford chuckled and pulled out a pipe from his pocket, poured the contents of a little paper bag into it, and lit it with a match he struck on the sole of his shoe.

"There's not much more than that."

"Well, what about your parents, friends . . . *close* friends?" Lord Stanford winked.

Corbin wasn't sure what or how much Lord Stanford wanted to know, or why. Everyone Corbin had always known already knew everything about him, so he had no practice in divulging information.

Lord Stanford leaned forward, his face engulfed in a cloud of smoke. "If you're worried about Princess Rose finding out anything more than you'd like her to know, don't fret. I barely speak to the woman, and only about legal matters." He leaned back and created more smoke clouds with his pipe.

Corbin shrugged. "I'm honestly not worried about that. It's just that there's not much to tell. I was born in Laurel, but raised by a kind couple in Claire. They . . ."

"Raised by a kind couple? You mean, they weren't your parents?"

Corbin smiled in understanding. "They were my parents, just not the ones that I was originally born to." Corbin chuckled, realizing that his upbringing was slightly untraditional. "They were good, hardworking people, though they were much older than my friends' parents. They were always favorites of the village children. My father would take scraps of metal and mold them into arrowheads, jewelry, and trinkets for the children. And my mother always had sweets for them. My father died when I was sixteen, and I took over his blacksmith shop, and just a few months later, my mother's health failed and she died."

"Oh, I'm so sorry. And you've been on your own since then?"

"Well, yes and no. I lived alone, but I had a close friend, Will. He was like a brother to me. And for a year before I came here, I was . . . e-engaged . . . until I wasn't." Corbin rushed forward with his story, ignoring Lord Stanford who opened his mouth to ask a question. "And then I made the decision to come here. I was planning on maybe looking for some clues about my family, but never really got the chance. I came to live here in the castle the day after I moved to Laurel." Corbin sighed. "But finding out about my past wasn't the only reason I came to Laurel. I came here to start a new life."

"Well, you got that." Lord Stanford laughed, Corbin joining in. "Engaged, eh? Did you love her?"

Corbin squirmed in his chair. "Well, despite what my present circumstances suggest, I wasn't in the habit of marrying people I didn't love." He quickly looked away, a wave of guilt overcoming him before he could understand why.

"But you left her?"

"Well, she left me first . . . in a way." Corbin tried not to ring his hands.

"Ahh." Lord Stanford nodded. "My, my. Well, you must admit, your life hasn't been dull. I would give anything to trade with you for a day." Lord Stanford stood and Corbin followed. "I know things are difficult. Just keep doing what you're doing and all will be well." After shaking hands, Lord Stanford headed for the foyer and Corbin climbed the stairs, feeling particularly tired.

When Corbin reached his chamber, Arthur was there as usual, but not to help him with cufflinks and cravats. Arthur hadn't been much use for weeks. Corbin didn't have the heart to tell the old man that he wasn't needed. Besides, he enjoyed their nightly chats, but mostly Arthur's mumblings as he headed out the door. Tonight's mumblings seemed to have an edge to them, though.

"Scruffy . . . dirty . . . no more a blacksmith, hardly a prince . . ."

Corbin felt his head hang a little lower as Arthur closed the door. He walked to the opposite wall of windows, passing the crown that hadn't been removed from its pedestal since that first night. He looked out one of the windows, hoping to be able to look out to the gathering storm outside, but since the candles were still lit, only saw his reflection.

In the glass, he saw what everyone else saw—a man who had given up. His clothes were tattered, his beard and hair unruly. But that wasn't who he was at all. He was trying—trying harder than he ever had in his life, and that was saying something. He had spent every waking hour out in that shop, fixing every broken thing, making it useful and beautiful again in the only way he knew how. But something was still missing.

He left the window with its disappointing reflection and stood by the conjoining door that led to Rose. Almost without his permission, his hand clenched and raised, as if it were ready to knock. He thought of her haughty smile, her demanding, unfeeling words, his overpowering and strange desire to see her smile . . . to understand her. Why did he feel this need to know her—a beast?

He was used to living alone, but not used to feeling lonely. There had always been something to do, someone who needed him. Why did he want to make her smile? Because it was a challenge? He shook his head. It was more than that. Through the closed door, Corbin could hear the rustling of sheets and bedclothes, the ruffling of book pages. He looked down and the light that flooded from beneath the door vanished as Rose blew out her candle.

CHAPTER 19

Corbin thought the windows would be dashed to pieces. Thunder rattled the entire castle. Icy rain pelted against the glass and stones, and Corbin expected the roof to cave in at any moment from the deluge of water. Still, to him, storms were exciting, fascinating. He stood at the window, mesmerized by the lightning and how each strike illuminated the countryside. Corbin let the fire die out so that he could more fully appreciate the heart-thumping storm. In the darkness, he could more easily see the contrast between the darkness and flashes of light, and hear the pounding of the rain.

Thunder rumbled again and quickened Corbin's heart. The thunder then became less rolling and more sharp, piercing through the darkness, the lightning brightening the sky in unison with the deafening booms.

A howl, an unearthly cry, wailed over the resounding thunder. Corbin hadn't heard this sound for a few nights, and each time he did hear it, it was almost instantly hushed. Perhaps it was because he was already alert, but this time he was positive that the sound came directly from Rose's adjoining bedchamber. The sound, terrible and tragic, carried over the storm once more and it was all Corbin could hear. He crossed the room and put his ear up to their shared door. There were more muffled cries and his heart pounded. It was Rose. It didn't sound like one of her tantrums. Was she hurt? Was anyone helping her?

He pushed against the door, but it didn't budge, the beam locking the door from Rose's side. Wearing only a nightshirt, Corbin hurried out into the corridor. A maid, one he didn't recognize, sat on the window seat, fast asleep. He walked over to her and gently shook her shoulder. Her head only lolled onto the windowsill, and an empty flask clanged onto the floor from her limp fingers.

Another cry penetrated the walls, accompanying the thunder that had taken on a new intensity; the only thing louder was the pounding of Corbin's heart in his ears. He took a step toward Rose's door, hesitated, then pushed it open.

With the door now open, Corbin could hear each whimper, each breathless sob. Slowly, he approached her bed. Rose thrashed in her sheets, her blankets in a heap on the floor. Taking tentative steps forward, he hoped she would wake and calm herself down before he reached her. To his right, next to the bed, sat a little side table with a book on top. It lay open and as Corbin's eyes adjusted to the darkness, he could see that in the crease lay a dried red rose.

He reached out his fingers and lightly touched the petals, certain it was the same one he had given Rose at the Gift Giving. The rose had never fully bloomed before it had dried out, but now the petals were perfectly preserved, their redness still deep and pristine. A few words were underlined on the open page, and even if it were light enough to see the words, Corbin still wouldn't be able to read them.

Rose sobbed and Corbin's head snapped up. Her fingers clutched her pillow, and when he looked at her face, it was obvious she was still sleeping, but not at all tranquil. Her eyebrows puckered and there were drops of moisture on her eyelashes. Never taking his gaze from her closed eyes, Corbin knelt down, slowly reached out, and touched Rose's hand that gripped the pillow. Immediately, her fingers let go of the pillow and clutched his hand in a desperate grip. She sobbed again, though it seemed more of a sad sound than a terrified one. With her eyes still closed, Rose rolled from her back to her side. If she had opened her eyes, she would have seen the face of the man she detested most in the world in her room in the middle of the night, holding her hand.

Thankfully, she only fell into a deeper, more restful sleep, though her hold on his hand never eased. Her face still seemed troubled, her breath still coming in sporadic sobs. Always watching her eyes, Corbin hesitantly lifted his free hand, and with a touch softer than the rose petals in the book, smoothed out the tenseness between her eyebrows, the tightness around her mouth.

When her breathing became deep and regular, Corbin slipped his hand out from hers. Her fingers lay on the bed, relaxed and still slightly rounded as if they still held his. He noticed that the storm had moved along and that he had missed it. But, he realized with a smile, he would take this quiet moment over a raging storm any day . . . or night.

Rose's breathing became slow and regular, and Corbin smiled at the sweet, feminine snores that she would be mortified to know he heard. He crossed the stone floor to the corridor and gently closed the door behind him. The maid was still asleep on the window seat and Corbin smiled at her too. A peacefulness and contentment had entered his heart and he was strangely grateful for this particular maid's decision to drink herself into a stupor.

He had been able to help Rose, though she would most likely never know it, and something about that comforted him. For now, he wanted to keep that moment to himself. He didn't want her reaction, which would most likely be furious and embarrassed resulting in misery for everyone, to take away from the happiness that helping her had brought to him—if only for a few minutes on a stormy night.

Corbin's old, tattered clothes lay in a heap in the corner of his room. He picked them up, his fingers tracing the burn holes, the worn, soft fabric, the frayed hems. They were the last things he had that connected him to his former life, and he knew he was clinging to them with an almost obsessive obstinacy. If he no longer had them, he was afraid he would lose himself completely.

But what if that was exactly what he was supposed to do?

Without allowing himself to really contemplate what he was doing, he stoked the waning fire in the fireplace and tossed his old clothes in the flame. A smile, stiff yet satisfied, stole across his face as he watched them burn.

When the morning came, Corbin dressed in his princely clothes as best he could—Arthur hadn't come to help him prepare for the day in weeks—fighting the urge to loosen the collar every few seconds. Arthur passed him in the corridor and an ecstatic smile lit his face. Then, he clicked his tongue, and straightened Corbin's cravat before continuing on his way.

Corbin ate breakfast in the kitchens, telling stories about his childhood in Maycott, laughing at Matthew's jokes, and being teased about his scruffy beard. He felt particularly cheerful, though the knot in his stomach wouldn't go away. What if Rose had seen him there last night? How was she going to treat him today?

He left the kitchens and found a window that overlooked the grounds. "Going out today?"

Corbin spun around at the sound of Rose's detached voice. If Corbin hadn't been looking at her so intently, and if he didn't know her face as well as he did, he would have missed the slightest flicker of sadness in her eyes. She wanted him to stay.

"No. I'm staying inside today."

"Pity."

Or so he thought.

She spun in the other direction and continued on her way.

There was a storm that night too. Corbin hadn't been able to go to sleep once he had seen the ominous clouds rolling in. He was wide awake, standing at his window when the cries began. Corbin rushed out into the corridor and saw that Maryann was the servant on night duty. She, too, must have heard the cries, and she stood from the window seat, yawned and stretched, and then shuffled toward Rose's door.

"Wait," Corbin whispered in the darkness. He was grateful Maryann was on duty tonight. They shared a certain friendliness since the day he freed her from prison, though she had never lost her uneasiness in his or anyone's presence.

Maryann shrieked, but quickly covered her mouth with her hand.

Corbin stepped closer, trying to speak quietly, but still be heard over the thunder and rain. "I'm sorry to startle you. The maid last night was . . . well, I was the one who helped Rose last night and I wanted to know what you do to help her."

"Y-you helped her? Did she see you?"

"No."

Maryann sighed in relief. "You are not supposed to know about her, um, dislike of storms."

"Do you mean her fear?"

Rose cried again, and Maryann glanced nervously in the direction of the closed door. "I must go help her."

"How? What do you do? What helps?"

"I don't know. I just go in and . . . shake her until she wakes up. It seems to agitate her even more for a few minutes. Sometimes she cries louder or throws things, but it stops the nightmares, at least for a little while."

Corbin pursed his lips in thought and rubbed his scruffy jaw. He had been hoping for something helpful, some tactic that had been used by people who knew her better than he did, but he realized in that moment that his technique had been much better. Rose had been able to stay unconscious, to conquer her own demons in her sleep where they belonged.

"Do you know what her nightmares are of?"

"She has never told me, of course, but sometimes she calls out for her parents, so it might have something to do with them."

Rose wailed again as the thunder penetrated the stones. "Maryann, I will take care of the princess from now on. I want one of you to sit on the window seat until she is asleep so she thinks you're there, but then you have my permission to leave . . . and get a good night's rest."

"We'll be hanged!" Maryann whispered, her voice high and strained.

"Oh, I doubt that." Corbin grinned and lightning flashed through the windows. Seeming to remember that she was speaking to her liberator, Maryann nodded and hunched into an exhausted curtsy. He smiled encouragingly as she glanced back before disappearing around the corner.

Corbin took a breath and opened the door, crossed the room, and knelt once more by Rose's bed. Sweat dampened her hair and her cheeks were wet with tears. He reached for her hand and she gripped it as she had the night before. Even sooner than the previous night, her breathing slowed, and with the help of his gentle fingers, her face smoothed.

The book lay open on the bedside table, the rose still marking the page with the underlined words. Corbin would give almost anything to know what was written on those pages. Perhaps those few words would give him a glimpse into her character. But even without the words, as he knelt down by her bed and held her hand, he felt that he was beginning to understand her just a little bit better.

She was afraid. Everything she claimed to hate, she really feared. Maryann said Rose disliked storms, but from what Corbin could see, she was terrified. He had seen her when she was angry—everyone had—but these cries and whimpers were nothing like her tantrums.

She also shirked her royal duties. Corbin had assumed it was because she hated the tedious work and responsibility, but could she somehow be afraid of that too?

Now, if only he could discover the meaning of her hatred for him. Did she truly hate him, or was there something about Corbin that she feared?

CHAPTER 20

Weeks dragged by. Rose never knew that Corbin came into her room to help her through her nightmares. Corbin began to look forward to those nights, though he felt a little guilty because he knew they were not enjoyable for her to say the least. In her sleep, once deep sleep finally came, he could really look at her and try to make sense of this woman he had married. Each night, it seemed that he came closer to her and even that his dislike for her faded away.

But the morning always came, and with it, the beast of a woman he had grown to detest, but even worse, to expect. The beautiful, stormy nights turned into miserable, endless days. Lord Stanford would sometimes appear—and then quickly disappear—fulfilling whatever duty he needed to attend to, talking to Rose in quiet corners about royal matters.

Corbin had lived in the castle for four months when Mrs. Whiting passed him in the corridor one dreary day, holding a stack of folded cloths in her hands.

"Oh, Prince Corbin! It's you. I didn't recognize you." She grinned. It had become one of her favorite jokes—teasing him about his thick beard, though she had become much more cheerful since he had abandoned his old clothes. She stopped and looked up at him, a little pucker forming between her eyebrows. "Are you sleeping well? Or are you sleeping *too* well?"

"I don't know what you mean," Corbin replied in a soft voice, unaccustomed to conversation.

"Well, when you first arrived, we would have to be in your room before dawn to light the fire. Now we stand outside your room, waiting for you to awake for hours. I just want to make sure you're comfortable and sleeping well."

"I'm sleeping well," he answered, though he didn't mention that he didn't sleep until after Rose was asleep. After that, he knew he was indeed sleeping *too* well. There was nothing to wake up for.

"You know, for years we have taken shifts watching over the princess at night to avoid exhaustion. While I admire you more than I can say for what you're doing for her, we will gladly help you."

Corbin shook his head. "No. It has to be me. It's good for me. It . . . it helps."

"But you seem so down, my little prince. More than just worn out. Is anything the matter?"

Was anything the matter? He was homesick for a home he didn't have. He missed his friends who didn't even know where he was or what had happened to him. He felt useless. He was married to a woman he didn't love, or barely knew—except what he tried to figure out on his own in the silence of her sleep—and she made no indication that she wanted to know or love him.

"No," Corbin said.

Mrs. Whiting placed her stack of cloths on the window seat and sat down, patting the spot next to her. Corbin couldn't help smiling a little as he sat next to her. After those awkward moments of their first meeting, Mrs. Whiting had treated him with respect, yet also with a friendly familiarity that always brightened his day.

"I can't imagine how hard this must be for you. When Princess Rose came home from losing Prince Kenton at the ball and told us of her plan to marry a commoner, I can't begin to tell you the worries that ran through my mind. All I could imagine when she told us was that she would end up with some ambitious man who only wanted a crown and the riches that came with it. I never imagined that she would bring home a man like you." Mrs. Whiting swallowed, and tears glimmered in her eyes. "You are good. You are strong. You're struggling right now, yes, and that is completely understandable. But, you can do this. It's in you, I know it. I'm sure you've done hard things before, and you can do this one. It won't always be like this . . . unless you want it to be, unless you can change. It truly is all up to you."

Lord Stanford had told Corbin to keep doing what he was doing and all would be well. Mrs. Whiting told him that he should change if things were going to improve. Which one was it?

Mrs. Whiting sniffed and looked around her. "I hope you don't mind my speaking to you so informally, Your Highness, but I have a feeling you'll forgive me." She winked and picked up her stack of cloths. The smell of cleanliness and industry floated past Corbin as she walked away. Suddenly he had an idea.

"Mrs. Whiting," Corbin called out. She turned to look at him. Corbin stood and walked near enough to her to whisper. He gnawed on his bottom lip for a moment before gathering his courage. "Do you write?" he whispered with a tense voice.

The gleam returned to her eyes, and she pursed her lips. "I'm sorry, my little prince, but no. I wish I did."

"That's all right. I was thinking about writing a letter to invite a friend to visit." The thought lightened his spirits so much, a genuine smile crept onto his face. It felt strange, like those muscles had been dormant for so long, they were rusty like an old hinge that needed oiling.

"That's a wonderful idea! You know, you could ask your wife to help you."

"And have her discover that the man she married is illiterate? Have her look at me with even more disdain? Not in a thousand years, but thank you."

She smiled in understanding. "I'm guessing she'll find out sometime, my dear."

"Not if I can help it."

"You know, it takes strength to admit when we're weak. I think opening up yourself to her in this little way might even soften her towards you."

"I can't imagine it."

"Well, then try it, and you won't have to imagine. What do you have to lose?" Mrs. Whiting grinned and spun in the other direction, her cloths in her arms.

At dinner, though his mood was greatly lightened, an uneasiness crawled around in Corbin's stomach that had nothing to do with what was on his plate. He stared down at the strange food—a grayish sea creature with tentacles—thinking only that he knew he would have to ask for help in writing his letter. He thought about asking one of the servants, but it was unlikely that any of them could read or write either, and he didn't want it to be common knowledge that the new prince couldn't write a simple letter on his own. And for that same reason, he couldn't bring himself to ask Lord Stanford, who happened to be traveling on some diplomatic journey anyway.

But, he was out of options. Corbin wanted to believe Mrs. Whiting—that somehow this could soften Rose toward him, but the very idea brought a cynical smile to his face.

"Is something wrong?" Rose said and Corbin met her eyes, the smile fleeing from his face.

"No. Why?"

"Well, you're smiling. Sort of. I thought you might be ill." Rose continued eating without waiting for an explanation. Corbin looked back down at his food. This was hopeless. But Mrs. Whiting was right. He had absolutely nothing to lose.

He took a breath. "I suppose I was thinking about what your reaction would be if I told you that I can't read or write."

Rose's eyes widened slightly, but she composed herself before she spoke. "I'm not surprised if that's what you're wondering." There was no kindness in her eyes, but there wasn't the disgust that Corbin had anticipated; no mockery or contempt. He couldn't help being encouraged by this.

"I was also wondering what your reaction would be if I asked for your help."

Rose placed her fork on the table and folded her hands in front of her. "*My* help? You mean you can't do everything?"

"No, and I never said I could." Corbin paused, fighting to keep his voice steady under her baleful expression. "I would like to invite some friends over for a visit."

"Some of your former, common friends?"

"No, some of my current, common friends."

"In this castle?"

"I'm common and I'm in this castle."

"Are you?"

Corbin couldn't make sense of her question, so he went on. "It would only be my friend Will and his new wife. They were both born upper class, if that helps. They just ran into some hard times in their lives. Will works at the palace stables. And Ella, well, she lost both of her parents when she was young . . . like you." Corbin feigned a cough when Rose's eyes narrowed. "They will both be able to read my letter when it arrives, if that tells you anything."

A trace of a sincere smile lifted the corner of Rose's mouth, and Corbin's breath caught. But then it was gone and Corbin was sure he had imagined it.

"Why do you need them here?"

Corbin swallowed hard. He hadn't thought he would have to give her an explanation. He wanted to tell her he was miserable here, that he needed to be with friends who brought the good out of him and help him figure out how that goodness could fit in with all this badness.

He was homesick, lonely, and miserable.

"Because," Corbin said.

Rose pursed her lips and a rare and momentary softness entered her eyes as she considered his trite answer. In that keen, yet contemplative look, Corbin knew that Rose heard more than he had said.

"Very well. Are you finished?"

"With what?" Did he have to explain himself further?

"Dinner."

"Oh. Yes, I am." He hadn't eaten a bite.

"Come with me."

Corbin wasn't sure where Rose was going until she stopped outside her chamber door. She looked up at him, a warning in her eyes.

"Don't touch anything."

"I wasn't going to."

She hesitated for another moment and then entered the room. Corbin had of course been inside Rose's room before, though she didn't know that. In the light, he could see the little feminine details—the cushioned window seats, the embroidered curtains, the roses carved in the bed-frame. Hairbrushes, jeweled combs and pins, and golden boxes that probably held small trinkets sat on a bureau to his left. A mirror hung above it, cherubs carved into the golden frame. He smiled at the unexpected sweetness of the room. He never could have noticed all these details with only the help of flashes of lightning. Besides, he realized that he had never cared to look. His eyes had always been steadfastly fixed on her.

Rose cleared her throat and he looked at her. She raised her eyebrows and a slow smile spread across his lips. He was surprised to feel a little heat on his neck. Grinning, he held up his hands in mock innocence.

"I'm not touching anything."

Another hint of a smile played at her lips, but she turned before Corbin could be sure. He followed Rose to a little writing desk in the far corner, passing her bed and next to it, the little side table. As always, the book lay on the table, its pages open, the dried rose marking her place.

He hadn't seen it on the nights he had been in her room, but across the room on a table sat a glass vase filled with the thirteen dried roses from her wedding bouquet. They looked less revolting there in a vase in her room than they had clenched in her white-knuckled hands at their wedding.

Rose sat in the chair and scooted it forward. She pulled out a piece of parchment from the small stack on the corner and placed it in front of her, smoothing it out on the writing desk. She studied the row of quills before her, finally deciding on a green-feathered one. Pulling the ink well closer to her, she dipped the quill inside and brushed the tip against the edge.

"What would you like to say?"

Corbin deliberated for a moment. He wasn't at liberty to express himself freely, or fully describe the strange turn of events that had led him here. He cleared his throat, choked by the awkwardness of the situation.

"Will," Corbin said, and Rose's quill scratched fluidly across the paper. Her writing was so elegant, even from what little Corbin knew. "I hope this letter finds you well. I want to congratulate you again on your recent wedding." He faltered, the next words particularly strange to say out loud, considering who his scribe was. "I, too, am married . . ." A small spot of ink splatted out into the page when Rose wrote the word, "and am extending an invitation for you and Ella to come and visit at your earliest convenience. You will find me at the palace in Laurel. I have included sufficient funds for your journey." He said the last sentence as a question, though Rose shrugged in acquiescence.

"You have all the money you want at your disposal," she said without looking up.

Corbin nodded, realizing he had never asked . . . or cared to ask. "All right. Well, I guess just end with 'Your friend, Corbin.'" Rose had almost touched her quill to the parchment when Corbin reached out, placing a hand on hers. "Wait."

Rose took in a quick breath of surprise and stared down at his hand on hers, but didn't shake it off. She shifted her eyes back to meet his.

Corbin smiled down at her, despite her astonishment. It had been a natural thing for him to reach out and touch her, especially here in this room where he had already spent countless hours holding her hands, brushing the tears from her cheeks.

Corbin let go of her hand and rubbed his bearded jaw.

"What is it?" she asked, sounding as if she had just run up a flight of stairs.

"I think I should give them a little . . . warning before they show up here and find that I'm a . . . the . . ."

"Prince," she finished for him.

"Yes. Although, it would be amusing if they looked for me in the kitchens or the stables. That would make much more sense."

"True." She pursed her lips as if to contain a smile. He wished she wouldn't.

"But they're going to find out sometime, so . . ."

"His Royal Highness, Prince Corbin of Laurel?" There was no contempt or mockery in her tone, and a wave of calm washed over Corbin.

"Yes."

Corbin knew there was really nothing he could do to soften the blow now. Will's old friend, Corbin the blacksmith, was now a prince. He would give anything to see Will's face when he read the letter. If Will and Ella didn't arrive within a fortnight, it was because they had died of shock.

Turning away, Rose blew across the letter, drying the ink, and folded it. She dripped a few drops of sealing wax onto the seam, then took a small metal object and pushed down on the wax. An intricate rose now decorated the seal. She held out the letter and Corbin lifted his hand to take it, his fingers brushing hers for the briefest moment.

"Thank you," he said.

The slightest blush of pink was rebelliously spreading across her cheeks.

Corbin's eyes darted to the bedside table. Suddenly, he was so tired of not knowing anything about her. He was tired of imagining who she was while she slept, and knowing nothing of the woman when she was awake.

"Rose . . ." Corbin cleared his throat, which seemed to be closing in on itself. "Is that the rose I gave you? Why did you keep it? What words are underlined on the page in your book?"

Rose's eyes darted to the book and the rose, and when her eyes met Corbin's again, they were troubled and shining with tears.

He stepped closer to her, in this room where he knew her best. "Please, Rose. Tell me."

Her mask fell and she forgot to be a beast, if only for a moment. Her lips trembled and opened slightly, though not enough for words to fit through.

She sat motionless on her chair at the desk, her eyes looking up at him, shining and pleading. Without thinking, he knelt down in front of her and rested his hand on hers.

"Please let me know you. I want to know you."

Rose blinked and her face became hard, her chin lifting slightly. She pulled her hands out from under his. "No, you don't."

She stood abruptly, marched to the door, and held it open for him. Corbin walked past her out into the corridor. She retreated back into her chamber, and he heard the unmistakable sound of a book being closed.

CHAPTER 21

Not much had changed between Corbin and Rose since she helped him write his letter, so he decided to keep his distance, spending his time out in the bitter cold as he waited for Will and Ella to arrive. He missed his old clothes more than ever, but Mrs. Whiting assured him, with a shrewd smile, that he could still work outside and not look like a vagabond.

Instead of working in the shops, Corbin now spent his hours in the garden. The weeds pulled up easily out of the sodden ground, and the soil left behind was rich and deep brown. Every servant, including Mrs. Whiting, said this was the coldest winter in their memory, but Corbin ignored the chill. Somehow working out in the garden had brought him satisfaction that working in the blacksmith shop had not. He was still working to improve the castle, as he had in the blacksmith shop—fixing and restoring things—but this felt different. This time, he wasn't shut inside a shop, trying to find himself and who he had been; he was out in the open trying to accept and grow into who he was supposed to be now.

At the end of a particularly exhausting day, Corbin chopped down the last of some overgrown, scraggly weeds that had covered a large portion of the outer wall. Behind them, hidden in their mangled branches and leaves, was a door—boarded up and rotten. It was built right into the wall and obviously led to the outside world.

Corbin gathered up the last of the weeds, their dried-out branches poking his arms and chest. He threw the last of the weeds on the enormous pile and set fire to them. As he watched the flames grow higher and higher into the darkening sky, he felt Rose watching. He turned and saw her on the parapet, the smoke almost obliterating her image. She held a white handkerchief to her face, though Corbin couldn't tell if it was to block out the smoke or to wipe her tears.

Corbin washed as thoroughly as possible at the well before entering the castle and then sought out Mrs. Whiting. He found her in the kitchens, where she was making sure dinner would be ready on time.

"Mrs. Whiting, when I was out in the garden just now, I saw a door that had been boarded up. Do you know anything about it?"

Mrs. Whiting paused for a moment, uttered a few more words of instruction to the maids, and then motioned for Corbin to follow her out into the corridor. She sat down on a window seat, and with the dim light of the setting sun resting on her face, seemed particularly tired.

"There have been many sad tales within the walls of this castle."

"Worse than the deaths of the king and queen?"

"Oh, my little prince, there are many kinds of deaths . . . and many kinds of births. The tale of the door involves both."

"Will you tell me?"

"I suppose it's time. It is good to learn the history of this castle, which has now become a part of your history. The tale I'm thinking of occurred many years ago. The princess wouldn't even be born for a few more years. This place used to be filled with life—parties, music, dancing, visitors from around the world. One such visitor was a duke from Hollow Mountain. He was just about twenty years old, and was charming as the devil. We scullery maids were all smitten with him, though he was a few years older than we were. We spent the days daydreaming and talking about him, but one girl took it further than that.

"This particular girl had a somewhat tragic history. Her mother wasn't married when she gave birth to her. When the king and queen— Princess Rose's grandparents—discovered the girl's secret, she was sent away and never heard from again. Only after the pleas of many servants did the king and queen allow the baby to stay, though she grew up without a family of her own. She longed for a family more than anything, and when the duke showed interest in her, well, it seemed that her dreams had finally come true.

"They were married, as she called it, in the garden one night. They made promises to each other, but couldn't tell anyone because of the duke's position. There were no witnesses, no priest, but the girl was convinced that their love was as binding as anything. When she told the duke about their baby that was to be born, he vanished. He didn't even tell the king and queen he was leaving. Nothing can describe her despair. It was one of the many kinds of deaths, perhaps worse than the death of the body. The servants all tried to help her, to comfort her. A few suspected that there was a baby coming, but never mentioned it to anyone. The girl had become a daughter to everyone and no one wanted her to suffer the same fate as her poor mother. She was a small thing and never grew very big. She stayed down in the kitchens, out of sight.

"The baby was born very early in the morning in the room next to the kitchen. There." Mrs. Whiting pointed to an open door down the corridor. "She was alone." Mrs. Whiting's voice caught and she dabbed at her eyes with the corner of her apron. "Forgive me, my little prince. The story still tugs at my heartstrings. The baby barely even cried. The girl stayed in the room all day and into the night. Everyone went about their business, but some slipped food under the door and offered their help. All were answered with silence.

"That night, she quietly slipped out of the room. Many of the servants were still awake, cleaning dishes, washing floors, but she paid them no heed. She clasped her tiny bundle to her heart, a look of quiet determination on her face. She passed by the cook's writing desk, picked up a quill, and held it over the parchment with trembling fingers.

"'Do you need help, honey?' The cook said, wrapping her arm around her thin shoulders. The cook was one of the literate ones.

"'I need to write his name,' the girl said, 'and I need to write it with my own hand.'

"The cook helped her write the child's name, which no one could hear but them. The girl kissed her baby's tiny head and pinned the ripped piece of parchment to his swaddling clothes. She stuffed a small basket into her shawl and without a word, stepped out into the night. The servants all watched her cross the garden and slip through the small door that led to the pathway to town. She knew that path better than anyone, she being the maid whose job it was to pick up needed supplies from local merchants and shopkeepers.

"Once she was out of sight, the cook sent one of the servants to follow her, making sure no harm came to her or the child, which it didn't. Thank goodness." Mrs. Whiting dabbed at her eyes again. "She returned just before dawn. Alone. There were a few who saw her return, all of them her friends, and they gathered around her inquiring after the baby. The only words she uttered, and she only said them once, was, 'I gave him back to God.'

"Her eyes were dry, her face blank, yet peaceful. She let everyone hug her and hold her. Then, her tears did come, and they didn't stop for many days. She developed a fever and it took her weeks to recover. She grew somber and often withdrawn and the rumors began to swirl. The king and queen—Princess Rose's parents—caught wind of it, though they never discovered who the girl was. Since everyone loved and pitied the girl, they all denied any knowledge of it. The king and queen boarded up the door as a warning against such behavior, unable to do much else. The bushes and trees became so overgrown that the door disappeared, and with it, the memory of the maid and her child."

"What happened to her?" Corbin asked.

"No one really knows. Only a handful of servants are still here who were here during that time, and many of them were never really certain who the girl was. Soon, she just became another face in the crowd. Just another maid. So many of the servants left soon after the king and queen died that all anyone could do was assume she was one of them."

Corbin looked out the window, his face thoughtful . . . which quickly became brooding. He turned back to Mrs. Whiting.

"What happened to the duke?" His eyes were fierce, his face flushed with indignation.

Mrs. Whiting's eyes were understanding as she patted his clenched hands. "Don't be too angry with him, dear. A few months later, he returned. Or tried to. His travelling companion arrived at the castle without him, reporting that the duke became very ill and died at an inn on his way here. All the duke had said was, 'Go to Laurel. Tell her I'm sorry. Tell her I was coming for her.'

"He had just been afraid. He died doing the right thing."

Corbin stood and exhaled slowly. "My story doesn't seem so bad now."

"It doesn't do any good to compare tragedies or hardships, or even joys or triumphs. We are all a part of each other's stories. That's what marriage does. That's what friendship does. That's what death and birth do. We are all weaved together, my little prince."

CHAPTER 22

Three weeks after Corbin sent his letter, Will and Ella arrived. When the wagon wheels were heard approaching up the front drive, Corbin was already out the door before the carriage came to a stop.

Will exited the carriage first and then reached up to help Ella down. Corbin almost gasped when he saw her. He hadn't known Ella well; her family had been upper class when he was young, and by the time he was older, she had become what Corbin saw as a recluse, if he noticed her at all. Will had secretly loved her for years, though Corbin wasn't aware until the week of Prince Kenton's ball. Will had always said Ella was beautiful, and it was true that her features were beautiful, but to Corbin she had always seemed a little too thin, a little too solemn.

But now, she looked like a different person. Her cheeks had filled out and were rosy. She smiled down at Will as he helped her out as if he were the only person alive. Her golden hair was pulled back into a twist, but Corbin could see that it was very short, and he wondered if it had been that short at their wedding, and at the ball. He couldn't remember. The only woman Corbin had noticed the night of the ball, and every night before, was Francine.

Will wore the same suit he had worn at the prince's ball, and Ella wore a deep blue dress that looked brand new.

Corbin ran to Will and grasped his hand. "How are you? *Who* are you?" Corbin laughed, gesturing to Will's suit.

"I was about to ask you the same thing!" Will laughed and released Corbin's hand. "Ella would never let me grow a beard like that!"

"As if you even could." Corbin laughed and turned to Ella. "Mrs. Hawkins, you are looking lovelier than ever. I don't know how you manage being married to this brute," Corbin said as he bowed over her hand and kissed it.

She laughed. "Well, someone had to." She winked at Will. "I figured it might as well be the one who was desperately in love with him."

Will took Ella's hand as soon as Corbin released it and kissed the top of her head. It was the first show of genuine affection Corbin had seen in months, and instead of making him feel comforted and hopeful, he felt a gnawing in the pit of his stomach. He couldn't imagine ever being that close to anyone again. He shook off the feeling as quickly as it came and walked into the palace with Will and Ella following behind.

As they entered the castle, Mrs. Whiting greeted them in the foyer.

"Welcome, Will and Ella!" She held out both her hands and grasped Ella's and kissed her cheeks. "Forgive my informality. It feels as if we're old friends." Mrs. Whiting let go of Ella's hands and looked around. "I'm sorry there's no one else here to greet you. I'm sure Princess Rose will be along shortly." She curtsied and left the room.

Will and Ella didn't seem to mind the lack of royal greeting. Ella was spinning in a slow circle, her face upturned as she took in the grandeur of the entrance hall.

"Nice place you have here. Kind of small, though," Will said, grinning.

Corbin chuckled. "I only get lost every few days now, instead of hourly."

Will shook his head in bewilderment, his voice lowering. "We heard that The Bea . . . Princess Rose had married a commoner, of course. Most of us assumed it was out of revenge for Prince Kenton marrying his commoner so soon after breaking off his engagement to Princess Rose. We never thought anything more about it until we received your letter. We never imagined it was *you* she married."

"I'm sorry. I meant to somehow send word as soon as I was settled. I suppose I'm still waiting to be."

Will's eyes became thoughtful. "Are you doing . . . all right? I mean, everything considered?"

Corbin knew Will was referring to his hasty decision to leave his old life—and former fiancée—and begin again in a new kingdom. Neither of them could have known that Corbin would be marrying a princess within a week of making that decision.

"I really don't know," Corbin finally answered. "I do know that I'm glad you're here, though."

Ella had joined them by then. She took Will's hand and smiled at Corbin, her blue eyes shining. Corbin was surprised that her tender look could bring moisture to his own eyes. Will seemed to notice and his expression became more concerned. Corbin knew he missed home, but didn't realize how much until he looked into the eyes of people who knew him.

"I'm sorry Rose didn't come to greet you. She isn't . . . around people much."

Ella reached out and grasped Corbin's arm. "Don't apologize, Corbin. There will be plenty of time for introductions."

Will and Ella were shown to their room, where they rested and changed after their long journey, then met Corbin in the Great Hall before dinner. Will had his same suit on, but it had been brushed and steamed. Ella's high-waisted gown was different than the one she arrived in, and it glistened faintly in the candlelight. She rested a hand tenderly over her abdomen, almost unconsciously.

Corbin couldn't contain his grin. "You look very nice, Ella."

"Thank—" Ella began.

"A compliment? I didn't know you were capable," said Rose's voice.

Everyone spun around to see Rose standing in the entrance of the Great Hall. Corbin didn't know if he should be embarrassed for Rose's behavior, or his. He had indeed prevented any compliments that had entered his head from ever exiting his mouth in regard to Rose, refusing to fan the flame of her ego.

But standing there all alone as she did, her head slightly bowed, her hands fidgeting with the fabric of her gown, Corbin could see the vulnerability past her scathing words. He detected none of the pride she usually carried around her like a torch that refused to be put out. Instead, she flickered like a candle, small and almost pleading for encouragement before she burned out.

Corbin walked toward her, something he rarely ever did, and longed to tell her she was beautiful, as he had so many times before.

She did look almost too stunning for words. Her hair was twisted up on her head, though the endearing curls were just beginning to escape at her hairline and fall onto her forehead. The candlelight brought out the gold in her hair, the brightness of her eyes, and the creaminess of her skin. She wore a deep-green dress that Corbin had never seen before. It was simpler than anything he had seen her wear. Only a single string of pearls adorned her white neck.

Corbin didn't realize he had been staring at her. Indeed, he was looking at her longer than he ever had—at least when she was awake—and she answered with a quizzical expression.

Quickly, he motioned toward the dining hall doors. "Shall we?"

The suddenly somber quartet shuffled to the table and sat down. With a silent sigh of relief, Corbin saw that they were not eating crab tonight. As much as he loved it, he was experiencing too many internal struggles to have to struggle with his food as well. Corbin looked up just in time to see Rose and Will look at each other and then back down quickly. For the first time Corbin could ever remember, Rose looked agonizingly uncomfortable, and it was obvious that it was more than the fact that she was dining with peasants. And Will's expression, though equally uncomfortable, was tinted with empathy and sorrow. Ella seemed to notice too, but had the tact not to pry. Corbin didn't.

"Rose, do you remember Will?" Corbin finally asked after Rose had dropped her eyes for the hundredth time. Corbin had not anticipated this. He had heard stories about her from Will from when Rose visited the palace at Claire, but he never imagined that Rose would even notice, much less remember, a lowly stable worker.

Rose jumped and her fork clanged against her plate, but Will spoke first.

"Yes, Princess Rose and I are old friends. I, uh, had the opportunity to assist Princess Rose with the horses when she would visit Claire. More recently, I saw her at Prince Kenton's ball. I retrieved her carriage for her when she was, um, leaving."

"You're very observant, Mr. Hawkins," Rose said with a false smile.

The awkwardness finally made sense. Will had witnessed what was surely one of the worst days in Rose's life—the day she lost her prince and decided to marry a commoner, just as Kenton had. She couldn't have known that the very man who had witnessed it would be sitting at her dining room table.

Rose and Will weren't off to the best start. But Corbin did wonder, however, if Rose and Ella might become friends. They had a very similar history, and Corbin hoped—though it was a small hope—that Rose might be comforted by that.

"Princess Rose, please forgive me. I honestly thought you wouldn't remember me, if you had even noticed me at all." Will was trying to meet her eyes, though Rose stared steadily at her plate.

"I can assure you I have a very good memory," she said to her roll.

"Yes, I'll be sure to remember that."

Rose looked up and Will smiled warmly at her, his subtle joke lightening the room a bit. Rose's face relaxed and her face softened slightly. Ella giggled, covering her mouth with a gloved hand. Corbin, shocked at how quickly Will could ease the tension in the room, joined in the laughter and grins with his own.

"A smile?" Rose said, meeting Corbin's eyes and smiling her own scornful smile. "A real smile?"

"You sound surprised." Will answered Rose before Corbin could speak. "Of course he's smiling. Corbin is the happiest person I know. In fact, the only time I can remember him *not* smiling was when—" Will stopped abruptly, then looked up at Corbin with a grimace and an apologetic smile.

"Is he?" Rose said, not seeming to notice Will's blunder. "Goodness! Peasants who dine at a king's table and husbands who actually smile. This night is simply full of surprises."

Will glanced at Corbin, his eyebrows raised quizzically. Corbin had undeniably become a different person since arriving in Laurel. Laughter was the last thing on his mind these days.

Rose didn't offer an apology for her rudeness, and no one seemed to expect one. The pity still lingered in Will's eyes, but a scrutiny accompanied it now, and Corbin could feel a chastisement coming. Though he hadn't heard it yet, a part of him knew he deserved it. Corbin barely recognized himself here, and he could only imagine how Will saw him.

Abruptly, Rose stood, her chair scraping across the stones.

"Good nigh—" she began.

"I would love to see more of your home," Ella said quickly before Rose could finish. "I am just stunned by the grandeur. The palace at Claire is beautiful, but it doesn't seem as immersed in tradition and history as yours."

Rose looked down at Ella with so much shock, Corbin was afraid she might fall over.

"Very well," Rose answered after an overly dramatic moment of deliberation. Ella smiled, unruffled by Rose's beastliness. She placed her napkin on the table and joined Rose. As naturally as if they were sisters,

Ella linked her arm through Rose's as they exited the room. Rose gaped at Ella as if she had sprouted another limb.

"The lily carvings that frame the front doors are absolutely enchanting. Were they always there, or . . ."

As soon as their voices trailed off, Will leaned his chair on its two back legs and rested his knee against the table. Corbin checked the doorway to make sure the women had left, then turned back to Will.

"So, *Papa*. When's the big day?" Corbin grinned.

Will couldn't fight the slow smile that spread across his face. "Summer. Ella says June. Maybe July."

"Boy or girl?"

Will laughed. "I don't know."

Corbin frowned. "Really? I just thought that was something married people told unmarried people."

"And I thought it was something women told men. But it's true. We really don't know."

"Strange." Corbin chuckled.

Will sighed, a smile of contentment on his face. He linked his fingers behind his head and looked at Corbin. "So, tell me about your blushing bride . . . and why she thinks you never smile."

Corbin knew this was coming. "First of all, she doesn't blush. The only time that she isn't pale, she's bright red with fury."

Will suppressed a grin, but Corbin knew that he understood exactly what he meant. "What do you two talk about?"

"How am I supposed to talk to her?"

"You open your mouth and words come out. You always have words. Even when you have no money or food or work, you have always had words."

"Well, if I do, I keep them to myself."

Will nodded. "All right. Well, if you don't speak, I know you have eyes. Have you noticed how she looks at you?"

"Yes. Like a cat watches a mouse, just waiting for the right time to strike."

"No. That's not what she looks like."

"Well, what *does* she look like then?" Corbin demanded, his jaw tight.

"I don't know if you want to know."

"I asked, didn't I?"

"That doesn't mean you want to know." Will's smile broke free, and he looked very satisfied with himself, though he hadn't said anything useful.

"How come you think you're so wise all of a sudden?"

"Because I'm married." He said this as if it were the most obvious thing in the world.

"So am I."

Will threw his head back and laughed, one hand slapping his knee. "Oh, you're not married, my friend. Not even close."

"What's that supposed to mean?" Corbin asked, his brows furrowing, though he knew exactly what that was supposed to mean.

"Have you even kissed her yet?"

"What, and have her bite my head off?"

"See? Not married." Will pulled his knee from off the table, and the legs of his chair slammed back on the floor. He looked straight back at Corbin, his fingers linked in front of him on the table, all the mirth drained from his face. "Corbin, she is always watching you. Every time she says something—or *anyone* says *anything*—she looks at you for your reaction. I think she wants your approval."

Corbin knew she watched him, had known it from the first time he walked inside the castle doors. But he had never put it in those words before and he didn't know how he felt about them.

"I really don't think she wants a blacksmith's approval."

Will shrugged. "Maybe you're more than a blacksmith to her."

This didn't make any sense. Of course he was a blacksmith to her. That's all he had ever been to her.

"So you just come in here, eat one meal with us, and tell me all about this woman I have been married to for five months?"

"Yes. Because I'm watching objectively. Do you know what I see when *you* look at her?"

"I don't think you're going to wait for my permiss—"

"Anger. Bare-faced, childish, brooding anger. I'm also going to throw in resentment, self-pity, and boredom. I barely recognize you. Back home, you were the one who always lifted everyone up who was down. Here, you're more like a storm that's constantly brewing. I think your lovely wife is a little afraid of you."

"How can a beast be afraid of a blacksmith?"

Will grinned. "Have you looked in a mirror lately?"

Corbin refused to be sidetracked. "That woman isn't afraid of anything," Corbin said, lying, the memory of Rose's anguished, tear-streaked face in the darkness flashing in his mind. He pushed away the image and the guilt for saying it.

"Don't call her 'that woman.' It isn't respectful."

"Do you have any idea how hard it is to respect someone who despises you? Who screams and pouts and throws people in prison for not keeping her food warm?"

Will thought about this for a moment, sympathy returning to his eyes. "She has earned her name, I'm afraid. I've seen it. I know. But there must be a reason for this. No one can be all bad. Can you think of anything about her that *isn't* beastly?"

After a rebellious moment of silence, Corbin finally answered. "Well, if it's true what you say about her looking at me for approval, I guess that could be something."

Besides what Will had pointed out, all Corbin could think of was how she never smiled and never laughed, how she looked at him with scorn and bitterness. But, reluctantly, the image of her curled up on her bed, crying, and holding onto him crept into his mind. He then remembered how she waited for him to return to the castle every night, though he had stayed away far past dark. He thought of how she helped him write his letter, and if she wanted to mock him for being illiterate, she held it in.

He thought of the few times she had blushed in his presence, though he told Will she never had; the times when she couldn't quite meet his eyes, and the moments she almost smiled, but never allowed herself.

Finally, he remembered her sweet and hopeful expression the first time he looked into her emerald eyes; how her brilliant hair had escaped her scarf and brushed across her forehead. He had willingly stepped forward and she had willingly taken his rose. Yes, things had changed almost instantly, but they had chosen their fate. They had chosen each other. Living with that choice was the challenge now.

"I don't even know where to begin." Corbin's voice was hollow, the anguish of the last few months weighing him down.

"That's because you're not wise yet." Will grinned, though his voice was soft with compassion. "I don't know Rose well. I only know you. And what I know about you is that you hate not having a plan. Whether that applies to a plan for your day, or for your life, it's the same. You hate floating. But what I'm looking at now is a floating man."

"Why is it always me who has to change?"

Corbin knew the answer was because only he could change himself. He couldn't change her. It had to be him.

Laughter drifted into the dining hall, and with it came Ella and Rose. Rose looked slightly less uncomfortable than when they had left, but still stiff. Ella was doubled over, trying to catch her breath to speak, but the laughter was winning.

"What's so funny?" Will asked, holding his arms out. Ella sat down on his knee as she wiped the tears from her eyes.

"I was just telling Princess Rose about the time you were trying to pull Lucy out of the mud and you fell . . . and . . ." Ella wrapped her arm around Will and was overcome with laughter.

Will joined in. "Well, if Princess Rose didn't know us before, she does now." Will smiled at Rose and Corbin. "Lucy is our cow, by the way. I fell in the mud and when I stood up, my boots were stuck in the mud, with my feet trapped inside. The mud was up to my knees. Ella had to tie a rope to Lucy and have her pull me out."

"And then I fell in the mud too. Oh, it was so miserable!"

While they spoke, Corbin laughed along with their story, trying to fight the jealousy that was building up inside him. They were so close, so comfortable. He thought of the addition they would be receiving in the summer and noticed how Will's hand tenderly rested on Ella's.

Corbin glanced over at Rose and saw that, as usual, she was already watching him. Her eyes twinkled in reaction to the story, but he also perceived the same jealousy on her face. When he caught her eye, she quickly looked away—familiar coldness erasing all the emotion out of her features.

Ella kissed Will's cheek, stood up, and sat back down in her chair.

"Somehow you were still handsome, even all covered in mud."

"That's because it covered his face," Corbin said and everyone burst out laughing, except for Rose, who simply lifted a hand to cover her mouth. There was more laughter in that one night in the castle than there had been in months, probably in years. The laughter quieted and Corbin looked once again at Rose. Her eyes glimmered in the candlelight, but she blinked away the moisture before Corbin could make sense of it.

Suddenly, Rose stood, and Will and Corbin quickly stood too. "I must wish you all good night."

Avoiding Corbin's eyes, Rose strode out of the room.

Corbin sat back down and sighed.

"What are you still doing here?" Will asked. "Go and follow your wife."

Instead of looking in his direction, Corbin looked up at Ella, suddenly needing some feminine reinforcement, not just Will's "wise married man" advice. She smiled encouragingly.

"She wants you to. Whether she acts like it or not. I promise."

CHAPTER 23

Corbin trudged up the grand staircase, using the banister to pull himself forward. The farther away he got from the center of the castle and closer to the windows, he realized it was raining, heavy drops pelting the glass and echoing through the empty corridors.

He was ready for a change; he needed a change, and he supposed Rose did too. These months of living like strangers had taken enough of a toll on him and he was tired of it. Tired of feeling defeated and lonely. Tired of feeling like an outsider in his own life. And, if he was being honest, tired of being an outsider in hers.

He wanted to know her. He wanted to know if the person he imagined in his mind while she slept—while she held his hand and was so easily soothed under his touch—really existed. He wanted to know what made her afraid, what made her happy, sad, hopeful, content.

After all this time, he was also acknowledging that he had put up a façade of his own, so it wasn't unfathomable that she had done the same.

When he approached Rose's chamber, he was surprised to see that her door was open. Will had reminded Corbin of his need to have a plan, and just the thought of talking to her instead of going straight to bed filled him with long-dormant optimism.

He took a step toward her open door and peeked inside. She sat across from him on one of the cushioned window seats, her arm resting on the windowsill. Taking a deep breath, he knocked softly on the door.

"May I come in?" he asked quietly.

Rose didn't seem surprised when he knocked; she had probably heard his heavy footsteps approaching from across the castle. She shrugged without looking at him. Light and warmth emanated from a low fire, though it didn't quite provide enough of either. Careful not to step too loudly, he crossed the room and sat down, joining her in staring out the window. The room was dark enough that he could barely see his reflection in the window, and he was able to see past the glass and outside to the gently falling rain. He raised a hand to the window and gasped quietly.

"Cold," he whispered.

"Cold." Rose also raised a hand to touch the glass, but she kept it there, leaving a foggy handprint on the window.

The silence—impenetrable and uneasy—stretched on and on and Corbin began to fidget on the seat, fighting the urge to leave. He turned away from the storm and looked at Rose. She had dropped her head to rest it back on her arms, though her gaze was still fixed on the storm.

"What are you thinking about?" Corbin's voice was quiet and sincere, and Rose looked over at him with slightly wide eyes, her brows furrowed. She didn't answer, but she didn't look away, either.

"Maybe I can guess." A playful smile tugged at the corner of his lips, and Rose glanced at his mouth and back to his laughing eyes.

She shrugged again, and returned to looking out the window, though a small smile was fighting its way to her face.

Encouraged, Corbin scooted closer to her.

"Hmm," he said, rubbing his chin. "You're thinking about how much you like my boots?"

Still looking out the window, she rolled her eyes, but her smile grew slightly.

"You're thinking about . . . crab? Door handles? How much you hate my beard? How much you secretly love my beard?" With each guess, Rose's small smile widened, though she kept her gaze on the window. There was no sarcasm on her face, only an uncharacteristic timidity that softened her normally severe expression. Corbin felt his breath catch in his throat and his voice lowered. "You're thinking about how nice tonight was?"

He thought of how she had looked at Will and Ella, remembered her face at dinner—the peculiar intensity in her eyes, the longing for . . . something.

"You're thinking about how much you like Will and Ella?"

She didn't meet his eyes, but seemed caught off guard by the question. Finally, she nodded subtly while looking at the stones at her feet.

"You envy them?" Corbin regretted the question as soon as he spoke it. Asking Rose if she envied Will and Ella was really only asking her to admit they were nothing like them. Taking a breath, he looked into her eyes—eyes that met his with a quiet fervor that made his heart pound suddenly. "I envy them," he admitted. "I envy what they have."

She didn't look away, though her face became steadily more pink. "I do too." She bit her lip, her gaze dropping as if weighed down by remorse.

Corbin laughed softly, hoping to lighten the mood and ease some of her obvious discomfort. "We really should confess all this envy to Father Goode. This is one of the deadly sins, you know."

Rose smiled sadly. "There are worse ways to die."

"What do you mean?"

"I don't know." She sighed. "I suppose I mean that it's better to die wanting something than to live never knowing what you want."

Corbin was shocked to see that her chin trembled for the tiniest moment before she hid it behind her arm still resting on the windowsill. She cleared her throat and turned to him, her eyes glistening like the rain on the glass. "Will and Ella, they . . . remind me of my parents."

"Tell me about them." Corbin scooted closer to her.

She opened her mouth and then closed it, turning again to hide her chin in her arm. "I can't," she said to the window.

That expression—that obstinate insistence to close herself off—he had seen it a thousand times. But without anger—hers or his—Corbin was able to see it for the fear it really was.

He cleared his throat and tried to make his voice sound nonchalant. "Maybe I can guess," he said, smiling, repeating his words from earlier.

"Maybe you can." The pleading intensity in her eyes belied her casual tone.

"Well, based on what little evidence I've seen," Corbin raised a hand, gesturing to Rose, "I would guess that they were very beautiful. Your mother had eyes like emeralds. Your father had a square, stubborn chin." Corbin paused to make sure Rose hadn't been offended, but the corner of her mouth lifted in a small smile. "They were both dignified and regal, wearing their royalty as comfortably as I wear my stomping boots." The other side of her mouth lifted. Corbin grinned, then became more thoughtful. "Your father was witty, but your mother was more subdued, shy even. She preferred the solitude of her music, and your father preferred hunting and the outdoors." Rose's glistening eyes widened. "They loved to go on long horse rides. They loved to travel. They loved parties and entertaining and reading. But mostly, they loved you."

Rose blinked, and for the first time that Corbin had ever seen, the first time anyone had seen in years, a tear escaped and slid freely down her pale, lightly freckled cheek.

"How did you do that?" she whispered in a trembling voice.

"I've been watching."

"Watching what?"

"You."

Rose dropped her gaze and breathed an unsteady breath. Tentatively and with slightly trembling fingers, Corbin reached over to brush away Rose's tear. She kept her head down, her cheeks now rosy and warm, and Corbin let his hand drop. "Everything they once loved, you now try to hate. I've seen the music room, all the instruments draped in sheets; the armory with rows and rows of dull swords, the bows and arrows hanging dusty on the wall. You didn't want me in either of those places. Those rooms weren't just locked away to preserve your parents' memory. They were locked away to conceal your pain."

Rose's head shot up and Corbin knew he had upset her. He had been too honest and he was sure that she would pull back.

He was wrong.

She moved closer to him, her body leaning forward. "How did you know what they looked like? How did you know I had her eyes and his chin?"

"I guessed," Corbin chuckled. "But it made sense to me. Your eyes are . . ." he stopped, trying to find the right words as he became suddenly very interested in the raindrops on the window. "Your eyes very often have a glint of unruliness about them—more often than not, actually— and I have wondered if your mother might have had just a little bit of willfulness about her if she had ever been allowed. With no one to *tame* you—if you'll forgive me—you have let that side of your nature have free reign. But, there are times when your eyes are soft and thoughtful and so full of feeling that . . ." he paused again, finally meeting her eyes, "that they are the most beautiful, gentlest part of you. Your father, on the other hand, was extremely disciplined. As a hunter and swordsmen, he would have to be. When I see the stubborn set of your jaw, I imagine that he—as strong a king as he was—would look shockingly similar."

Another tear slipped down her cheek, but when she spoke, her voice was light. "You've been busy."

"No, just observant. I can't help it." He chuckled. "And maybe a little bored."

Something like shame flitted across Rose's face, but she tossed her head and turned back to the window.

Corbin instantly recognized Rose's habit of shaking off any painful feelings and turning them into indifference. "If you feel guilty for marrying me and then leaving me to wander the castle all alone for months, you have my permission to feel that way." Rose met Corbin's eyes and he winked before she could lash out.

Her mouth opened in shock, but then broke into a surprised grin. "How dare you . . . No one has ever . . ." She pursed her lips, her shoulders shaking as she held back a laugh.

Corbin took advantage of her stammering. "But first, I would like to apologize for wandering around, brooding like a spoiled child. I'm sorry I spent every waking moment out in the blacksmith shop, looking to my past when I should have been embracing the present. I . . . I'm sorry I didn't tell you every time I thought you were beautiful." He stopped, his voice becoming grave. "And, most importantly, I'm sorry I pretended not to like crab because, I must admit, it's my favorite thing in the world."

Rose had been listening intently, her eyes wistful, until he spoke his last sentence. And when he did, Rose laughed so freely, the sound danced through the air. It echoed off the walls and was the most joyful, beautiful laugh Corbin had ever heard. He heard a door open somewhere, and he knew that the whole household had been surprised by the sound.

When he became vulnerable, he exposed her vulnerability, and the result—incredibly—was laughter.

A spell had been broken.

Rose wiped her eyes and her laugh quieted. Soon, all was silent and she looked at him with a somber expression. Her brow softened and her eyes melted into pools of regret. "I'm sorry," she finally whispered.

Her gaze faltered and she crossed both her arms to rest on the stone windowsill and laid her cheek on them. The rain had hushed to tiny, gentle drops and frost had begun to form on the corners of the glass.

Corbin shifted his body closer to her. Rose's legs were curled up under her skirts, her eyes misty, her cheeks still slightly pink. She rubbed her head where one of her many pins must have been poking her. Every fold of her gown, every jewel was always perfectly placed and coordinated. He realized then what a burden that must be—to never relax, to never let yourself really breathe around anyone else.

Hesitating for a moment, Corbin raised his hand and touched Rose's hair. She flinched slightly under his touch, but didn't move besides that. He ran his fingers over her braided, twisted-up hair until he found a pin. Grasping it with his fingers, he pulled, and her hair fell down around her shoulders. He thought he heard her sigh. He found all the pins he could, placing each one he found on the window seat, and watched with fascination as her hair fell all around her like a shroud. Once her hair was down, she let her head fall deeper into her arms.

Her head still resting, she met Corbin's eyes. Her face was haloed by billows of red curls and she smiled. Really smiled. He raised a hand and placed it softly on her cheek, his thumb brushing away the last of the moisture from when she had cried.

What had happened to them in just a matter of moments? He could touch her, with only the slightest hint of hesitation. She allowed him to, with only the smallest indication of reluctance. And when he looked at her now, she met his eyes with only questions—no accusations, no judgements.

"Rose," Corbin whispered with an unexpected and overwhelming earnestness, "I want to love you."

Her eyes widened and, without seeming to think about it, she placed a hand over his that rested on her cheek. She let another tear escape, and Corbin felt it slide onto his fingers. When she spoke, it was less than a whisper.

"I want to love you, too."

Corbin smiled and Rose rested her head on her arms once more. No more words needed to be said. Besides, Rose seemed exhausted from the effort it took to open up as much as she had.

The rain had become soft *plink plinks* on the glass, and nothing had ever sounded more like a lullaby. With each drop, the tension of the last few months lifted off Corbin's shoulders. Soon, Rose was sleeping deeply, her breathing slow and steady, her body twitching every once in a while. Corbin stood, walked across the room, and pulled a blanket and some pillows off Rose's bed. He draped the blanket over her and, carefully, lifted her head and tucked the pillow under it. He placed a pillow against the wall and leaned against it.

The last thing he saw before he drifted off to sleep was Rose—her mouth soft, her eyes closed and untroubled, her lashes resting on her cheek. Her hair cascaded all around her, hopefully providing some added warmth against the cold night.

He had finally seen her smile in what looked like genuine, sincere happiness. Her lips were smooth and relaxed now, no tenseness or sarcasm, not even a hint of the sadness that usually touched them in her sleep. More than ever, he wondered what it would be like to kiss her—to kiss this woman he had married. But he knew he could never just claim them. They had to be freely given. And he was willing to wait.

When Corbin awoke, it was to a peculiar silvery light. He squinted against the strange brightness, and through the slits, he could see that the castle grounds, the trees, and the surrounding countryside was blanketed in brilliant white. The clouds from the storm had moved on, and the morning sky was clear and clean. The sun hadn't quite risen, but the first hints of light shattered off the snow like a million tiny diamonds.

Corbin looked over at Rose and saw that she still slept. She had barely moved in the night, except for one of her arms, which had fallen by her side. No nightmares. No fear. Her face was the picture of contentment.

Her neck was bent at a strange angle, and Corbin thought she might be more comfortable in her bed. He stood and, smiling, gathered her in his arms, careful not to jostle her. Her hair tickled his cheek and she murmured softly, but didn't wake. If there was one thing he absolutely knew about Rose, it was that she was a deep sleeper. He carried her to her bed and carefully removed her shoes before pulling a thick blanket over her.

Corbin knelt down next to the bed to watch her sleep, his hand gently holding hers, just as he had so many times before. But now, everything was different.

They wanted to love each other. And in admitting this, Corbin wondered if, somehow, they already did . . . just a little bit.

The same book lay open, the dried rose still on the page. She must have opened it again since the day she had closed it. Corbin lightly ran his fingers over the crisp petals, smiling.

Corbin stood, brushed the hair back from her face, and leaned down to touch his lips to her cheek.

The sun rose steadily higher, and with it, the light became blinding. Looking down at her tranquil, unguarded face, Corbin said farewell to the beast.

CHAPTER 24

ROSE

Sometime in the night or early morning, Rose opened her eyes. A peculiar gleam shone through the windows and cast a cool, glimmering light throughout her chamber.

Someone was with her. A man. He was kneeling next to her bed, though she couldn't remember going to bed. His gray eyes, glistening in the soft light, were focused on her hand, which he held on her pillow. His black hair fell across his forehead, and Rose recognized the straight nose, the faint burn scar across his cheek, the strong, bearded jaw, the subtly smiling lips.

A breath later, her eyes closed, and when she opened them again, he was gone.

Just a dream.

Rose awoke with her hand cradled against her cheek. Rolling over, she blinked against the morning light that streaked in through her windows; the curtains had never been closed. The last thing she saw before she had drifted off to sleep on the window seat was the blacksmith watching her with an intense, piercing expression, mingled with an uncharacteristic tenderness. She remembered being cold, then some jostling, then being so warm.

She looked down and saw that she was still wearing her green gown, but that her shoes had been removed and placed side by side on the floor next to her bed, and that a blanket had been pulled over her. How did she get here? Sitting up, Rose pulled the blanket up to her chin, suddenly feeling very exposed. She fought through the bleariness in her mind and tried to remember what she and the blacksmith had talked about the night before.

Her cheeks warmed as she recalled how he had spoken so kindly about her parents he had never met . . . how he had spoken about her. He had called her beautiful. Did he mean all those things? Was the gentleness in his eyes sincere, or would he return to the brooding, melancholy man he had been for the past few months?

And what about her? She had not only spoken civilly to him, but had been open and honest—even vulnerable. What had brought about this change, and would it last?

She blinked against bewildering tears that merged the light with the darkness in her chamber. He had said he wanted to love her. She had told him the same.

Footsteps approached from behind her closed door. They were still, then the door creaked open slowly. Rose's heart pounded.

Maryann's head peeked in from the open door. "Oh, Princess Rose. You're awake! Forgive me. I'll run and fetch your breakfast."

Rose heard her footsteps retreat, pause, and then hastily return. Her head popped back in the doorway. "Did you see the snow? It's glorious!" After her unusual outburst, she ducked her head slightly, then bowed into a quick and awkward curtsy. Rose cringed when Maryann slammed the door in her nervousness.

Once Maryann's footsteps faded away, Rose waited to make sure she was gone, then leapt up out of bed. She flew across the frozen stones and stopped in front of the window on the opposite side of her chamber. Through disbelieving eyes, Rose squinted against the brilliant sunlight, the bright blueness of the sky, and the dazzling white that covered all the browns and greens with cleanliness and sameness. Everything, from the tallest tree to the smallest blade of grass, had been given a fresh start—and all were equally pure.

Rose could tell by the dramatic slant of the shadows against the snow that she was awake earlier than she had been in years. Except, she didn't feel tired. On the contrary, a strange energy filled her whole body, causing her heart to fly like hummingbird wings. A warmth and brightness seemed to be radiating from her heart to her head and down to the tips of her toes.

The next door down the corridor—Corbin's door—opened and then closed and Arthur's familiar whistle reached her ears. Rose, grateful she was still dressed—though she knew her hair was a fright—ran to her door and pulled it open. Arthur came walking past Rose's door, carrying a bucket of old, charred wood and ashes.

"Arthur, is the blacksmith awake yet?"

"Awake? Of course, Your Majesty. Since dawn." He bowed quickly mid-step, eager to rid his bucket of the soot and ashes, and to be out of her presence as quickly as possible . . . as usual. As he trudged down the corridor, Rose could hear his muted mumblings. "Awake and not even noon yet . . . strange . . . mane like a lion, she's got . . ."

Just then, the heart-pounding sound of masculine laughter echoed from around the corner. Was it always this loud and lively in the castle before midday? Rose unexpectedly felt slightly forlorn, realizing that she had been missing out on a whole history of mornings.

The laughter belonged to the blacksmith, and the stable worker, Will Hawkins, was speaking. As silently as she could, Rose pushed the door closed before they saw her. She didn't know what to do. Was she supposed to greet the blacksmith? And what about his guests? Was she obligated to mingle with them—those commoners who were infuriatingly kind and surprisingly well-mannered? They were nothing like she was expecting, and she was completely baffled by them.

After a moment of deliberation, Rose quickly returned to her bed and pulled her blankets back up around her chin.

"Oh, Will! Look at the stables!" Ella's soft voice landed on Rose's ears. A pleasant, comforting warmth spread through Rose, and again, inexplicable tears swam in her eyes. She shook her head and blinked against the tears, which had quickly become tears of frustration. She couldn't be feeling fondness for this stranger, this peasant. It didn't make any sense. Nothing made sense this morning.

"Yes." It was Corbin who answered. "There are stables, but no horses. There haven't been horses here in years."

"Oh, really? That's too bad."

"Well," Will said, "if you ever want to start filling those stables up again, you say the word. I'll send you my best."

Corbin chuckled. "You'll be the first to know."

"Where is Rose, Corbin? Is she feeling well?" Ella's voice sounded as if it was right outside Rose's chamber door.

Corbin cleared his throat.

"Rose? Well, she likes to . . . I usually don't see her before . . ." He obviously didn't want to share that Rose had a propensity for sleeping until noon.

Rose flung her legs out from under her blanket and put her feet on the floor, then she marched to the door and flung it open.

All three were standing at the window across from her room and turned to stare at her in the open doorway. She felt her cheeks warm, and then burn, when she realized she was wearing the same dress as yesterday and that her hair was as wild as it had ever been.

"Good morning," she said with a hint of defiance.

Ella blushed and Will stifled a grin. Rose couldn't make herself meet Corbin's eyes, but was forced to when he left the window and stepped toward her.

"Rose! Good morning." His arms had been crossed, but they dropped limply to his sides. His mouth fell open slightly and then lifted in a wide, reassuring grin. "It's nice to see you so . . . early," he finished awkwardly.

His warm, welcoming smile and the way his sky-gray eyes looked from her face to her wild hair and back again made her forget that she had the ability to scowl. He walked forward, leaving Ella and Will, who suddenly became very interested in the view of the snow-covered gardens.

"Look at all the bushes! Have you ever seen so many bushes? It's so bushy here!" Will muttered in what sounded like feigned astonishment. Ella elbowed him and giggled, but they both kept their eyes focused on the landscape.

"Did you sleep well?" Corbin's tone, his mannerisms, and his smile were all touched with an endearing shyness, taking all the words from Rose's mouth. "I hope you don't mind that I carried you to bed. I was afraid you would have a sore neck today if you stayed on the window seat all night." He grinned, then raised a hand to run his fingers through his hair. His face was freshly shaven and smooth, his hair slightly damp. She could smell the soap on his skin and the freshness of his clothes.

In contrast, her clothes were rumpled, and she knew that her face was blotchy from the ridiculous tears that kept springing to her eyes all morning—as they did now. She stood in her bare feet on the stones, and her hair dangled in front of her eyes. She knew she looked the most like a peasant of any of them. But Corbin didn't seem disappointed. He looked at her with tenderness and a gentle smile that seemed to encourage her exasperating tears.

"Well," Corbin said when Rose didn't respond, "I wanted to show Will the shops, and Ella would like to explore the castle." Rose stood silently, her words unable to find a way from her mind to her mouth. Corbin grinned and bent his head closer to hers, his fingers brushing away the hair that covered her eyes. "And Rose, you look beautiful in the morning."

All Rose could do was blink slowly, the heat in her cheeks spreading disobediently across her face. Corbin's smile widened, a dimple appearing on the left side of his mouth as he turned to rejoin Ella and Will.

If it had been difficult trying to detest him when he was distant and withdrawn, Rose couldn't imagine how difficult it would be now that he was charming.

CHAPTER 25

Rose stared back at her reflection as Maryann pinned and braided her hair. She barely recognized herself. Her eyes were too bright, too wide, too full of excitement. There wasn't even a hint of scorn in the small smile that lit her face. She couldn't deny that the pink in her cheeks was most alluring, though too often it turned deep red and spread all the way to her hairline, but only when she thought of the blacksmith—how he had wiped her tears, smiled at her, complimented her, and had carried her to bed. She closed her eyes in mortification and delight as her heart fluttered . . . until something sharp and painful jabbed into her head.

Rose gasped and touched her fingers to where Maryann had just poked her head with a pin.

Maryann backed away from Rose's chair, her hands at her mouth, her eyes wide and brimming with tears. "Please forgive me! Oh, please forgive me. I am so terribly sorry."

Rose pulled her hand away from her head, and Maryann shrieked when she saw that Rose's fingers were wet with blood. Rose had thrown Maryann in the dungeon for less than this.

Familiar fury filled Rose. Her fingers were covered in blood and sharp pain radiated through her head. Would this girl ever learn to do Rose's hair without disaster . . . or bloodshed? Rose knew very well, though she could never admit it aloud, that no one else from the village would come to replace Maryann if Rose sent her away. She knew her reputation as well as anyone.

"Well, I would send you to the dungeon for this . . ." Rose said, looking at Maryann in the mirror.

Maryann whimpered, but Rose rolled her eyes and continued.

"But we both know that the blacksmith will simply release you, so . . ." Rose sighed, her anger melting. "Here." She picked up a pin off the bureau and held it out for Maryann to take. Maryann remained where she was, trembling and pale. "It's all right, Maryann. It . . . it was an accident." Rose could barely comprehend her own words.

Out of relief, gratitude, or utter confusion, Maryann's tears began afresh, coursing down her blotched cheeks. "You mean . . . I'm not going . . . t-to the dungeon?" she sobbed.

Unsettling and unnatural shame burned in Rose's chest. Maryann was terrified—even more terrified of Rose's forgiveness than of her wrath. Rose didn't know how to respond. She didn't know herself.

How could Corbin's kindness toward her—and her acceptance of it—change everything?

Rose shifted in her chair, though she couldn't quite manage a smile. Besides, Maryann's eyes were too blurred with tears to see it if she had.

"No," Rose said slowly, her voice barely a whisper, "you're not going to the dungeon."

The snow steadily melted throughout the day under the rays of the brilliant winter sun. Corbin and Will braved the cold and spent much of the day out in the grounds. Will mended planters and pruned bushes and trees, while Corbin cleared walkways and patched one of the shop roofs. Even Ella joined them after exploring the library and the Great Hall all morning. She knelt right down in the snow and inspected the health of the laurel bushes.

Rose watched from inside the castle feeling utterly useless. She didn't know anything about gardening, and less than nothing about mending roofs. Normally, she would be content to watch the peasants work—though why they *wanted* to work was an absolute mystery to her. But as she watched them, she felt strangely envious. They joked and laughed, in spite of the mud and cold, and seemed to even be having deep conversations. The grounds became increasingly beautiful and decluttered as the day progressed, and even though Corbin had spent much of his days working in the grounds and shops, so much was accomplished with the help of his peculiar friends.

From where she stood, she could also see Lord Stanford's house. She looked at the roof, the quaint windows, and the neatly placed stones that made up the outer wall. When her eyes finally made it to the door, she gave a little start when she saw Lord Stanford standing there, still as a statue, his eyes fixed on the castle. Rose smiled and chastised herself for being so alarmed by his sudden appearance. She blinked, and the next thing she saw was the door closing behind him.

Corbin and his friends worked throughout the rest of the day, stopping every once in a while to sit on the benches and eat the sandwiches brought out to them by Mrs. Whiting. Rose could see them from the parapet or through the windows as she walked by. Although, she would duck out of sight when Corbin would look up toward the castle. His eyes seemed expectant and, though she could have imagined it, disappointed when he couldn't find her.

Mercifully, dinner was a much less taxing affair that evening. Corbin greeted Rose in the Great Hall with a genuine smile and compliment. She blushed under his gaze as he approached her, and more deeply as he kissed her hand, his lips lingering on her skin.

Will and Ella wore the same clothes they had dined in the night before, though Rose wasn't surprised, or even bothered. Rose chose to wear one of her more simple gowns—a high-necked gown of pale pink— and decided to forego the jewels.

Once they were seated, Corbin and Will discussed their plans for the rest of the week—what they would work on and fix up, and what needed the most attention.

"I've been wanting to secure the beams in the stable, but it's a two-man job at least," Corbin said before taking a bite of his roll.

"Yes, I noticed that. That roof wouldn't be safe for any horses," Will agreed between spoonfuls of chowder. "After that, we should secure those loose stones in the outer wall in the garden. That's an accident waiting to happen."

They didn't seem overwhelmed by all they wanted to accomplish. On the contrary, their eyes were lit with excitement and purpose. Corbin spoke animatedly and Rose couldn't stop watching him. And when he met her eyes, there was none of the previous acrimony of the past five months. Once, he winked at her and smiled as her cheeks burned.

Ella looked at Will and Corbin as they spoke like they were mischievous little boys, an affectionate smile on her gentle face. Where did such peace come from? Rose remembered that Corbin had told her that Ella had also lost both of her parents. How was she so filled with warmth and tenderness? How had she overcome that tragedy with such grace?

Suddenly, more than she had ever wanted anything, Rose wanted to feel that peace.

CHAPTER 26

Ella's eyes widened as she absorbed the grandeur of the Throne Room. "I love the ancient feeling of this castle. So ornate and elaborate. Claire's castle is stunning and has a certain vitality about it, but it almost seems to lack the maturity and steadiness of this one," Ella said after they had explored the second floor.

The night before, Rose resolved to spend more time with Ella. After Corbin and Will ate breakfast, they went out to work in the grounds, and Rose invited Ella to tour the castle. Ella had consented with sparkling eyes and an ecstatic smile.

Ella's fingers traced the pattern that had been carved in a nearby stone pillar. "Roses. Beautiful." She walked over to the wall and admired the molding. "Oh, and irises. Were they carved when your great-grandmother was born?"

"Yes, they were, as a matter of fact," Rose answered with a hint of disbelief. Somehow, Ella knew almost as much about the kingdom as Rose did. It was tradition in Laurel to name each princess after a flower or bush, but Ella seemed to already know this. Rose's mother's name was Marion, her grandmother was named Lily.

"I've always wondered," Ella said, smiling, "where did your mother's name come from?"

Rose grinned, remembering how her grandfather would tell her the story when she was a little girl. "My grandfather came here from another kingdom. When he learned that our princesses are named after bushes and flowers, he thought it was kind of silly. After my mother was born, my grandparents couldn't agree on a name. She was their first child, and my

143

grandfather was surprised by how quickly their tiny baby grew. He said she grew as fast as his marionberry bush he had when he was growing up and began calling her Marion. The name stuck."

"How sweet!" Ella said. "I love how the history of the kingdom is engraved in every detail. The paintings of the laurel bush, the lilies carved in the garden benches, the irises that line the front walk . . ."

"How do you know so much about the history of Laurel?" Rose couldn't stop herself from asking, and couldn't quite keep the surprise out of her voice. Ella's calloused hands and sunburned cheeks contradicted the air of refinement and intelligence about her.

Ella laughed and then sighed. "Before my father died, I had the best tutors money could buy. I learned more in those years than I even realized at the time, and I guess it has all stayed with me."

By now, they had descended the grand staircase and had walked out the back doors to the crisp afternoon sunshine. They walked out into the garden, and Ella smiled at the sound of hammering and sawing coming from one of the shops. "I know that your kingdom is named after the laurel bush because of its hardiness and its ability to survive for hundreds of years." She walked over to one of the freshly hedged laurels and caressed its cold, silky leaves between her fingers. "It provides shade and protection from the sun, as well as beauty. In cold weather, the laurel curls in on itself, protecting it from the effects of the cold. And every summer, it blooms white and purple blossoms."

Rose nodded and smiled in remembrance, her own lessons from her youth filling her mind. She hadn't thought about them or cared to think about them in years. She looked up at the window she used to gaze out of when she sat through hours of lessons. As a young girl, she used to long to be outside, feeling and smelling the things she was reading about. But soon, she preferred the books and was content to simply observe from a distance.

Ella walked away from the laurel and knelt down in front of a nearby planter. Her gloveless hands glided over the damp soil. "When I was little, I remember learning about a princess who lived just across the sea. She was about my age, and she was named Rose." Ella smiled and looked up at Rose, blinking against the sun. "My mother died soon after I was born and I lost my father ten years later. I remember walking into town one day . . . I must have been about thirteen years old . . . and I heard about the deaths of the king and queen of Laurel. Everyone was so sad for them, understandably. But all I could think about was the princess named Rose who had lost her parents like I did."

Ella stood, her eyes glistening with unashamed tears. Rose turned away, but didn't know where to look. No one spoke to her about her parents, except for Corbin only a couple of nights ago. Mrs. Whiting used to try to comfort her. She used to try to hold her close and tell Rose that she understood her pain, but that was impossible. No one understood. No one else could understand pain that ripped you open and sucked you in, pain so unbearable you actually wished it would swallow you whole, pain you could touch and feel and taste.

It might have been possible that Mrs. Whiting understood, but Rose refused to believe back then that anyone could. But now, years later, as she looked at the tear-filled eyes of this woman who was a stranger and somehow a friend, Rose felt that Ella might understand.

Rose looked down at the planter and saw the littering of dried rose thorns—the only remnant of the beautiful rosebushes that used to guard the garden. "They named me after their favorite flower—the rose. Only . . . I'm more thorns than flower." Rose closed her mouth, shocked at her own candor. She wanted to toss her head and shake off the emotion that overcame her then, but couldn't quite manage it.

"You have known tragedy, Princess Rose. You have suffered. You were so young when you lost your parents, and in such an unexpected way. You didn't even get to say goodbye. No one can judge you for that."

Rose's chin quivered. "Maybe not," she said with a hushed voice. "But what about all these years after? I have become a beast. I don't even know how to change. It's been so long, I can't even remember who I used to be. This is all I know."

Rose turned away as she brushed away disobedient tears. She had never dared to admit to anyone that she didn't want to be a beast. The task of overcoming that once-small part of herself—which now consumed every other part of herself—was too monumental.

Ella, as naturally as if Rose was her own sister, gathered her in her arms and smoothed Rose's hair.

"You poor thing," Ella murmured. A week ago, if anyone had dared to call Princess Rose "poor" and a "thing," they would have been thrown in the dungeon until all that was left of them were bones. Perhaps it was because of Ella's natural kindness, and the fact that she didn't see Rose as something to be feared or hated, but Rose didn't push her away. Corbin had invited his friends to come, Rose assumed, to help and comfort him in his loneliness. But Rose never imagined that she would be comforted by them too.

Ella pulled back and grasped the tops of Rose's arms with gentle but steady hands. "Rose, it doesn't matter how long you have been what you are. When my parents died, I became a different person too. I became quiet and solemn at times, but people needed me, and it helped me heal, even if I didn't realize it at the time. Find someone who needs you and take care of them." Compassion still lingered in Ella's eyes, but there was a conviction there that blazed.

Rose nodded, but remained silent. How could she care for someone else when she herself was so broken?

CHAPTER 27

The snow was almost completely melted by the end of the week. Only a few patches remained—those that had been protected in dark and icy shadows. Working out in the wintry sunshine, Corbin and Will became more and more sunburned with each passing day and Ella now knew as much as Rose about Laurel and its history. It was surprisingly enjoyable telling Ella all about this kingdom Rose had been born to rule. She was reminded of the richness of her heritage and the legacy of those who had gone before her. A sense of pride and duty had been reawakened in Rose that both excited and terrified her.

A week after Will and Ella arrived, the sky began to grow dark again. Rose had almost begun to think that the rainy season had ended early. There had been no nightmares, not since the night that she and Corbin had spoken by the window. But by the time they all met in the Great Hall before dinner, the sky was heavy with thick and ominous clouds churning in the distance.

"I think we better leave first thing in the morning," Will announced over the main course. "We've already been gone almost two weeks now and there's no way to know how long that storm will last."

"So soon?" Corbin's voice was steady, but Rose noted a hint of panic.

"I wish we could stay longer, but it's a lot to ask for the neighbor boy to look after things for too much longer. We still have a three-day's journey."

"True. I understand." Corbin, who had been eating his crab with unabashed enthusiasm, now poked at the claws with his fork.

Though Ella and Will reminded Rose of her own parents, there was a very significant difference. As rulers of a kingdom, Rose's parents were often away on diplomatic visits and assignments. They almost always left Rose behind, telling her it was dangerous for children to travel so much and that it was no life for a child to live. They always promised they would be back as soon as possible, though their trips often lasted months. Until the time they never returned . . .

Ella watched Will and Corbin speak and kept looking in Rose's direction, but Rose couldn't meet her eyes. She knew they were all thinking the same thing. How much would change once Will and Ella left?

Matthew, who stood at Rose's elbow, placed a plate of custard on the table in front of her. She lifted her fork and methodically took a bite, her mind preoccupied. She grimaced as she bit into something sharp and crunchy that shattered unpleasantly between her teeth.

She threw her fork down at the table. "Matthew! There is an eggshell in my custard! Send for the cook!"

Ella gaped at Rose. Will paused mid-bite, his eyes wide and questioning. Corbin closed his eyes, but didn't make any other movements. The same foreign shame Rose had felt when Maryann had poked her head with a pin earlier in the week came flooding back. Ella and Will resumed eating, or at least pretending to. Corbin opened his eyes and was now looking at her. He wasn't angry. He wasn't embarrassed. His piercing, expectant gaze held Rose's steadily.

The chef was summoned and arrived, breathless, in the dining room. His face was redder than usual, and though it had been a while since he had been sent to the dungeons, he didn't seem surprised. He bowed, and waited silently.

Ella stared awkwardly at her plate while Will looked between the chef and Rose with interest. Corbin's eyes never left Rose.

Rose took a deep breath. "I wanted to thank you for this delicious meal."

The chef's mustache twitched. "Pardon me, Your Highness?"

"I wanted to thank you for this delicious meal." She tried to smile, but her face was too tense.

"W-why, it's my pleasure, Your Highness."

Rose nodded and the chef exited the dining room as quickly as he came. Before he closed the door, he threw an exultant smile at Corbin.

She didn't know what to do. She wanted to run from the room and escape the terrible awkwardness, the judgement, and her own mortification. But she knew it would only make things worse. Too much had changed too quickly and Rose was struggling to keep up.

Thankfully, Corbin addressed Will. "So, you'll have to leave first thing in the morning? I'll have Baines send for a carriage."

"Wonderful. Thank you," Will answered as he leaned back in his chair. "I think the best way to spend our last night here is for me to tell embarrassing stories from your childhood to your new wife."

As they stood, Corbin looked over at Rose and winked. Rose smiled and her tense face relaxed, and she felt, once again, gratitude for these people she never would have had anything to do with five months ago.

Ella crossed the room and linked her arm through Rose's as they walked to the drawing room.

"Well done, Rose."

That night, as she did every night, Rose fought against sleep, though she was thoroughly exhausted. She had never had such a good time and was surprised by how much she enjoyed hearing stories about the man she married. Everyone had laughed and talked, including Rose, and her eyes were once again opened to the character and goodness of the man who had given her the rose. But once all was quiet and she was alone in her room, she read until her eyes watered and burned. The wind had begun to howl outside, and as soon as the first of the raindrops began to fall, Rose reluctantly closed her eyes.

The nightmares came, as did Rose's usual frustration—frustration that she was still afraid, frustration that they still came. Lately, though, they seemed to end more quickly than usual. A peace and tranquility drove them away, without her ever waking.

CHAPTER 28

The next morning, Rose woke early. She didn't know when Will and Ella would leave, but she wanted to be up to say goodbye. At the first stirrings in the castle corridors, Rose rang for Maryann and dressed quickly, hurrying to the front doors.

The clouds hung heavy and dark, and the air was filled with the dusty-sweet smell of rain. Corbin stood on the steps, watching as the carriage pulled up to take Ella and Will to the harbor. When Ella noticed Rose, she rushed over to her, pulling her close in a sisterly embrace.

"I'm going to miss you, Rose. I'm so glad I got to meet the princess across the sea."

Rose's couldn't speak, but could only mouth the words, "Thank you."

Once Ella let Rose go, Corbin kissed Ella's hand and gave a basket overflowing with food to Will.

"For your trip. Mrs. Whiting packed extra roast beef," Corbin said with a smile, and he closed the door of the carriage after they climbed in.

Ella and Will pulled the carriage curtains back and waved until they were hidden behind the hill. Corbin watched as they disappeared, and Rose observed Corbin from the steps. She thought about all that had been revealed about this man in the last week with his friends here. He had laughed until his eyes twinkled with tears. He was filled with a vitality that made Rose a little breathless to be around. He moved a little more quickly, much like when he had first arrived, only then it had agitated and exhausted her, making her heart beat a little too rapidly. Her heart still beat too rapidly, but she was slowly learning to keep up.

She looked down at his hair he had trimmed the day after their conversation at the window, at the profile of his smooth, freshly shaven jaw, and at his shoulders that were so broad they were almost vulgar. He sighed quietly and placed his hands in his pockets—ungloved hands that were covered in burns and scars; hands that would envelop hers if they ever held them.

A feeling of abandonment had drifted over her, and Rose wondered if Corbin could sense it too. Her cheeks warmed as she thought about their conversation that had seemed to change so much—how sincere and open he was, how vulnerable she was, yet how safe she felt. How could they recapture that when all she felt now was detachment and hesitation?

Corbin raised a hand to rub the back of his neck and turned to look at Rose, the expression on his face mirroring hers. Rose saw the unease she felt, the trepidation about how to move forward.

Corbin walked up a few steps so that his face was level with hers.

"May I ask you what you're thinking, Rose?"

His voice, soft and deep, somehow had the power to inspire infuriating blushes and fill her heart with a strange tightness. She had been in the same castle with him, but had missed him since their last real conversation a week ago.

"You may."

His dimple appeared and she had to catch her breath. "What are you thinking, Rose?"

Rose had never had problems speaking her mind, but it usually didn't involve speaking her heart. Now, the words were blocked in her throat and she felt that if she uttered them, this safe little space they had created would be shattered. But in his eyes was only gentleness. On his face was an almost desperate, exposed expression that seemed to plead with her to be honest.

"I'm afraid," she whispered.

"I am too."

"What are we going to do now?"

Corbin swallowed, then shrugged his shoulders. "Breakfast?"

She smiled a little, relief making her dizzy. "That's a good start. I haven't eaten breakfast out of bed in years."

"You haven't eaten *breakfast* in years." Corbin laughed, though he watched Rose with a guarded expression.

Rose tried to scowl, but it was half-hearted and a smile escaped instead. "How about after breakfast, I teach you to read?" The words had tumbled out before she had thought them through, and she fought the urge to slap a hand over her mouth.

"Read? If you're trying to punish me for my teasing, a good eye rolling would suffice." Corbin chuckled as he held the door open for her.

Mrs. Whiting entered the foyer just then and Corbin stepped forward. "Wait, Mrs. Whiting. Would you mind setting two places at the breakfast table?"

Rose had noticed that Corbin and Mrs. Whiting had formed a friendship, and she couldn't help smiling at their closeness. It had brought a warmth and pleasantness to the castle that even she had felt. When Corbin finished speaking, Mrs. Whiting nodded, her face cheerful and pleased. She scurried off and disappeared around a corner.

They laughed a little tentatively at Mrs. Whiting's reaction as they walked to the morning dining room. When they entered, Corbin walked over to a chair where one of the place settings sat on the table, and just before Rose thought he would sit down, he pulled the chair out for her. Feeling suddenly awkward, but pleasantly surprised, Rose walked over to the chair and sat down. Corbin cleared his throat and sat at the other place setting that had been hastily laid out.

Silence entered the room and neither one could meet the other's eyes.

"Sorry," Corbin finally said. "This is just all so . . . different." Corbin lifted his fork and stared at his food as if he had forgotten how to eat. After a moment, he met her eyes. "Rose, that night at the window, this morning, these are new beginnings. Let's just take as many as we need."

From the first time she met him, Rose had noticed the intense steel gray of his eyes. When he was in a foul mood, they seemed darker, almost in a shadow. When he laughed or smiled, which had been rare up until the last couple of days, they shimmered like rainclouds reflected in a pond. Now, as he fell silent and pensive, they matched the gray clouds before a storm. Only the color wasn't tempestuous and angry; it was calm, like a protective shroud giving the world a brief respite from the glare of the sun.

CHAPTER 29

The soft, sleepy light of the library glistened off the dust motes and warmed Rose's fingers as they traced along the spines of the volumes of leather-bound books. Corbin hovered in the entrance, his hands in his pockets, feet shuffling. Rose tried not to smile at his overwhelmed expression and couldn't help noting how endearing his nervousness was. He bit the corner of his lower lip and sighed quietly every few seconds.

"Here, this should do it," Rose announced as she walked toward an overstuffed chair, carrying half a dozen books.

"Why do we need all of those?" Corbin still lingered in the doorway. His voice was nonchalant, but his eyes were anxious, the hands in his pockets clenched in tight fists.

"I just want to see what your preferences are. It's not enjoyable reading something you don't like."

She sat down, choosing a chair rather than the settee. Corbin shuffled forward and plopped down on the chair that sat opposite the little table beside Rose's chair. She spread out the books in front of her on the table, her hands trembling with excitement.

"First, maybe you should tell me what you know. Do you know any letters?"

"I've learned their names, and most of their sounds. But, I just don't recognize them and I get their sounds confused. I know my name starts with 'c.' I can recognize 'o' but I get 'p' and 'q' mixed up, as well as 'v' and 'w.' Beyond that, it's just a bunch of lines and curves and . . ." Corbin looked away from Rose's face and out the window. "I don't think I can do this."

An abnormal and overwhelming sense of pity twisted in the pit of Rose's stomach. This was the first time Corbin had ever shown any sign of weakness, or even fear. He could be aloof sometimes, and even moody, but never weak. Never afraid.

He took a breath, "I will try, I promise. I just need a little fresh air first."

The air in the library was indeed oppressive, their sudden closeness strange and disquieting. Corbin stood and hurried out the open library doors. Rose watched from the library window as he walked through the garden toward the shops and disappeared. As he walked, she could almost feel the tension melt off him in the morning sun.

A low chuckle preceded the footsteps of Lord Stanford as he entered the library.

"I'm told that it has been a very enjoyable morning here. The blacksmith is winning you over, it sounds like." He walked forward and joined Rose at the window.

Rose reluctantly pulled her gaze away from the gardens. "We've just decided to be a little more civil to each other. Living in such incessant animosity is arduous."

"Did you tell that to the prince?"

Rose was silent for a moment. "Perhaps not in those exact words."

Lord Stanford nodded, a small smile underneath his goatee. "No, I should think not." He reached into his breast pocket. "I just came to have you sign a few more things."

Rose sighed. "Very well."

Lord Stanford reached for a quill off a nearby table and handed it to Rose who signed the documents lethargically.

"Very good. Thank you, Princess Rose. I'll be getting back to my duties."

For the first time, Rose felt a twinge of guilt as Lord Stanford left the library. The sense of pride that she felt while showing Ella the castle and teaching her about Laurel's history gripped her uncomfortably. She had willingly relinquished her duties after her parents' deaths, but seeing Lord Stanford doing work she should be doing—setting the tax rate, making laws, overseeing the general welfare of the kingdom, going on diplomatic mission in her stead—weighed heavily on her mind.

In the months after their deaths, Rose had removed her parents' portraits from the walls, covering them in sheets and putting them in abandoned rooms, so that she couldn't see the reproof in their eyes. But for the first time in many years, she could envision them now. They weren't angry; they were disappointed. And it was infinitely worse.

The sound of approaching footsteps brought Rose out of her reverie. Mrs. Whiting entered the room carrying a tray of food and placed it on a table.

Mrs. Whiting's naturally kind, soft voice instantly calmed Rose. "Hello, Princess Rose, dear. I've brought you some tea and cookies."

She could have thrown her arms around the woman. That was exactly what she needed. Rose left the window and sat down, taking a bite of a cookie and feeling the tea trickle down her throat and warm her from the inside.

Mrs. Whiting had always done her best to take care of Rose, and for as long as she could remember, Rose had adored Mrs. Whiting. She had always been a kind woman, though prone to solemnity. And as Mrs. Whiting had no children, she doted on Rose . . . until Rose, in her grief, shut her and everyone else out.

When Rose announced that she had decided to marry a commoner, Mrs. Whiting had pleaded with her to keep with tradition, reminding Rose for the millionth time of her duty to rule her kingdom in honor as her parents had. But she had eventually accepted Rose's decision in silence and meekness, especially when she had been threatened with dismissal for her flagrant resistance to the princess's wishes.

Rose knew perfectly well then, as she knew now, that Mrs. Whiting's opposition was really just concern for Rose's well-being. Rose had been in no state of mind for marriage. Prince Kenton had just broken off their engagement and had announced a ball, which Rose had rushed to, hoping to win him back. He had refused to see her, and before Rose had even crossed the sea back to her own kingdom after his ball, he had already married a commoner. When Rose returned, Mrs. Whiting recognized the blaze of vengeance in Rose's eyes and had counseled Rose to wait. But after Rose had chosen Corbin at the Gift Giving and was dressing for her wedding, Mrs. Whiting had come to Rose with red-rimmed, swollen eyes, wet with contrition, and apologized for her previous disapproval.

"Thank you, Mrs. Whiting," Rose said before Mrs. Whiting left the library.

Mrs. Whiting turned to face her, and Rose hoped she knew that her gratitude wasn't only for the tea.

"You're welcome, my little princess. You're very welcome." Mrs. Whiting left, but not before Rose saw the sheen of tears in her eyes—tears

Rose had seen many times before whenever Mrs. Whiting felt a particular fondness for the often unlovable princess.

After Rose ate a cookie and drank a cup of tea, she left the library and wound and weaved her way to the parapet on the fourth floor. The smoke billowed from the blacksmith shop and she knew that's where he was. But when the smoke waned, her heart pounded, knowing that he would soon be returning.

Finally, Corbin appeared in the garden. The cold, rainy season was still upon them, and she could see his breath as he piled up the branches he had trimmed. Royal life had not softened him, and she found herself being glad of it. If anything, his skin seemed impossibly darker, scratches and scrapes from weeding, trimming, and digging joining the burn scars that glared angrily on his skin.

She had been captivated by the simple, dirty blacksmith with the rose from that very first day. From the first moment she saw him, he awakened something in her that had long been dormant. And yet, she had been cruel to him. Out of habit, out of choice. But he had stayed, when so many others had left.

Tears came so easily to Rose these past couple of days, and they slipped freely down her cheeks now. She let them fall, hoping they could wash away some of the guilt that seemed to burn her from the inside.

It was a strange kind of remorse. It didn't pull her down into despair. Rather, it lifted her up and gave her courage and determination not to repeat those mistakes again. Corbin had said they should take as many beginnings as they needed, and Rose knew that this would be one of her own.

As Rose waited for Corbin to return, she felt the same peculiar eagerness that she had the first time the blacksmith had ventured out into the grounds. The feeling had been so strong, and so familiar—even though *he* was not at all familiar to her.

As a child, she had waited, watching from the parapet, for her parents to come home every time they left. Always, when she would see their carriages rise up over the hill, she would run down to meet them, lightness and relief moving her tiny feet forward.

She couldn't understand or explain why she had felt that same feeling when she watched Corbin return from the grounds. It didn't make any sense and was so unlike her—to feel so deeply and to wait so patiently; to be overcome with relief when he met her eyes at the end of every day, the same question on his face. The question he had asked her that first night.

Why? Why did she choose him?

Today, as the afternoon sun shone off the blackness of his hair and the same eagerness lit Rose from within, Corbin met her eyes as always. The same question was on his face, but today, he lifted a hand in greeting.

She knew why she chose him, but didn't know if she could tell him. It might bring him closer to her than anyone had ever been, and that terrified her.

A realization washed over her then as she gripped the splintery railing. He had become her family—not just in marriage, but in this new and beautiful closeness she felt for him. But she had lost her family before, and she knew that by accepting him as hers, she was also accepting that he, too, could be lost.

CHAPTER 30

A s Corbin washed at the well, Rose hurried down from the parapet, through the castle, and was standing at the back doors when he walked inside. His skin was bronzed from working outdoors and his hands, though freshly cleaned, had fresh dirt stuck underneath the fingernails.

He grinned down at her, his dimple appearing on his tanned cheek. "What is it?"

She was staring. Trying to act nonchalant, she dropped her gaze from his and glanced out the window. "Oh, it's nothing. I was just wondering if you're too tired for a reading lesson. It's been a long day."

He was shaking his head before she finished. "No, no. I'm better now. A little fresh air always helps. Oh, u-unless *you're* tired . . . or something. We don't have to . . . I mean, I'm fine if . . ."

A smile was fighting its way to Rose's lips, and Corbin stopped stammering.

"We're an awkward pair, aren't we?" he said with a reluctant smile.

"Yes. A little."

"No. A lot." He laughed and ran his fingers through his hair. "I'm fine going to the library if you are."

"I am."

"All right, then." Corbin chuckled. "After you."

Rose turned in the direction of the library, and Corbin followed, eventually falling into step beside her. When they reached the library doors, Corbin stepped forward and pushed one open, standing aside to let her enter first. Rose raised her eyebrows, a small smile on her face.

"Who is this gentleman and where did he leave the blacksmith?"

Corbin laughed. "Can't I be both?"

"Apparently," she said, surprised that this didn't bother her.

As she passed by Corbin, she felt a warm touch on the small of her back as he led her into the room.

She forced herself to act casual, but her pounding heart had other plans. Suppressing a smile and trying to breathe normally, she made her way to the nearest line of bookshelves. Corbin stood close to her, his eyes looking at the titles of books, though he couldn't read the words.

"Before we start with actual books, let's just go over the letters and their sounds." Her fingers traced along the spines of books on a low shelf. She smiled. "Ah, here it is. I learned my letters by this book."

The spine was split and the pages were tattered. She sat down on a chair and opened to the first page. Each page had one big letter with a picture over it.

Corbin scrunched up his face. "This book is for little children." Corbin plopped down on the chair next to her, a little table separating them. "I'm too far behind. This is impossible."

"Well, some of us were too far *ahead*. I spent my entire childhood with tutors, sitting indoors, my face in books. Does that sound preferable?"

Corbin shook his head. "I wouldn't have survived that."

"See, now? You're going to do just fine. Besides, I've heard that adults sometimes learn to read more quickly than children. They've had more experience with words, letters, sentence structure . . . things like that. You might be surprised by how much you know."

He sighed. "You might be surprised by how much I don't."

She placed the book on the table between them. "Let's see who's more surprised, then, shall we?"

They bent their heads close together and looked down at the first page. "Well, everyone knows that one," Corbin said.

"All right, how about this one?" Rose turned the page, and the next, and the next. With each new letter, Corbin would almost always know its name, and often its sound. Soon, she let him turn the pages so that he couldn't see the trembling of her fingers.

Rose had been engaged before. She had shared moonlight kisses with suitors over the years, most of them princes and other royals. But none of them—not their kisses or love letters—had affected her this way. This man had never kissed her. He couldn't write her a letter even if he wanted to, and yet she felt a nearness, a bond with him. It was more than the fact that she had chosen to marry him. It was more than the fact that he had chosen to step forward and then to stay with her despite her beastliness.

She was helping someone, even if it was in such a simple way. And this small act of service seemed to endear him to her, to connect them to each other. No one had been able to see past The Beast long enough to know if she was even capable of kindness. Until he came.

By the time they reached the end, only a few letters and sounds had given Corbin trouble.

Rose sat back in her chair and crossed her arms with a satisfied smile. "So, who's more surprised?"

"Well, I can't speak for you, but I'm about to fall out of my chair, I'm so surprised."

"I told you."

He grinned. "You did." He picked up the book and flipped through the pages. "Thank you. I've always been too afraid to discover how much I didn't know."

Rose nodded. She knew exactly how he felt. She was supposed to be ruling this kingdom—something she knew almost nothing about. So little, in fact, that she was too afraid to find out. But something told her that she couldn't rely on Lord Stanford much longer.

CHAPTER 31

A thirteen-year-old Princess Rose stood on the parapet in anticipation. Her mother and father had been gone for nearly three months, and she had watched for their return almost as soon as they left. Mrs. Whiting had kindly suggested that Rose might want to play her instruments or read, so that she could occupy her thoughts with other things. Rose had refused. The sun was setting on yet another day, and she couldn't endure the feeling of abandonment any longer.

Thunder rolled—profound and ominous—the lightning flashing across the sky, its thin, white fingers frantically grasping for things Rose couldn't see.

She couldn't hear the horse's hooves over the thunder, but Rose's heart pounded at the sight of the lone rider coming up the distant hill. She looked past him for signs of the king and queen, but soon her face fell in disappointment. He was alone.

He reached the gates and the soaked guards flung them open. Without stopping, he raced toward the castle, barely slowing his panting horse before jumping off the saddle. Rose, her face whipped by the angry wind, her slippered feet freezing, couldn't make herself move. She didn't want to know why the man had rushed to the castle in the pouring rain. She didn't want to know why her parents weren't with him.

Moments later, indistinct, anguished cries reverberated off the castle walls behind Rose until they reached her ears. Suddenly, she couldn't hear the thunder or feel its resonating wrath.

Rose had been safely sheltered from the rain on the parapet, but she felt the wetness now, though it only touched her cheeks. Clenching the railing in front of her, she opened her mouth to cry out, but only a muffled whimper escaped.

"They're dead! The king and queen are dead!" Hysterical servants ran through the corridors, pounding on doors, making certain that even the stones were aware. Rose stood anchored to the railing, feeling that she had heard the dreadful news a thousand times before. For, indeed, she had. In a thousand nightmares before this one.

Now, her cries finally came—as they always did. She waited for the dream to end—as it always did. For years, it ended with Rose being shaken roughly, her cries shattering the stillness of the night, the memory that had become her nightmare always mercilessly following her into wakefulness.

But recently, in the worst part of her familiar nightmare when she couldn't cry loud enough and there wasn't enough pain for her to feel, she would dream that someone was holding her on the stormy parapet. Sometimes it was her mother, sometimes her father—though Rose knew it was impossible. Sometimes it was Mrs. Whiting, or Maryann, though Rose knew that Maryann was terrified of her and it made no sense.

She would try to make herself dream that Corbin was there, to try to call out to him. She wanted him to hold her and to comfort her, but it was never him who did. A part of her knew that it would hurt too much if she had dreamed he came, only to wake and feel the distance between them. For now, she had to be content that someone was there to comfort her and that she was able to leave her nightmare in her sleep, to let it stay where it belonged.

Now, her dream ended when someone's gentle fingers brushed away her tears, smoothed her hair from her damp face, and kissed her wet cheeks. Sometimes she would look down at her hand, thinking she was grasping someone's hand, but see that it was really rose petals she clutched.

And then, the next thing she knew, it was morning.

Rose slept late again the next day, but it was still technically morning when she found Corbin in the library. He stood at the window, and though the sun shone, the glass was splattered with raindrops, and gray clouds blanketed the distant sky. Corbin held a small, leather-bound book in his permanently blackened hands, a finger tracing the lines of words on the page. The strength in his rough hands and fingers seemed to contradict the gentle way he cradled the weathered book.

With one movement, Corbin closed the book and ran his free hand through his hair and rubbed his neck. After a moment, he turned and saw Rose and a hesitant smile lit his face.

"Good morning. Did you sleep well?" Corbin smiled, the dimple appearing as he placed one hand in his pocket. His face seemed a little weary, but his eyes were alert and even piercing.

"I don't know," Rose answered, trying to gauge her level of fatigue. "You?"

Corbin shrugged, his gaze dropping and concealing his intense expression. "There was another storm last night."

"Yes. But the rainy season is almost over."

Corbin's expression darkened slightly at those words, though Rose couldn't understand why. She always looked forward to the clear—and silent—nights as soon as the first raindrops hit her window.

He took a deep breath. "Well, I think we can go over the letters and sounds again, and maybe I'll be ready to move on to books by the end of the day. Maybe?" He grinned, then left the window and sat down on a chair near the fire, and Rose sat on the chair next to him. She waited for him to open the book in his hands, but he sat staring at the cover.

Corbin looked at her and smiled, seeming surprised that she was there, and so close. "First, I have a question that I have asked once before and I'm going to ask it again."

Rose's defenses went up, her eyes going blank and her chin lifting out of habit.

"The book on your bedside table. What is it?"

Rose met his eyes evenly. "*Paradise Lost.*" How was he still concerned about a book he had only seen once or twice?

"*Paradise Lost.* Hmm." Corbin's eyebrows pulled together. "You know, that doesn't help me at all."

Rose smiled. "Help you what?"

"Get to know you better."

"Oh." Rose laughed quietly.

Corbin grew serious. "Don't you want me to know you?" He leaned forward in his chair and looked so deeply into her eyes, she was afraid that he already did.

Rose stood and walked to stand by the window.

"Is that a *no?*" Corbin asked. Rose could hear the smile in his voice, though her gaze was steadily on the droplets on the glass.

"I don't know. I barely know myself these days."

"Is that a bad thing?" He seemed on the verge of laughter, and Rose had to admit that getting to know the unbeastly side of herself had been much more enjoyable than she had imagined.

"No, it's . . . good. Just confusing. Also," she hesitated, afraid of saying too much, "I don't think you'll like what you learn about me."

She heard him stand from his chair and take a few steps forward. "The rose marking the page in your book—is that the rose I gave you?"

Rose inhaled quickly, the warmth on her cheeks spreading to her hairline, to her ears, and down her neck. He saw too much.

He took more steps toward her, his voice softer. "If it is, I don't think it's anything to be embarrassed about." Corbin's voice was close now and Rose knew that he was standing right behind her. He cleared his throat and Rose could hear the hesitation when he spoke again. "Is there anything special on the page you marked? Does it mean anything?"

Abruptly, Rose spun away from the window and tried to walk around Corbin to the door, but his hands seized her arms and stopped her.

"Rose." His voice was gentle and low.

He dropped his hands, an encouraging smile on his face, and Rose stayed where she was. She met his eyes—now steel gray—and bit her lower lip as she deliberated.

"It *is* your rose."

Corbin's smile spread to the rest of his face. "May I ask why you kept it, and what is on the page of the book it marks?"

"You may ask, but I won't answer. Not today."

"Someday?"

"Perhaps."

"That's good enough for me." He grinned down at her, the tension in the room easing a bit. "Now, teach me to read."

Rose exhaled, wishing she could cool her burning face against the glass. "What is the book you have now? Maybe we can start with that."

Corbin turned the book over in his hands. "I don't know. I saw that it had big, fat letters and pictures in it, and thought it might be a good place to start." He smiled.

Rose took the book and the corners of her mouth lifted in remembrance. "This is *Chanticleer and the Fox*. This will be perfect."

She sat back down on her chair and Corbin sat in his. Each holding half of the book, they started out with Rose saying a word, and Corbin repeating after her. They moved to sentences, and by the end, Corbin could read small words on his own.

Over the next few days, Rose waited for her usual impatience to emerge when Corbin struggled with a word. She wondered when she would finally lash out when he couldn't remember the sound a letter made. But she couldn't even imagine doing it. He was trying so hard, his face screwed up endearingly as he struggled to put the sounds together to make words, the words to make sentences. He would look up at her in triumph with every small victory and she praised every accomplishment.

They had been working for hours one day when Mrs. Whiting entered the library to announce dinner. Her usual smile was on her face and Rose smiled back, pleased to see that Mrs. Whiting seemed so content these days.

When she left, Corbin sighed, stretched, and rubbed his weary eyes. "How do people do this for hours on end?"

Rose smiled. "It gets easier, I promise. You may get to the point where stopping is a burden."

He laughed out loud. "I can't imagine." He looked down and straightened the stack of children's books on the table between them. "Though I could get used to this."

Rose looked up at him, wondering what he meant, and when she met his eyes she understood . . . or hoped she did. His eyes were brimming with tenderness and gratitude. He reached out, took her hand, and held it to his lips.

CHAPTER 32

The dream came as usual, though it seemed Rose was viewing it through a thick fog—the memory and nightmare slowly, hopefully, fading in the glow of her newfound happiness. She knew that after the wailing and tears, the sweet peace and comfort would come. Invisible hands would hold hers, unseen lips would brush away the tears from her cheeks, and she would fall into a deep sleep. She found herself quietly yearning for the dream—though she hated and feared it—knowing that the beautiful ending would come.

Rose took extra care in preparing for the day. Maryann almost lovingly pinned Rose's hair to her head, her fingers particularly gentle, though Rose asked her to leave half of it down. Corbin seemed to watch her more when her hair flowed down her neck and back, Tose remembered with a smile.

As Corbin and Rose ate breakfast in the morning room, they talked about what books Corbin would try to read that day. He had been reading for almost a month and had made astounding progress. Rose had always assumed that commoners were less intelligent than royals, but she was discovering she was wrong. Like many of them, Corbin had simply never been given the opportunity. He learned more quickly and absorbed everything with more enthusiasm than she had ever seen in anyone—including herself. He had graduated from children's books and was moving on to more difficult literature—Shakespeare's sonnets and Blake's poetry. Rose would read the longer, more challenging words, while Corbin read the shorter ones he now recognized by sight.

166

Not once did Rose laugh at him . . . unless he laughed first. Some mistakes were so comical, a little humor was a welcome relief from the laborious learning, and Corbin had no problem laughing at himself.

When they were finished eating, they retired to the library and settled in for yet another day of reading. The sun shined so brilliantly through the windows, and Corbin's restless eyes kept shifting to look outside.

"It's such a beautiful day," he said with longing.

Rose felt her spirits drop. She had thought Corbin was enjoying the time he spent with her. They had laughed and talked for days, spending every waking moment together, and she had cherished it. Not once had he hinted that he wanted to escape to the shops or the garden, but obviously, he had had enough.

"Let's go read out in the garden," he said, his eyes twinkling with excitement.

Rose nodded and smiled, too relieved to speak. He didn't want to leave her. He wanted her to come with him. Grinning, a new vitality moving his body, Corbin rushed to the doors.

Too stunned and happy to move, Rose's feet remained fastened to the floor. Before he left the library, Corbin paused. He turned and saw Rose still standing at the window.

"Don't you want to come with me?" His eyes darkened in what looked like pain.

"Yes, of course I do." She hoped he couldn't hear her breathlessness.

He crossed the library in three strides and offered her his arm. "Then, come on." He laughed, clearly not seeing or understanding how affected she was by him as she linked her arm through his. She was glad he faced away from her, leading the way to the doors that led outside so he couldn't see the furious blush spreading across her face.

As they passed the corridor that would lead to their chambers, Corbin paused.

"Rose," he said, still holding her hand, "can we read *Paradise Lost?*"

Rose stammered, hoping that Corbin couldn't feel the sudden dampness on her hand through his sleeve. "It . . . it's very advanced."

"I think I'm ready." He straightened his arm that was linked through hers, and her hand fell, but he caught it in his. "With your help, I'm ready."

"All right," she answered, her eyes unable to meet his, "but you have to read it in order. No skipping ahead."

She felt the touch of his hand under her chin as he lifted her face up toward him.

"I promise."

She met his eyes for a moment, then looked down, and just as she had imagined a thousand times, his brown hand enveloped her white one.

His hand, so sure and strong, its roughness strangely comforting, tugged at her memory. She knew she hadn't held his hand before, but in her mind, almost in a dream, she felt that she had clung to it as the only real thing in the world.

Rose squinted against the bright sun that fell across the pages, fighting the desire to lie down on the grass and sleep. The pleasant heat tickled the top of her head and trickled down her body like liquid. She and Corbin sat close together on a stone bench in the garden, their heads bent over the pages.

"What in me is dark i-illumine, what is low raise and . . . s-support; That to the hee . . . hig . . ."

"Height," Rose whispered.

"Height," Corbin repeated, incredulous. "Why does it take so many letters to make such a small word?" Rose giggled and he continued. "That to the height of this great . . . ar-argu-ment I may assert this . . . eet . . ."

"Eternal providence . . ."

"Eternal providence, and j-justify the ways of God to men."

"You did it! Your first page!"

"Well, let's not forget all the pages I read of *The Flea*, *The Little Good Mouse*, or my favorite, *The Goat-Faced Girl*."

Rose laughed. "Be nice! I learned to read by those books."

"I did too. I have the utmost respect for them. But I must admit I get a little bit more out of Milton."

"And I must admit I'm relieved."

Corbin laughed and then sobered. His gaze was fixed on the little garden in front of them, particularly on the dried rose thorns on the soil. "Rose, those roses in the vase in your room—the dried ones. Who gave them to you?"

Rose met his eyes, but found no questions there. He seemed to already know the answer.

"My father did."

Corbin's eyes softened, a kind smile on his lips. "And when did he give them to you?"

Rose swallowed against the tightness in her throat, the aching tears that choked her. All she could see were her father's kind and wise eyes, a single rose held between his fingers.

"Every spring." Her voice caught and she turned away. Why did it still hurt? Why did it feel like her father had died yesterday, and also a hundred years ago? How could she still hear his perfect voice, speaking to her with such affection, and yet had somehow forgotten the meaning behind his words?

"For thirteen springs?" Corbin whispered.

Rose nodded.

Corbin closed the book and put it on the bench between them. "Can you tell me about it?"

Could she? It was a hallowed memory—sacred—and she felt that if she shared it, it might lessen its importance. Or, would it increase it, sharing it with someone else who, at the moment, seemed to want nothing more than to be close to her?

"I never met my mother," Corbin said when Rose didn't answer. "I never knew my father. I was raised by the best people on earth. They took care of me and taught me all I know, but there is a part of me that wonders about where I came from—who my parents were and what they were like, and if I'm like them in any way. You have been given a tremendous gift. You know exactly who you are and what has always been expected of you. Or, you once knew."

Did she still know? She closed her eyes, allowing her memory to reach back past the haze of pain, and spoke before she gave herself permission. "When I was born in mid-summer, my parents had rose bushes planted in the borders around every garden. That spring, before I could even remember, and every year after, my father would inspect every bush, waiting for the first bloom. As soon as it appeared, he would pluck it—red, pink, white, or orange, it didn't matter. He . . . he would run and find me. He would kneel down, hold the rose out for me . . ."

Rose paused. The similarity between the story of her father giving her a rose and Corbin giving her a rose was too similar . . . for both of them. Suddenly, they felt too close, too quickly.

"It's all right," Corbin said. "You don't have to finish."

But she wanted to. More than anything. "'Rose,' he would say, 'may you ever rule this kingdom as this rose rules the garden. Like its roots that grow deep and sure in the ground, may you never forget where you come from. Like its petals, may you ever look upward and seek for light and truth. Like its thorns that are fierce and sharp, may you defend your people with strength and boldness. Like its leaves, may your arms reach outward to your fellowmen in friendship and goodwill. And, like its stem, may you stand proud in defense of what is right and noble.'"

Rose didn't cry. She smiled. She could hear the words, could feel them, as if they had been whispered in her ear at that very moment. Corbin was watching her intently; she couldn't even hear his breath, and she looked up. The questions had returned to his eyes—reflecting her own.

Where was that little girl who had been born and raised to be a queen?

CHAPTER 33

R ose, that's . . ." He looked down at the cobblestones at his feet. "Is that why you chose me? Did I remind you of him?"

When she spoke, it was no more than a whisper. "Yes. And, you reminded me of who I was born to be . . . who they wanted me to be. I had forgotten. And even when I was reminded, I fought against it. I still don't know what to do." His hand, sturdy yet gentle, gripped hers, which had been entangled in the folds of her gown. "So, now you know why I chose you. What I still don't understand is why you stepped forward, why you didn't run away when the others had."

Corbin nodded, his face becoming thoughtful. "Oh, you saw them, did you?" He smiled at the ground, then met her eyes and held on more tightly to her hand. "I did what I had come to do. Yes, I could have escaped. No one would have condemned me. You were, well, a . . ."

"Beast." She smiled.

Corbin laughed softly. "Well, no one would have condemned me . . . except myself. I would have gone home and lived the new life I had planned for myself—alone, hoping to find what I had come here for . . ."

"What had you come here for? To Laurel?"

Corbin grinned and bit his lower lip, seeming to understand something that had just dawned on him. "I came here to find my family. I was born here, and I hoped to find out where I belonged."

Rose didn't dare to ask him if he had found either of those things. It was too much to hope that he had found family in her, that he felt he belonged here. But as far as she was concerned, she suddenly couldn't imagine life without him.

"I think . . . I hope I had found those things in deciding to step forward. I felt peaceful in that moment, like I was . . . like it was the right thing to do. It's as simple as that."

"I'm sorry I made that decision hard to live with."

"*I* made that decision hard to live with. I looked back instead of appreciating what was right in front of me, and what lies ahead. And doing that has made all the difference."

Rose's chin started to quiver, and she spoke to hide it. "What lies ahead for us now?"

"For *us*?" Corbin's smile lit up his face. "We need to help you do what you were born to do."

Familiar terror filled Rose at those words. She hoped it wouldn't come, but she had fought against that responsibility for too long and fear had become a habit.

"I-I'm going to go rest for a while before dinner." She stood from the bench and picked up *Paradise Lost*. She avoided Corbin's eyes, though she managed a small smile. "Well done. Wonderful reading today."

She heard him say her name as she walked away, but pretended not to hear. Rushing to her room, she closed the door, knowing she was being absurd, without really caring. So much had been revealed about both of them in so short a time. They both knew why they had chosen each other, which was a relief. She felt closer to Corbin than she ever had. But she also felt closer to her fate than she ever had. And she now saw that they were intertwined.

Dinner was announced, but Rose remained in her room. She wasn't hungry, nor was she ready to face Corbin, who would certainly want to discuss her hasty retreat from the garden. She didn't answer when Corbin's gentle knock echoed through the corridor, nor when he whispered her name through the door. A part of her wanted to—desperately— but the same fear that had held her back for the past ten years held her captive now.

Corbin entered his chamber, and she listened to his footsteps until sleepiness threatened to close her eyes. For the hundredth time, she read the words in *Paradise Lost* that she had found as soon as she returned from the Gift Giving. She smiled, tracing the words with her fingers, until the words blurred and almost disappeared. There was no light or sound coming from Corbin's chamber, and she knew he must be sleeping. Thankfully, it wasn't raining.

A soft knock on her door made Rose jump so suddenly, her book closed on her lap. After a moment of stunned silence, she quickly placed the book on her table, blew out the candle, and covered herself in blankets.

"Rose." Corbin's whisper traveled through the door and quickened her heart. She was being a coward, a foolish coward. She was trying to hide from who she was meant to be beneath a pile of blankets.

After another gentle knock, the door creaked open. "Are you pretending to sleep?" There was a smile in his voice, and she pulled the blankets over her guilty face.

His footsteps crossed the floor, and even through her closed eyes, she could feel where his shadow blocked the dim light flooding in from the corridor.

"Rose. I know you're not asleep. For one thing, you're too upset to sleep. For another thing . . . you snore when you're really sleeping."

Rose shot up in bed, all pretenses abandoned. "I do not snore! How dare you! Princesses do *not* snore."

Corbin laughed as he crossed his arms over his chest. "This one does, but only when she's very tired. But don't worry. They're . . . kind of pretty snores."

"How do you know this?" Her voice a squeaky, mortified whisper, Rose pulled her blanket up to her nose.

"We share a wall, Rose." He chuckled, but then became somber. "Will you meet me in the library?"

She sat in the bed for a silent moment and then nodded. Abruptly, Corbin left the room, closing the door behind him. Before she could change her mind, Rose slid her feet out from under her warm quilts and onto the stone floor, pulled her wrapper around her shoulders, and made her way to the library.

When she pushed the library door open, Corbin was sitting on a settee in the darkness, lit only by the cool moonlight filtering in through the stained glass. He was hunched over, his elbows resting on his knees, his head bent over his clasped hands.

Without speaking, Rose went to sit on the cushion next to him, a shiver overtaking her. Corbin looked up, a sad smile creeping onto his face.

"Rose, I need to know why you're afraid."

Rose turned away and rested her chin on her hand. The old Rose—the beastly one she and everyone else knew so well—would have thoroughly chastised him for prying into such personal matters. But this new Rose—the one no one knew, especially herself—was fastened to her seat, her heart reaching out to him in a way that forced the breath from her lungs and the scorn from her face.

Corbin continued, talking to the back of her head. "Every time I feel close to you, one or both of us pulls away." She felt his warm touch on her hand. "You aren't a beast. You're hurting. You wanted everyone to be afraid of you so you could hide your own fear. Without that mask on, you're exposed and you don't know what to do."

Rose turned to him. In the moonlight, his eyes shone with a gentle blueish gleam. "But why do I do it? Why doesn't anyone else?"

Corbin surprised her by laughing softly in the darkness. "We all do, I promise. We all have little beasts inside of us. Sometimes we let them grow into huge, frightening beasts, but that doesn't mean we can't beat them back down. And usually, it's because of fear that we allow our beasts to grow. Do you think I avoided you for all those weeks because I'm really a childish, unhappy, brooding person? No. I was afraid. I was afraid of this new life and the expectations."

"Of me?"

Corbin grinned. "No. I was never afraid of you. Not from that first day. Not ever." He chuckled. "Perplexed? Yes. Annoyed? Absolutely. Infuriated? Undoubtedly. But never afraid." Without taking his eyes away from hers, he reached out and caressed her hair, then cradled her face in his hand. "Rose, I'm sorry to disappoint you, but you are anything but frightening."

CHAPTER 34

Neither one of them seemed eager for sleep, so they stayed in the library and talked until the sky turned a deep, smoky violet. Rose told Corbin all she could remember about her mother—her gentle laugh, her love of reading and music, the way she tucked Rose in tightly at bedtime. She spoke about her father—his courage and strength, his humor and often recklessness.

With reluctance, she admitted that it hurt her when they left on their extended trips. She grew to resent their royal duties that called them away so often. And when it came time for her to rule—much earlier than anyone had anticipated—she rebelled against it, and eventually utterly refused.

She had been content to delegate her royal duties to various advisors, and eventually to Lord Stanford when the others grew tired of her tantrums and lack of concern for her subjects. Lord Stanford had taken the task, and Rose had been silently grateful ever since.

Suddenly, Corbin sat up, a pucker forming between his eyebrows. "Rose, who sets the tax rate?"

"Well, technically I do."

"Technically?"

"I've let Lord Stanford handle all that for me."

Corbin nodded, his lips pursed. "Hmm. I don't know if he's doing a very good job. Based on what I saw in town even in one day and what I heard from the villagers, there is a lot of room for improvement."

"What do you mean?" Her eyes widened.

Corbin seemed to force a smile onto his face. "We don't need to worry about it tonight. Just make sure you know what you're signing when he brings you those documents. Now, tell me more about your family."

He listened for hours, smiling when she smiled, concern on his face when she frowned. The sparks—tempestuous or otherwise—from earlier in their relationships had cooled to a friendly ember that warmed Rose from the inside.

When she was finished speaking, Rose yawned and shivered, the cold-ness of the room finally seeping through her nightgown. Corbin stood, reaching over her to retrieve a blanket that hung over the back of a chair behind her, and draped it over her, tucking it snugly underneath her chin.

"Are you ready to sleep now? Or at least take a little pre-breakfast nap?" He grinned sleepily.

"I'm ready to go to bed, but I don't know if I'll sleep."

Corbin looked out the window at the orange, cloudless sky. "I think you'll sleep well enough."

And whether it was because she was so exhausted, or because the sky was clear as glass, Rose slept a dreamless sleep.

In the morning, Rose found Corbin looking through some legal docu-ments and tax codes.

"A lot of these words are too big for me, but the numbers make sense," Corbin said when he showed Rose what he was reading. "I've spent my entire life working and paying taxes, and based off of what I've been able to read today and what I saw in the village, rules have either been bent, or downright broken."

"Who has been breaking them?"

Corbin shrugged, though he wouldn't meet Rose's questioning eyes. "I think we need to learn all we can before making any accusations or assumptions."

They spent the morning going through document after document, learning about recent changes made to laws, taxes, and legislation. Corbin told her about the condition of the village, the baker warning him about their high taxes, and the dilapidated roads and buildings. Only, neither Rose nor Corbin could determine where all the money was going. Rose feared the answer might be obvious, and she wondered of Corbin knew it too.

Rose's brows puckered as she read about the latest tax increase on grain. "This can't be right. I know I didn't authorize this. At least, I don't think I did."

Corbin bit his lower lip nervously, but said nothing.

Mrs. Whiting entered the library with a plate full of sandwiches.

"Thank you, Mrs. Whiting," Corbin said as he stood. He looked down at Rose. "I'll be right back." He followed Mrs. Whiting out into the corridor, and Rose continued reading while they spoke, catching only snippets of their muted conversation.

After a few minutes, Mrs. Whiting was answering a question Corbin had asked. "Well, I think the best time is in the dormant season, as long as the ground isn't frozen, which it usually isn't." Mrs. Whiting paused and Rose could hear her shift the linens in her arms. "It's a beautiful thing you're trying to do, a very beautiful thing."

Rose leaned in her chair to get a better look. Corbin was smiling down at Mrs. Whiting.

"I hope so. Here," Corbin reached out and took the linens from Mrs. Whiting, "let me carry these. What rooms do they go in?"

Mrs. Whiting put her hands on her back and stretched. "Oh, all right. Just this once. Thank you, my dear. I was going to make some of the beds in the north wing."

Corbin looked back at Rose, winked at her, and mouthed, "I'll be right back," before following Mrs. Whiting down the corridor.

Rose sat in uncomfortable silence until a moment later when Lord Stanford entered the library. He bowed at her and Rose stiffened. She watched him warily, though she tried to appear nonchalant. He had never seemed menacing to her before, but if her suspicions were correct, he was not to be trusted.

He held out his usual stack of documents. "Just a few more for you to sign before I leave."

Rose took the quill Lord Stanford offered her and touched it to the parchment . . . then paused. "And what am I signing?"

Lord Stanford's head snapped up, his brows furrowing. "Oh, yes, of course. It's nothing, just that we need to raise the price of wheat again. Last year was so dry after the rains left and production went down, which greatly affected our increase. If we raise the price of wheat by a mere five percent, this should protect us should we suffer another dry season."

"What will the five percent be added to?"

Lord Stanford shook his head and grinned. "What do you mean?"

"I mean, how many times has it been raised? Is it five percent above the base price, or five percent above the last time it was raised?"

"Your Highness has been studying." He beamed at her, though a shadow passed over his eyes. "Well, you actually approved the last increase about two years ago. We had to raise it seven percent that time, so this is actually quite good."

Rose's brow furrowed. "I don't think I'm going to sign this, not until I can do a little more research on the subject."

"Research? Forgive me, Princess Rose, but I have spent my life researching for the good of this kingdom. I need you to trust me that this is for the benefit of all concerned."

"It's not that I don't trust you, Lord Stanford." She didn't meet his eyes. "I just feel that I have been . . . neglectful of my duties and guilty of placing too much of a burden on you."

"Have I ever complained, Your Highness?"

"No, but . . ."

"Exactly. It is an honor and a privilege to serve my princess. You must allow me to continue with the duties you have entrusted to my care and judgement."

Rose squared her shoulders and looked Lord Stanford in the eye. "As I have already explained to you, I have been neglectful of my duties. I have shirked them for far too long, and I don't need to ask your permission to resume them. I appreciate all you've done, but it's time to return to how things *should* be done. Besides, the new prince has a good grasp on the numbers, and he has worked his whole life as a laborer. He knows what's fair and he will help . . ."

"Ah, an excellent point, Your Majesty. But if I may . . ."

"You may not."

Lord Stanford smiled, then continued as if she hadn't spoken. "Have you considered where his loyalties lie? He has only lived here for a short time. It is no secret that he pines for his home, for the . . . *people* he left behind. Have you heard his history? Do you really know this man? I certainly don't. And I don't think I'm alone."

Rose stood, fury filling her, and for once, she was grateful.

"You have forgotten your place, Lord Stanford, and you will not be making that mistake again."

She walked across the room and rang the bell pull. While she waited, she glared at Lord Stanford who looked back at her, infuriatingly composed. Finally, Baines entered the library.

"Baines, you will take Lord Stanford to the dungeon."

Baines blinked hard a couple of times, then looked at her with wide eyes. "I will?"

"Do *not* question me! Take him immediately!"

But Baines didn't move. His gaze slowly moved from Rose to Lord Stanford, his eyes seeking confirmation. Lord Stanford grinned and walked over to stand next to Rose. "Baines, you may leave."

Without questioning—but with a small bow and grateful smile—Baines hurried out of the library as Rose gaped.

The closing of the door seemed to rouse Rose from her shock. She rounded on Lord Stanford, her lips a white line of fury, her eyes blazing. "How dare you undermine me in front of a servant! How dare you dismiss him when I ordered you to be taken to . . ."

Lord Stanford raised his hands and bobbed them up in down as if soothing the air in front of him. "I did it for your own benefit. I didn't want you to feel foolish."

"Foolish!"

He continued speaking in a cool, polite tone. "I hate to be the bearer of bad news, Princess Rose, but you signed away your authority to imprison me about three years ago. I couldn't help noticing your tendency to throw anyone in there who didn't meet your extremely high expectations. I could produce the actual document for you, but it will only waste time and I really must be getting along."

Rose stood silently, shaking with anger and humiliation. Lord Stanford stepped closer to her, his voice almost warm in its kindness and contrition.

"My dear princess, please don't be angry. Things were different then. And please forgive me for what I said about the new prince." He glanced toward the door. "Anyway, I'm sure that the carriage is waiting outside for me. Is there anything you would like me to tell the king and queen of Claire . . . and their son?"

Rose's anger boiled at the off-hand mention of Prince Kenton, but she met Lord Stanford's eyes squarely, not fooled by his overly innocent expression. "Tell them it will be my husband and me who will be on the next diplomatic visit."

Lord Stanford nodded, almost expecting those exact words. "I will, gladly, my princess. But first—and I only ask this for the good of the kingdom and our foreign relations—have you asked your husband who he was engaged to before he came here and why the engagement was broken off?"

After years of practice, it was not difficult for Rose to keep her face deceptively smooth despite feeling like she had just been doused in ice water. She even smiled, and that smile grew as Lord Stanford's face paled. "Tell the king and queen *and* their son that it will be my husband and me who will be on the next diplomatic visit."

CHAPTER 35

Lord Stanford bowed politely and exited the room. Corbin appeared in the doorway at that exact moment and accidentally bumped into him.

"Oh, forgive me, Lord Stanford," Corbin said.

Lord Stanford only bowed again and smiled, his lips tight, before hurrying on his way. Corbin shrugged and joined Rose who stood in the middle of the room, but then he looked more deeply at her. "Is there anything the matter?"

Rose couldn't meet his eyes. They had grown so close over the past few weeks, but now it felt as if they were starting over. How could Corbin have left out this crucial information about himself? He spoke about his parents—the people who raised him. He told her countless stories from his childhood and even invited his friends for a visit. How could she not know he had been engaged?

She forgot about the taxes and diplomacy, laws and tariffs, and Lord Stanford's disrespect towards her and Corbin. All that mattered now was this.

"He told me that . . . y-you were engaged before you came here."

Corbin exhaled slowly, his countenance falling slightly. "Oh." He took a moment to think before continuing. "I'm sorry, Rose. I wasn't trying to keep it from you. I honestly just wanted it to stay in my past where it belonged. I hoped that by leaving it there, it couldn't affect me now." He took her cold hand in his and led her to the settee by the fireplace.

Rose was finally able to find her words as she sat down. "I'm not upset that you were engaged before. Everyone knows that I was too. I just wished you would have told me."

"I'm sure I would have eventually. But honestly, since you and I have grown . . . closer, it just hasn't been on my mind. It was such a relief to be free of her, to be free of a past I shared with someone else."

"Will you tell me about her?"

Corbin looked down at Rose from where he stood at the fireplace. His hand gripped the mantle, but his grasp seemed to ease when he met her eyes.

"Her name is Francine. We had been engaged for a year when we heard about Prince Kenton's ball and that he would choose his wife from among his subjects. She changed that day." Unexpectedly, Corbin laughed softly. "She even fainted right there in the street when the announcement was made." He sobered and looked at the cold fireplace. "Our wedding was supposed to take place on the night of the ball, but she decided to postpone it, hoping for a chance to marry the prince. It broke my heart, watching her chase after him when she had been so in love with me . . . or so I thought. At the ball, Francine was chosen to meet him, but Prince Kenton fell in love with another. Once she lost him, Francine tried to win me back. She showed up at my shop when I was about to leave. She begged me to stay, but I was too broken by then. Our love hadn't been enough. We had no real foundation, and I had to watch it crumble right from under our feet."

He chuckled. "Interesting how things work out, isn't it? If Kenton hadn't broken off his engagement to you . . ." Rose was pleasantly surprised that she felt no pain as he said this, "and then chosen to marry another, you wouldn't have felt the need to hurry home and marry a commoner to spite him. And if Francine hadn't chased after him, I wouldn't have left to start a new life without her." He sighed again, finally turning to face her. "I feel that our pasts might help us understand each other better than most others would, to help each other through the pain that hasn't quite healed."

"So . . . do you still love her?" Rose couldn't hide the hurt in her voice.

Corbin left the fireplace and sat close to her on the settee. "No. Truly, I don't. I never thought it was possible, but I have gone hours, then days, then weeks without thinking of her. When I arrived, every thought revolved around her. I was so frustrated with myself. I even wondered if I had done the right thing in leaving her. I wondered if I had been selfish and cowardly. But after a lot of thinking—too much thinking—I realized that when I left, I wasn't abandoning Francine. I wasn't running away. I was leaving something that wasn't good for either of us."

Rose knew instantly what he meant. She and Kenton had never been good for each other, and she had known it all along. Letting go of him had been easier than she ever would have imagined, not only because they could barely stand each other, but because she didn't—or hadn't—ever let herself feel anything too deeply . . . until the blacksmith came.

"And what about us? Are we good for each other?" Her voice was not timid. Her eyes held his boldly. She wanted to know. She needed to know. She knew he had helped change her, had helped her begin to heal and begin to embrace who she was meant to be. He had brought sunshine and warmth and laughter back into this castle and into her life. This simple blacksmith had taught her how to be a princess. He respected the servants, he freed the innocent men, and he fixed things that were broken with his determined and capable hands—including her.

Corbin leaned closer to her and held both of her hands in his. He leaned his forehead down until it touched hers.

"Yes, Rose. We are."

Rose told Corbin all about her conversation with Lord Stanford and how she had signed the document that took away some of her authority over him. Corbin seemed concerned, but not distraught.

"Let's just keep learning all we can so that when . . . *if* the time comes to take more serious action, we can be prepared. We certainly need to be wary of him, but while he's gone, let's focus on making sure we're strong."

Rose nodded, but then ducked her head in shame. "I did this. If I hadn't given him all my power, he wouldn't have so much power over me."

Corbin grinned and lifted her chin. "Everything will be fine. We'll figure it out." He picked up a book from off the table. "I promise we'll study laws and . . . royal things, but sometimes it's nice to take a little break, don't you agree?"

He opened *Paradise Lost* and began reading, his words slow and deliberate, though becoming steadily smoother. She smiled, feeling the tension roll off her shoulders, her breathing return to normal.

Corbin read *Paradise Lost* almost constantly over the next couple of weeks, as well as books on royal duties, traditions, and laws. A few times a day, he would escape to the gardens and shops, and when he would return, he was filled with fresh energy.

Rose sat close to him, loving the sound of his voice, surprised by how quickly he learned, and grateful for his calming presence. She closed her eyes as she listened to his deep voice become less hesitant, more effortless and confident. She smiled as he read words like, "'The mind is its own place, and in itself can make a heaven of hell, a hell of heaven,'" and, "'What hath night to do with sleep?'" After he read this, he looked up at Rose, a slow grin lighting his face.

"You said this. Remember? That night I was stomping in the corridor."

Rose nodded. "Yes. Unfortunately, sleep hasn't come easily for me in many years. Though, I have to admit, it has been a little better lately. Sometimes, when I wake up . . ."

"Which is actually in the morning now," Corbin interrupted, then laughed as Rose elbowed him in the side.

". . . I actually feel like I've slept."

Corbin reached for her hand and kissed it, his eyes gentle. "I'm glad."

Days later, he read, "'His wonder was to find unawakened Eve with tresses discomposed, and glowing cheek, as through quiet unrest; he on his side leaning half-raised, with looks of cordial love hung over her enamoured, and beheld Beauty . . .'"

Corbin stopped reading and blinked at the words, his hand holding the book trembling slightly. "While she slept, he saw Beauty," he whispered.

CHAPTER 36

"So parted they, the angel up to heaven from the thick shade, and Adam to his bower.'" Corbin leaned back in his chair, grinning while rubbing his eyes. "We finished Book Eight."

Rose looked up from the book and smiled over at him. "Well done, Corbin. I am very impressed. Book Nine is my favorite." Even after all these weeks of reading, Corbin had stayed true to his promise and had not read ahead. But now, Rose felt an overwhelming urgency to continue, to discover the words that she hadn't allowed him to read yet.

The storm that night seemed furious, bent on getting out all its rage while it still could, before the dry season arrived. When Rose awoke in the morning, she felt particularly exhausted, her nightmare increasing its intensity with the storm.

She tried to go back to sleep, but realized that what had woken her in the first place was a commotion out in the grounds. She slid out of bed and crossed her chamber, opened the door, and looked out the window that overlooked the gardens.

The sun had just risen, and through the misty rain she saw that four large wagons filled with brown, oddly shaped objects had been driven back there. Corbin and a few other servants had formed a line and were unloading the objects and spacing them evenly in the planters that bordered each garden. Rose squinted and looked closer at the objects, but the thick glass made it impossible to see what they were.

Running back to her room, she rang for Maryann and quickly dressed, not bothering to eat. She hurried out the back doors and then stopped. Corbin was digging in the sodden ground, his sleeves rolled up to his elbows. His hair was soaked and rain dripped down his focused face.

Rose stepped forward, her slippered feet squishing in the mud, and looked at the objects. They were bushes. Hundreds of them. No more than a foot or two tall each. Their roots were wrapped and protected in coarse, brown fabric, and poking out of the fabric were thick, woody stems. Rose bent down and felt along the branches. They were smooth and young, their prickly thorns still pliable.

Roses.

Her eyes wide and swimming with tears, Rose looked up to meet Corbin's smiling face. He winked at her and continued with his digging.

For the entire week, Corbin dug, planted, and inspected each rose bush. Rose watched from the parapet, and every so often, he would glance up at her and smile.

As a grieving child, Rose had cried in anguish when the roses had been pulled up and burned—though it had been her doing—and she cried with joy now that they were restored.

While Corbin worked outside, Rose worked inside. When she was able to pull herself away from watching the roses be planted, she had the music room opened up, the sheets removed, and all the instruments polished, dusted, and restrung, and had even begun to play some of them again. Tears wet her cheeks and a smile lit her face as the familiar, comforting sounds filled the castle once again. Doors that had been closed were opened, and sunshine and warmth enlivened the rooms and corridors.

The rainy season had refused to go quietly, the days and nights were dark and furious . . . but no one had ever seemed happier. Laughter, playful banter, and industry filled the castle and lifted everyone's spirits. At the end of each day, Rose and Corbin ate dinner together and then read in the library.

One night, he looked up from his reading, his voice grave. "Rose, it says here that a chief governor can only be dismissed if he commits an act of treason."

"Really? I don't think I've ever known that. Well, Lord Stanford was rude to me before he left, certainly, and he hasn't been handling the finances well, but I can't imagine him committing treason."

"Well, let's hope we won't have to worry about it. In the meantime, we'll get the taxes under control, and once the rains leave, we can get to work on the roads."

She grinned as she pretended to read her own book. She could just imagine it, Corbin working day and night, bent over as he worked, his face gleaming with exertion and contentment, working side by side with the people of the kingdom. His kingdom. And she knew then that she would be there too—out of the isolating confines of the castle, working with her people.

When she looked at him a moment later, he had fallen asleep on the settee, the book open across his chest.

Smiling, Rose closed the book and placed it on the table. She draped a blanket over him, placed a pillow under his head, and carefully lifted his legs onto the cushions. Rearranging her skirts around her, she knelt next to him and studied his handsome, tranquil face. His eyelashes were long for a man, and they brought a softness to his tanned face, which was now covered in end-of-the-day stubble. Even in his sleep, she could see the indication of his endearing dimple next to his smooth, untroubled mouth.

His lips smiled faintly, even as he slept. Tenderly, and with slight hesitation, she traced his lips with the tip of her finger. He twitched and lifted a hand to rub his mouth before settling back into deep sleep. Rose laughed softly. She wondered when, or if, he would ever kiss her. He offered her his hand all the time now, and his arm as he led her into dinner. But not his lips. Not yet.

But she was willing to wait. Their friendship was warm and growing and for now, it was enough. She bent over and touched her lips to his forehead. She kissed both of his hands that lay folded across his chest—hands that had been working to save her from the moment she met him.

Standing from her kneeling position, she sat on the other end of the settee, and fell into a dreamless sleep.

On the final day of planting, Rose was there waiting when Corbin entered the castle, drenched with mud and rain. He left his boots in the entry and thanked the servant who took his shirt and replaced it with a dry blanket. He was rubbing his hair when he spotted Rose. His face broke into a wide smile and he walked toward her, the hem of his sodden pants dragging on the ground.

His hair dripped onto his shoulders, soaking the blanket. "What do you think? Of the garden, not of me." He glanced up at his wet hair and grinned.

She stepped closer to him and pulled the blanket more tightly around his shoulders. She would love to tell him exactly what she thought of him.

"You have done a beautiful thing," she whispered, her voice soft with emotion.

He smiled, his face weary but happy, and pressed his lips to her forehead. Water dripped from his hair onto her face and down her cheeks.

CHAPTER 37

In Rose's nightmare, the messenger on the horse was just about to enter the castle and announce that Rose's parents were dead. The wind howled and the rain pounded, its wetness only landing on Rose's cheeks, as always. Her desperate fingers clutched the railing, which was rough, but strangely malleable. She looked up into the churning, unruly sky, and for the first time she could remember, the raindrops that fell from the somber clouds were joined by flittering snow-white rose petals. They fell gently, even amid the frantic wind, and landed all around her—brushing her cheeks and wiping away her tears, covering and warming her bare feet, landing in her hair like a crown.

She reached her hands out and one by one they fell into her palms, the weight of them making her body pleasantly sleepy. The petals surrounded her and blanketed the parapet where she stood. She smiled, her cheeks suddenly warm and, with one last caress of a petal on her face, tearless.

The petals enveloped her like an embrace. There were no cries, no mourning voices, no frantic footsteps, no pounding hands against closed doors. All was peaceful. All was well. She lay down in the petals, allowing them to cover her body and cradle her head. The sun broke through the heavy clouds and shone on her face with such intensity she knew she had to be dreaming. She stared at it, but it didn't burn her eyes. The warmth tickled her face and spread to her fingers and toes, and she sighed.

She wanted to stare at its brightness forever, but finally, two petals brushed over her eyes and she slept.

Rose stared out the window of the library, silently pleading for the storm to end, to fade away before the night came. Her dream had ended so beautifully the night before. But, as beautiful as it was, she wished she could experience that beauty without always having to feel the familiar pain and fear that preceded it.

She heard footsteps approach her from behind and jumped a little when Corbin's warm hands gripped her shoulders. Willingly turning her gaze away from the storm, she faced him, questions in her eyes.

His jaw was tight and his eyes stared down into hers. He moved his hands from her shoulders to her waist and pulled her closer to him. She didn't know where this was coming from, but she didn't exactly mind.

"Rose," he whispered.

Resounding thunder that seemed to shake the very stones of the castle was accompanied by a blinding flash of lightning. Rose ducked her head against Corbin's chest. His arms wrapped around her.

He spoke, and Rose could feel his lips brush against her hair. "Rose, you need to let go of this fear."

Relief and embarrassment brought tears to her eyes, and she hid her face against his shirt. "I don't understand why I'm still afraid. It was so long ago."

"That doesn't matter. Unless we can conquer them, our pain and fear only grow." He pulled back and placed his hands back on her shoulders. He looked out into the darkening sky and the lightning in the distance. He dropped his hands, but grasped one of hers. "Come on!"

Before she knew what was happening, Corbin pulled her out of the library, up some stairs, through a door, and out onto the parapet. Rain soaked her hair, her dress, her shoes, and thunder pounded in her ears.

She looked beyond the gardens, her hand still clutching Corbin's, and could almost imagine the messenger riding up the hill, crying out that the king and queen were dead.

"I need to go inside!" she cried, hot tears now mingling with the rain on her face.

"Wait." Corbin's voice was swallowed up by a clap of thunder. He pulled her close to him, his own arms trembling. She clung to him, her breath now coming in sobs. He held her so tightly, and he was the only steady thing in the world.

He leaned down and whispered in her ear, his voice soft and soothing. "You don't need to be afraid."

The storm only grew stronger, the wind beating against them, angry raindrops swirling around them. Lightning lit the sky and thunder threatened to break them apart with its fury. But Corbin didn't move. And Rose could only cling to him. Soon, her trembling ceased. She let herself be enveloped in his warmth and stability, and her sobs stopped.

His hand smoothed her dripping hair, his lips brushing her forehead. He spoke calming words, his voice rumbling in his chest like thunder.

"It's over now," he whispered, though the trembling in his arms had returned. The rain had softened to mist and the thunder and lightning had surrendered. "I don't want you to be afraid. You don't have to be afraid."

He pulled back just enough to smile down at her, raindrops falling from his dark eyelashes. His fingers brushed the rain and tears from her face, and the feeling of his fingertips on her skin was somehow as familiar to her as breathing. He looked away from her eyes and to her lips, leaning closer to her face.

"A visitor, Your Highness." Baines's voice called from behind them. "Oh, excuse me. I didn't know . . . that is . . . I'm terribly sorr . . ." Baines walked slowly backward, his face turning a deep purple.

"Thank you, Baines. I'll be right in," Rose answered, her voice weak.

"Pardon me, my princess. But this is a visitor for His Highness, Prince Corbin," Baines said almost ominously.

Rose looked up at Corbin questioningly, who looked just as surprised as anyone.

"For me?" Corbin's eyebrows disappeared under his dark hair that fell across his forehead. He looked down at Rose, his face apologetic, his eyes dark with disappointment. The moment had passed. He backed away from Rose, but still grasped her hand as he walked back into the castle, muttering something about Will and Ella and someone named Bart.

Burning with curiosity, Rose followed Corbin through the corridors, down the grand staircase, past the drawing rooms and dining rooms, and to the foyer, following the trail of water he left behind him. Her sodden skirts slowed her down, and she jogged to keep up with his long stride and heavy footsteps, gripping his hand to help propel her forward. Abruptly, the sound of his clomping feet silenced. An arm length behind, and still clasping his hand, she turned the last corner and ran right into the back of him, though he didn't even budge. Somehow, he had turned to stone and it appeared that he would never move again.

Rose followed his chilling gaze to the front door, and there stood a woman—her wet hair stuck to her face like the tentacles of an octopus, her traveling clothes dripping, the water forming a puddle around her on the stone floor. She was breathing as if she had run all the way there from wherever she had come. She shivered, but smiled at Corbin as if she were seeing the sunrise for the first time.

"Francine," Corbin whispered.

CHAPTER 38

"Francine?" Rose repeated to no one.

The visitor, soaked to the skin and shivering, sneezed daintily and then walked forward, her arms outstretched.

"Corbin! Look at you! Such a gentleman." She turned to Rose. "Your Majesty." She curtsied low and bowed her head. "Please forgive the lateness of the hour and my . . . soggy condition." She laughed and then sneezed again.

This woman seemed to think that her presence was in no way a shock to the entire household. Rose, unaccustomed to false sincerity, made no attempt to hide her astonishment.

"Why are you here?"

"Why, Corbin's letter, of course." A hint of panic widened Francine's eyes as she spoke. She looked over to Corbin for validation.

Corbin's mouth dropped open, but he said nothing. Francine stared at Corbin for a moment, beseeching him to say something, but he only gaped. He wore the same expression on his face from when Rose had begun teaching him to read—dread and uncertainty on every feature.

Just when Rose felt like she would scream from the tension, Mrs. Whiting arrived out of nowhere and stepped forward, her hair blown out of place. Someone must have summoned her, and she breathed heavily as if she had run the entire length of the castle.

"A visitor. How lovely. Princess Rose, Prince Corbin, shall I show this young woman to one of the guest rooms?" Mrs. Whiting said, her eyes tight, her smile a little too wide.

Corbin didn't move. Not even one muscle on his face indicated that he heard Mrs. Whiting speak. Francine's panicked eyes still pleaded silently with Corbin, whose gaze now seemed forever fixed on the floor.

Rose nodded to Mrs. Whiting, not out of hospitality, but confusion and curiosity.

"Come, dear, we must get you out of your wet things before you catch cold," said Mrs. Whiting in her most imperious voice. Without waiting for Francine to comply, Mrs. Whiting took her by the arm and propelled her out of the foyer.

Finally, Corbin turned to look at Rose. His face was ghostly pale and his eyes so full of unabashed agony that Rose had to catch her breath.

"I thought I'd never see her again." Corbin's voice was too quiet to be discernible. Rose couldn't tell if she heard relief or despair in his words.

"Corbin." Rose stepped closer to him, daring to slip her hand into his. His hand was like ice, like stone, and didn't grasp hers back. She fought the urge to grab his shoulders and shake him awake. He had been hers—only hers—just moments before, and for some inexplicable reason, his past had shown up at their door, presumptuous and soaked.

Rose couldn't bear his baffling silence, and she began to pull her hand away from his limp one. His stony grip pulled her to a stop.

"Don't leave me." His voice was a strangled whisper. Corbin gathered Rose into his arms and held her all alone in the cavernous foyer. "Please don't leave me."

Rose, too stunned for words, clung to him. He was supposed to be the strong one. He was the one who helped her conquer her fears. She wasn't ready for this. To be strong when he was weak. To be calm when he was troubled.

She fought against the pain, knowing that this person could still affect him so powerfully, even after all this time. But she cast the pain aside. He hadn't followed Francine. He had stayed with Rose, and held onto her, pleading with her to help him.

The rest of the evening was endless. Francine was dried and changed and asking for Corbin's audience, always receiving no answer. Rose burned with curiosity, but she let Corbin decide if or when he would speak to Francine.

After they quickly changed into dry clothes, Corbin stayed with Rose in the library, the doors closed, until a late dinner was announced. His agitation comforted Rose, strangely. As positive as Francine had been that Corbin had written a letter inviting her here, it seemed that her sudden appearance was the last thing Corbin was expecting. A small part of Rose wondered if he had invited Francine a long time ago, when he and Rose weren't even on speaking terms. Perhaps he had chosen a different scribe than his wife for that letter.

Rose had been cruel, and he had been lonely and homesick. Was it so preposterous a notion that he would want to contact someone from his past, someone who had loved him? She looked up at Corbin as he paced the library, his hands in his pockets, his gaze focused on the stormy sky. Yes, it was an absolutely preposterous notion.

Corbin refused to eat in the dining room, so instead Mrs. Whiting brought a plate up to him in the library, which Corbin didn't eat a bite of. Rose ate very little, and assumed that Francine must be eating alone in the enormous formal dining room. The whole situation was too bizarre for Rose to feel any pleasure when she pictured the strange woman sitting at the great table with no one to talk to.

When darkness fell, Corbin peeked his head out of the library door. Without a word, he reached behind him for Rose's hand and hurried through the castle to their corridor.

"Corbin," Rose whispered, out of breath from walking so quickly, "what's the worst that could happen? If she sees you, you can just tell her to go away. Or you can just ask her why she's here."

Corbin was shaking his head before she finished. "I can't talk to her. Not now. I know her. I-I know myself. I'm not afraid of her. I'm afraid of what I might feel if I allow it." He grimaced as if in pain, but also regret. "That . . . that sounds bad. I'm sorry. She's just very . . . cunning."

When they reached Rose's door, Corbin stopped and pulled her tightly to him. For the first time, she was afraid. She had been thoroughly perplexed by Francine's sudden appearance, and more than a little angry, but now as she felt Corbin's trembling arms and his rapid breath on her hair, she was afraid.

Who was this woman and why was Corbin so completely diminished by her presence? Rose wrapped her arms around him, and she felt him rest his head on hers.

"It's all right. Everything's fine," he mumbled into her hair. She wasn't sure who he was talking to.

He let her go and hurried to his chamber, closing the door behind him. When Rose entered her own chamber, Maryann was waiting, holding

Rose's nightgown in front of the fire so that it would be warm when Rose slipped it on. But the normally comforting warmth eluded Rose, leaving her anxious. She dismissed Maryann and began to pace her room.

She was never one to pace the floor as she had seen others do. She always found it silly and even overdramatic, but pace she did. No corner of her room held answers. No wall comforted her. The fire only crackled in response to her growing unease. There was no one to talk to, no one to confide in. But she knew that the only person she could and should talk to was the distressed man in the next room.

The beastly Rose writhed and stirred just underneath the surface. She could feel it in the rage that welled up inside of her that made her teeth and fists clench so tightly the only way to release the anger was to scream.

But she resisted. For the first time in her life when she felt such fury, she held it in. She hoped that it would subside, but it didn't. It changed. It transformed into a hurt so deep, she almost wished she had screamed and cried, hoping to set a little of it free.

A knock so gentle it sounded more like someone tapping their finger against the door almost made Rose cry out. She looked toward her door, but the quiet tapping was coming from the door that conjoined hers and Corbin's chambers.

Her heart in her stomach, Rose ran to the door, lifted the beam she had forgotten about, and opened it.

Corbin's face was remorseful, yet urgent. "May I stay in here tonight?" He glanced over at his door. "I-I'll sleep on the floor, but I just . . . need to be here."

Rose didn't move or speak, and Corbin only stood for one more second before walking past her and closing the door behind him. He had a blanket slung over his shoulder, his feet bare, his shirt untucked. Corbin walked over to the fire and laid out the blanket on the floor. Without a word, he stretched out his body on the blanket, linking his fingers beneath his head and using them as a pillow.

Corbin rolled over and faced the fire, and Rose stepped closer so she could see him. His jaw was tense and his eyes stared unblinking into the flames. She wished she could smooth the anxious lines on his face, the tenseness around his mouth and eyes.

She looked over at the six fluffy feather pillows on her bed, walked over, and grabbed one, then tossed it to him. It hit him right in the face.

"Oh!" Rose covered her mouth and tried to stifle a giggle, the comical situation releasing some of the tension that had become excruciating.

196

Corbin pulled the pillow off his face and looked over at Rose, the dimple appearing on the side of his mouth, illuminated by the fire. "Thank you."

He slid the pillow under his head and sighed a short, uneasy sigh as his eyes closed. Some of the stress faded away from his face and his breathing slowed. The overwhelming anxiety from just moments ago had almost completely faded, and the warmth from the fire and Corbin's soft breathing were like a lullaby. Rose pulled her blankets over her and nestled into bed.

She was just beginning to doze when a soft knock echoed through the corridor and into the room. Corbin, who appeared to be almost asleep just moments before, shot up and stared in the direction the knock had come. The knock hadn't been at Rose's door. The only other two doors near enough were the one that led down to the washing rooms . . . and Corbin's. Silence followed the sound and Corbin lay back down, his back toward Rose, his face toward the fire.

The knock echoed again, and the blinding fury that had become dormant welled up inside Rose. It was undeniable where the knock was coming from. *Someone* was knocking on Corbin's door in the middle of the night. Rose flung the quilts off of her, ready to strangle that woman and have the guards remove her, when she looked over at Corbin. One arm was curled around his pillow, his hand clasping it so tightly his knuckles were white, even with the orange glow of the fire on them.

"Corbin?" Francine's whisper accompanied another knock on Corbin's door. His fingers clenched the pillow tighter, and he pulled his legs up tighter toward his chest. Rose got up from her bed and tiptoed across the room so that she was standing above him. His eyes were clenched shut, anguish distorting every feature. In that moment, he was the most important thing. Francine could pound on the door all night if she felt like it, but Rose wouldn't leave him.

The rain had started to fall harder, joined by bursts of light and booming thunder. Rose didn't even think to be afraid. She sat next to him, her legs tucked underneath her nightgown. The rage she felt at the sound of this audacious woman knocking and whispering to her husband melted away into a crushing wave of sympathy for him, mingled with unabashed adoration. He knew Francine well enough to know what she was willing to do to win him back and he would not allow it.

He had fled.

And Rose loved him for it.

Rose lifted her hand, surprised to see that it was steady, and placed it on Corbin's broad shoulder. He flinched at her touch, but almost immediately, he let go of his pillow, reached back, and grasped onto her hand fiercely.

After a moment or two, Francine whispered Corbin's name once more, a desperate, angry edge to her voice. Rose looked down to see what Corbin's reaction would be, but his face was smooth and calm. Corbin, his hand still gently curved around hers, his breathing soft and regular, had fallen asleep.

CHAPTER 39

A soft, crackling sound invaded whatever dream she was having and Rose's eyes fluttered open.

She was lying on the floor, a blanket draped over her, a pillow under her head. Blinking against the soft morning light, she saw that Corbin was placing a log on the growing fire.

"I know I'm not supposed to do this, but you were shivering." He winked. "Don't tell Arthur." He stood, brushed his hands on his pants, and smiled down at her. "Thank you for taking me in."

"Were there any more . . . whisperings?"

"I don't know. I was sleeping." His voice softened and he left the fire and sat down next to Rose, his hair disheveled, his jaw scruffy.

Rose shook her head. "May I ask how you're handling all of this so well?"

Corbin chuckled. "You think I am? I don't know about that."

"Well, yesterday was a little . . . difficult, but you seem better now."

"I think that has something to do with you."

"I was here yesterday, and it was still difficult."

"That was my fault. I didn't know if I could ask for your help. But once I did, everything changed." He sighed and looked toward the closed door that led to the corridor. "This looks bad, I know. I'm going to figure it out. I don't blame you for being confused and even upset. For some reason, she thought she was invited."

"Could Will and Ella have mentioned something to her?"

"It's not impossible, but I doubt it." He pondered for a moment. "But why would she say she received a letter from me? Why did she feel so comfortable showing up out of nowhere?"

"I don't know. What I do know is that she seems quite relentless when she wants something."

"You have no idea." Corbin's eyes were far away. "She has always wanted what she couldn't have, or what seemed almost impossible to attain. She loved the challenge."

"She *loves* the challenge," Rose corrected, more meaning in her words than she intended.

A soft knock at the door made them both jump, and Corbin stared with wide eyes at the closed door.

"Breakfast," Maryann's voice floated through the crack in the door.

"Come in," Rose called.

The door creaked open, and Maryann entered with a breakfast tray balanced on each hand. She placed the trays on a table and was almost to the door when Rose spoke.

"Maryann, where is our visitor?"

Maryann's eyes shot to Corbin and back at Rose. There was a flicker of accusation in her expression that wasn't lost on either of them. "She has just eaten downstairs and has requested an audience with Prince Corbin. Multiple times."

Corbin met Rose's eyes, irritation on his face.

"Thank you, Maryann," Rose said, and Maryann closed the door behind her.

Once Maryann's footsteps faded, Corbin spoke. "Maryann doesn't believe that I didn't send for Francine. Of all people, I thought *she* would believe me."

"Servants talk, and Maryann is easily swayed." Rose shrugged, defeated.

"I need to tell Francine to leave. I couldn't face her last night, but I'm ready now." Corbin marched toward the door.

"No, not now. Besides, you aren't exactly decent." She looked pointedly at his rumpled shirt and bare feet. "We need to know why she came here. We can't just send her away without her telling us why she came in the first place. If we tell Francine to leave without putting an end to this, we'll always be afraid that she'll show up again. Every knock at the door, every unexpected letter will bring this all back again. When she leaves it has to be for good."

Corbin nodded slowly, reluctantly. "You're right. But I'll need you there."

"Oh, I'll be there."

As Rose picked up a bunch of grapes off her breakfast plate, an unexpected thought hit her. Had she not done the exact same thing Francine was doing? Rose had gone to Kenton's ball and had thrown a royal fit, right there in his palace, demanding that he reconsider his idiotic plan to marry a commoner instead of her. They had been engaged and he had broken it off and brushed her aside, and she had been cut to the very center. She even came home and married her own commoner, just to spite him.

The only—and very important—difference between Francine and Rose was that while Rose had gone after Kenton at the ball, he hadn't been married yet. Corbin was married. It wasn't a perfect marriage, and to everyone else they probably looked more like acquaintances who lived in the same castle, but he was still married and Francine had still come.

Rose had never considered herself a pillar of morality, but this was beyond even her.

Still, she saw that she and Francine had both acted irrationally, and it was because they had been hurt. Rose understood Francine against her will, and that understanding told her that if Francine was ever going to let go of Corbin, she had to do it on her own.

Corbin returned to his own chamber when Maryann came to help Rose prepare for the day. He was waiting in the corridor for her when she emerged, dressed and ready. A wary expression shadowed his face, and he looked up and down the corridor again and again.

"Library?" Rose said as she slipped her hand into Corbin's.

He looked down at her and smiled. He gripped her hand more tightly and nodded. "Please."

Once they were in the library, Corbin relaxed, his usual, steady expression resuming its rightful place on his face.

"All right. Let's send for her and get this over with."

Rose walked over near the fireplace and tugged on the bell pull. A moment later, Baines appeared.

He bowed. "What can I do for you?"

Corbin stepped forward. "Hello, Baines. Will you please send for Miss McClure?"

Baines, like Maryann, was unable to keep the accusation out of his eyes. But unlike Maryann, there was an edge to his accusation, something more sinister beneath the surface. After Baines left, Rose looked at Corbin, and Corbin looked back with troubled eyes.

"Baines too," he said, his voice strained and low.

A few minutes later, Baines returned, his gaze focused on the window behind Rose and Corbin. "I'm sorry, Your Highnesses. She has refused to come."

"Refused!" Rose stood and crossed the room. She stared up at Corbin and his eyes were piercing.

Corbin addressed Baines evenly, though his face grew more flushed with each word. "Then send her away. We don't even want to know how this all came to be. If she won't speak to both of us, then she must leave." Baines nodded and left the library, closing the doors behind him.

Rose gaped. "Do you really think that she won't come because you're with me?"

"I do." The muscle in Corbin's jaw tightened.

They sat in silence on the settee, holding hands and looking out the window. After an agonizingly long wait, the sound of a woman's footsteps approached the library, and they both stood, their eyes wide and expectant.

Mrs. Whiting knocked and then entered. "Miss McClure has been packed and sent on her way." There was a note of triumph in her voice. She spun out of the room, a skip in her step.

Rose laughed at Corbin's dramatic sigh of relief. He sank back onto the settee, his hands covering his face.

"What a nightmare!"

Rose sat next to him and smiled. "It seems we're both well-acquainted with nightmares."

Corbin dropped his hands from his face. "Thank you for helping me through mine." He lifted her hand and kissed it.

"My pleasure." Rose sighed and smiled, then looked out the window, her eyebrows knitting together. "I know it sounds strange," she said, shaking her head, "but I wish she would stay, at least long enough to explain herself. This feels so . . . unresolved." And, if she was being honest, she wanted to know what kind of woman Corbin had run away from, who had broken his heart into so many pieces. So far, Rose couldn't see the allure. "Aren't you at all curious?"

Corbin was still for a moment and finally nodded. "I've known Francine for years. I've seen her be more conniving and manipulative more times than I can count. She will persist until she gets what she wants. That's always been her way." He sighed, his eyes troubled. "But I didn't think she was capable of this." Corbin stretched and rubbed his hands over his eyes. "Anyway, it's over now."

Rose couldn't quite share in his relief. "Yes, it looks like the storm has passed. Maybe you should get some fresh air."

"Oh, that sounds perfect. It's almost like you know me." He winked. "Almost."

His voice became tender and he squeezed her hand. "More than almost." He stood and walked toward the door, but stopped before he touched the handle. When he turned back, his eyes were twinkling. "Rose, do you want to come out to the shop with me?"

Rose beamed, surprised by how the prospect of spending the afternoon in an old shop made her heart pound excitedly in her chest. "I would love to!"

Corbin crossed the room and took her hand, pulling her up to follow him. He led her out of the library, down the grand staircase, and out the back doors, a wide grin on his face.

As they passed by the gardens, Rose noticed that the little rosebushes were covered in tender green leaves. She smiled. Soon, this garden would be covered in blossoms and everything would be perfect.

When they reached the shop, Corbin opened the door and let Rose in first. He followed in behind her, walked over to a woodpile in the corner of the room, and started tossing logs onto the fireplace. "This may take a while. And it's going to get very hot. You're going to want to stand back."

The flames started low, transforming the logs into a deep orange. Then, no longer willing to be enclosed in the confines of the logs, they leapt up and crackled pleasantly. At first, Rose welcomed the warmth. It chased away the cold in her fingers and cheeks and eventually even her toes, a lovely tingling sensation taking its place. The flames continued to grow, seeping through her skirts and being trapped against her legs, feet, and arms. Her face began to flush and she felt sweat bead up under her hair and on her forehead.

The flames seemed to become angry then, licking the stones of the fireplace, snapping and grasping desperately, furiously. Rose found herself across the room, her back against the wall opposite the fire. But she was still too close. Her face burned and the heat became almost unbearable.

Corbin stood close to the fire, apparently accustomed to the swelter-ing heat. He was looking at a variety of metal rods, inspecting them. He grinned up at her, the dancing flames reflected in his gray eyes. "I've been bringing broken things here from the castle, fixing them, melting off the excess, and saving it for when I might need it. Thankfully, you didn't have to be here for the melting of the metal. If you think this it hot . . ."

He chuckled, though Rose couldn't quite manage a smile. The heat seemed to sear her mouth, her throat, her lungs. She was being burned from the inside.

"How . . ." she coughed, attempted to swallow, then continued, "how can you bear this heat?"

Corbin looked up, concern on his face. "Oh, I'm sorry!" He put the rods down on a big, flat metal object and crossed the room. He placed a hand under her elbow and led her out into the crisp, light air. The rain-saturated breeze crept invitingly across her face, and she gulped in the coolness. She brushed her forehead with the back of her hand, her hair sticking to her skin. "I'm sorry," Corbin said again. "I guess I don't mind the heat because I know it's necessary. Here, you can watch from the doorway."

The flames leapt impatiently out of the fireplace as Corbin returned to them, anticipating whatever they were about to do. He picked up one of the rods with some kind of large pinching tool and held it in the flames. The heat still prickled on Rose's face, but the coolness of the outside blew across her neck mercifully. Slowly, the rod turned a deep red, then a whitish-yellow.

"Perfect," Corbin whispered. He returned the rod to the metal block and turned to Rose, his face shiny and slightly blackened from the fire. "You may want to cover your ears."

She didn't need to be told twice. Corbin raised a heavy, rounded hammer and pounded on the glowing metal, turning and shaping it. Rose had heard these pounding sounds from across the grounds, but hearing them up close was another matter entirely. She jumped with each swing of the hammer, her ears ringing.

But as hot and cold as she was, and though her brain felt as if it would shatter from the sound, she was mesmerized. Corbin's face was intense and focused, the muscles on his arms illuminated by the firelight. Sweat trickled down his face as his strong hands molded and shaped the metal into compliance.

Within minutes, the rod had become almost as thin as parchment and Corbin had cut and shaped it into what appeared to be an open-faced flower, like a daffodil or buttercup. He repeated the process until he had multiple flower-like objects, with holes cut into the centers. Sliding the flat pieces onto a thin rod, he began shaping and hammering each individual petal up and around the rod as he twisted it against the flat metal surface.

Over and over, he stuck the flower back into the flames, only taking it out when it glowed orange, and repeated the shaping and curving. He took a sharp object and hit the back of it with the hammer, cutting sharp thorns into the stem.

He inspected the flower for any flaws, pounding and reshaping as necessary, until finally, he dipped it into a barrel of cool water. A satisfying sizzle and a burst of steam escaped the water and Corbin smiled.

"That's my favorite part." He pulled the pinching tool out of the water and placed the perfectly formed rose on a table.

Rose stood, one arm across her waist, one hand cradling her chin. Her eyes were soft and contemplative as she stared down at the pristine rose in the brilliant firelight. She stepped forward and reached out her hand to touch it, her fingers hovering above the petals.

"Don't worry. It won't burn you," Corbin said, glancing over his shoulder as he put things away.

Carefully, Rose touched the smooth, sharp edge of a petal, then, hesitantly, pricked her finger softly against the tip of one of the thorns.

She felt Corbin watching her, almost warily. "Do you not like it?"

It took a moment for her to find her voice. "I love it," she whispered, "but . . . does it have to have thorns?"

Corbin smiled knowingly. He hung the pinching tool on a hook and crossed the room to stand by Rose.

"You know, I've been reading a little about roses. We have always been taught to hate the thorns, to fear them. They hurt us, repel us, and might even detract from the beauty of the petals. But, I've learned that they can serve another purpose. Certain coastal roses use their thorns to trap sand as it blows by."

"Why?"

"The sand reduces erosion, which then protects the roots." He grinned. "That's why I kept the thorns."

His steel-gray eyes were intense, just as they had been when they shaped and pounded the metal. But there was a gentleness there too.

Without timidity or hesitation, Corbin took Rose by the shoulders. Her arms dropped by her sides for an astonished moment and then reached up to wrap around his neck. Corbin freed a hand to trace her face with his fingers—across her cheek and jaw, along her hairline, and then through her hair. He smiled as she wrapped her hands tighter around him and pulled his face closer to hers.

CHAPTER 40

"Why, Princess Rose, are you getting *indecorous* notions?" Corbin laughed huskily.

Rose smiled. "*In*decorous? Certainly not. My notions are quite decorous, I can assure you . . ."

A voice carried over from somewhere in the gardens. "Princess Rose! Are you out here?"

Corbin sighed, the muscle in his jaw tightening. "This," he leaned his forehead against hers, "is getting ridiculous."

Footsteps crunched in the grass and gravel and soon Lord Stanford appeared. "Oh my. Forgive me. I didn't mean to interrupt."

"Sure you didn't," Corbin mumbled, pulling away from Rose. He looked up at Lord Stanford. "When did you get back?"

"Just barely." He looked at Rose and smiled. "And princess, I've been thinking about our conversation that we had before I left and I hope there are no hard feelings."

Rose shrugged. "Of course not." She honestly hadn't had much time to think about it. It almost seemed silly now. No harm had been done.

"I had hoped that you might be able to help me with something. Consider this a first step in regaining the power you have bestowed upon me. Honestly, I'll be glad to be rid of it." He chuckled, and Rose and Corbin smiled, though Corbin's eyes were tight. "Anyway, I have a man in the dungeons who was belligerent to me in the village on my way back to the castle. If you'd like, you could talk to him and let me know where we should go from there."

"Very well." Rose began to follow Lord Stanford with Corbin right behind her.

Lord Stanford stopped. "Oh, Prince Corbin. I don't mean to take you away from whatever you're working on in here. We won't be a minute."

Corbin stopped. "Oh . . . Yes, I suppose I should put the fire out anyway."

Rose turned back to the shop, picking up the warm rose from off the table and touching it to her lips. "Thank you," Rose whispered, her eyes glistening. "I love it."

Lord Stanford spoke before Corbin could answer. "Excellent. We'll be right back, Prince Corbin." He walked off in the direction of the castle and Rose followed.

The guards opened the doors as they approached.

"Lord Stanford, wait here," Rose said when they passed by the staircase.

"Princess Rose, the prisoner is waiting."

Rose ignored Lord Stanford's protest and hurried up the stairs and to her chamber. She laid the iron rose next to the open book on her table and touched the cooled petals and thorns. It was perfect, permanent.

With a smile on her face, Rose returned to Lord Stanford and followed him through the castle to places she hadn't been in years. She hadn't cared to spend any time in the dungeons and was overwhelmed by the dankness and revolting smells that greeted her even as they descended the stairs.

"Lord Stanford, the first thing we should do is make the dungeons less horrible." Rose held her sleeve up to her nose.

"For the prisoners?" Lord Stanford chuckled, his laugh echoing against the stones in the damp darkness. "What do you have in mind? Flowers? Musicians?"

"Cleanliness at the very least. They *are* human beings, after all."

"Are they?" Lord Stanford said quietly.

Finally, they reached the dungeon, and Rose tried as hard as she could to keep her breakfast down. "*This* is where I've been sending people? It's absolutely atrocious!"

"Well, now you can see why people aren't exactly fond of you."

She glared at him, shocked by his harsh words, but then sighed. She couldn't deny the truth. "Where is this prisoner?"

"Right over there." Lord Stanford walked forward. "It's too dark to see, but he's in that cell to your right."

Rose squinted in the darkness and crouched slightly. She tried speaking to the prisoner, though she could hear no sound other than her own anxious breathing. "Hello? May I speak to you for a moment? It's Princess Rose."

She took a few more steps along the wet floor in the darkness, her hands reaching out in front of her, though she was met with only emptiness. Suddenly, a rough shove on her back hurled her forward and into an open cell, the iron door slamming behind her.

CHAPTER 41

CORBIN

Corbin prodded the small, glowing embers with the toe of his boot, smothering out the last of the heat. The raindrops had become deafening, and Corbin glanced once more toward the castle. Rose had not yet returned. He placed the chisel and hammer on a shelf and stepped out into the storm.

The pelting rain was as purifying as it was painful. Every drop felt like a stinging pinprick on his face and shoulders, and Corbin quickened his steps. He wasn't just trying to escape the downpour, but to return to Rose who he knew would be waiting for him.

She had always been waiting for him. Waiting for him to return from working in the shops and the garden. Waiting for him to figure out his place in this castle. Waiting for him to let go of his past he hadn't realized he was clinging to.

But now that Francine was gone, a weight was lifted off of him that he didn't know he carried. That impalpable, infuriating barrier that had prevented him from fully moving on was now obliterated.

By the time he reached the gardens with their tall hedges and young rosebushes, he was as wet as if he had jumped into the lake fully clothed. Corbin decided to cut through the garden instead of walking around it, eager to be inside and with Rose. As soon as he entered and was surrounded on every side by the laurel bushes, his way was inexplicably blocked by the resolute figure of a soaked, honey-haired woman.

Francine McClure.

Corbin stopped so suddenly his wet boots slid on the sodden ground, his mouth gaping in disbelief.

Francine gripped a shawl tightly around her shoulders, her teeth chattering.

"I thought you . . . why are you still here? You were sent away." Corbin was too shocked to move.

Francine set her jaw, and her knuckles became white as she clenched her shawl. "I traveled for three days to get here. I defied my mother and snuck out in the middle of the night. I crossed an ocean. The wagon got stuck in the mud. I have been soaked by rain and hail. I expected a warm greeting and have only received a cold shoulder." The fury fled from her face, and she looked up at him with an obstinacy he was quite accustomed to. "I will not leave until I speak to you."

"I was willing to speak with you, but you wouldn't come."

"I need to speak to you *alone*." She stepped toward him, her eyes darting around her to make sure they truly were alone before resting on him again. "I know you can't be completely honest with me in the presence of that beast. Everyone knows she tricked you into marrying her and that she has held you captive all these months. And *you and I* know that if she hadn't connived you into marrying her out of spite, *we* would be married by now."

Corbin's anger flared, but he refused to be sidetracked. "Why did you expect a warm welcome?"

He thought of their final goodbyes in Maycott outside his shop. His mind grazed over the memory of her face filled with longing, the way he kissed her before he left. He hadn't thought of it in weeks and was grateful for how little the memory affected him. Still, he wouldn't allow himself to look into her eyes—eyes that he knew were chestnut brown with five little flecks of gold in the right, and three in the left.

"Your letter!"

He met her eyes then and was relieved that he felt nothing but confusion. "I didn't write a letter. I can't even write." Well, he could write his name and a few small words, but that was a recent development.

"I-I assumed you had taken lessons."

"I did, but . . ." He shook his head. "None of this matters. I didn't write you a letter. It doesn't make any sense. Please go back home." He glanced up nervously at the castle. "I need to get back inside."

Corbin stepped forward, but Francine clutched his sleeve. "Corbin, my darling, I know you still love me. You can barely look at me because you love me so much. Come back with me. You can't stay married to that beast."

Corbin's head snapped up. "Stop calling her that!"

"It doesn't matter what I call her. It's still true. Her reputation is legendary."

"You don't know her."

"Neither do you!"

A couple of months ago, Corbin might have silently agreed with her. He knew he didn't know Rose as well as he knew Francine, but that didn't mean he wasn't trying. Unfortunately, that didn't matter at the moment. All that mattered, all that people would see, was that Corbin was out in the garden with his former fiancée, alone, while his wife waited inside the castle for him.

He shook Francine's hand off his arm and moved as quickly as he could to get out of the confines of the garden, Francine on his heels. She was so close to him, he felt the warmth of her breath on his neck, and he lengthened his stride.

"Corbin, come back with me. I've come to bring you home, to save you from this hopeless situation. No one will blame you for leaving."

Corbin ignored her as he marched forward. He looked up toward the castle. This was the absolute worst situation he could be in right now. The servants already looked at him with distrust, despite his efforts to stay away from Francine. He and Francine were the only ones outside in this miserable storm, hidden by the tall hedges. He looked up again to the place from where Rose always watched him, but it was still empty. There were no witnesses. The thought terrified him.

"Francine, please leave. This doesn't . . . look right."

"No! I'm trying to talk to you and this might be my last chance."

"No, Francine. Your last chance was when you left me at the ball with the hope of marrying the prince." Corbin continued to walk forward, though Francine jogged next to him, struggling to keep up.

She pursed her lips and let her shawl fall slightly. "You never denied that you still love me, you know. You're afraid to be alone with me." Corbin remained silent and kept walking, weaving through the too-tall hedges. "I understand you're upset. I was swept up by the idea of marrying a prince and you were hurt. Now you go off and marry a princess and I'm not allowed to be hurt like you?"

Corbin's steps quickened almost to a run when he saw how close he was to the castle doors.

"What keeps you here? You don't even love her! I love you and you love me. You got your revenge, but this has gone far enough." Francine ran ahead of him and grasped his arms, her fingers hard and tense. "You probably think you're being honorable, staying here in a castle you hate with a woman you barely know, but tell me, how honorable is it to deny your own feelings and stay with someone you don't love? Where's the honor in that?"

Finally, Corbin stopped, his jaw tight and his eyes blazing.

"I'm glad I didn't marry you." Corbin stepped around her, wrenching out of her cold, clinging grasp.

But she seized him. With one last look of pure, desperate determination, she threw her arms around his neck, holding him tightly to her. He reached behind him, trying to pry her wet fingers loose.

"You're obviously under some spell here. She's poisoned you against everything you love. I've come to set you free."

She brought her face closer to his just as he untangled her hands. He wrenched away from her and she teetered on her feet, but Corbin reached out to grab her before she fell into the mud. His arms were still around her and her feet were barely steady when the door to the castle flung open.

CHAPTER 42

"M y, my. This is unfortunate." Lord Stanford stood in the doorway. His voice was full of regret, but it didn't mask the strange glint of triumph on his face. He was surrounded by servants—Baines, Matthew, Maryann, the chef—and they all looked at Corbin in either silent accusation or downright disbelief.

Nothing made any sense. How could they all accuse him so quickly? How could they think the worst of him after all these months? Corbin had had enough. He pushed past them, leaving Francine out in the rain. His teeth chattered, and every bit of his skin felt cold and raw, his frozen clothes clinging to him and trapping in the chill.

As he passed by the servants and their silent accusations, he stopped his determined steps and turned to face them. "I know what this situation looks like. I know you don't know Miss McClure, but I would have hoped that you would know me better than this by now."

Lord Stanford offered Francine his arm and led her into the castle. Baines closed the door behind them. No one looked at Francine. All accusatory eyes were on Corbin. They knew him better, and in their eyes he had farther to fall.

He turned to Maryann in the silent crowd, though she wouldn't look up at him. "Maryann, will you please get this woman some dry clothes?" Maryann didn't move, but her eyes shifted nervously.

"Maryann!" Mrs. Whiting's voice carried over the terrible silence as she made her way to the front. "You heard the prince. Take Miss McClure and get her into some dry clothes. Immediately!"

Maryann curtsied unsteadily and then walked to stand by Francine, who planted her feet on the floor. Her face was wet from what Corbin assumed was only rain, but her chin trembled in defiance and hurt.

Well, if she wanted to stay wet and freezing, Corbin wasn't going to argue with her. He had said all he could say to her and she still refused to move. He searched the crowd and found Baines. He was looking at Corbin, but his eyes darted around the room every few seconds. "Baines, will you please send for a coach? Miss McClure is leaving."

"Out in that weather?" Baines protested, gesturing to the rain pouring down the window. Matthew, standing just behind Baines, looked at Baines with astonishment.

"I don't care if it's raining!" Corbin shouted, walking to the door and opening it for Baines. The sound of rain plinking against the stones and ground was a welcome relief from the agonizing stillness. Baines simply stared back at Corbin, his eyes grim.

Corbin, resigned, slowed his breathing and marched past the disparaging glares, eager to change out of his wet clothes and end this grueling day, though it wasn't even sundown.

All he had to do was find Rose and everything would be fixed, everything would be made right. But she was nowhere to be seen.

He met Mrs. Whiting's eyes, and she looked back at him with such resolved reassurance that his spirits lifted. She believed him. She knew him the best of all the servants, and somehow, her approval meant more than all their disapproval combined.

Corbin was almost through the crowd when he turned to face everyone. "All right, we'll get this all sorted out in time. For now, I will go find Princess Rose and you can all resume whatever you were doing before this misunderstanding."

Lord Stanford spoke clearly over the low hum of now-muttering voices. "I don't see the point in obeying this man who isn't even worthy to be a prince. He sent for his fiancée and has been caught in an indecent situation." Lord Stanford appeared strangely calm, even reluctant, though there was a glimmer in his eyes. "Yes, the blacksmith came here—selflessly, perhaps honorably—and straightened our hinges and fixed the roofs of our old shops." He paused for a few hesitant chuckles. "He tamed that beast of a princess into something almost human. But hinges and roofs and taming of beasts do not justify impropriety, especially when it smacks of treason." His grew somber. "And we do *not* know this man. Anyone can appear to be whatever they want for a few months. But you *do* know me. You have reported to me, trusted me, and confided in me for the last ten years. Don't allow this charlatan to deceive you."

Lord Stanford stopped speaking and let his words weigh down on the tense air of the Great Hall. Everything Lord Stanford said could be perceived as truth, only, he had twisted it into a tainted version of truth. He sighed. "I hate to be the bearer of bad news, but . . ."

"Do you?" Corbin interrupted.

"But, in light of recent events, I hereby banish this treasonous black-smith from this castle and kingdom."

Mrs. Whiting placed a trembling hand to her mouth, and Corbin stepped toward Lord Stanford in outrage.

Lord Stanford raised his hands. "Before you give us one of your speeches about authority and right and wrong, blacksmith, I should tell you that only a few weeks ago, Princess Rose signed away her authority to banish to . . . let's see here." He unfolded the document, Rose's signature clearly signed at the bottom. "Me."

Some servants gasped, and Mrs. Whiting's stoic face paled.

A few—including Matthew and Arthur, his white hair quivering—protested, but Baines and some others nodded in approval. Maryann's eyes darted from face to face, clearly not sure who to side with. Corbin didn't react. He wasn't even surprised. He only needed to see Rose.

"Where is Rose?" Corbin finally said. How had she not made an appearance yet? The entire household was gathered and had already taken sides, and she was nowhere to be seen.

Lord Stanford nodded. "I suppose this situation is two-fold in its misfortune. You see, I was speaking with Princess Rose when we both saw you out in the garden with this beautiful young lady, here. The princess saw you take Miss McClure in your arms and she burst into tears. She has not been seen since."

Corbin turned to Lord Stanford, skepticism on his face. He had seen how the chief governor could twist the truth and had no intention of believing him.

"It's true. I saw the whole thing." Baines spoke up, his red face defiant. Despite the terribleness of the situation, Corbin couldn't fight the sardonic grin from spreading over his face. It seemed Lord Stanford had worked on securing quite the following, though for how long, Corbin might never know. Baines's eyes shifted, unwilling to meet Corbin's steady, incensed glare.

"You see? It's time you were leaving, blacksmith." Lord Stanford stepped closer to him, but Corbin moved back.

"Lord Stanford, I believe you have the authority to banish me, and I will leave. But I need to speak to Rose first."

Lord Stanford reddened and his mustached bristled. "No, you will leave now. I have banished you, and you will not defy—"

Corbin ignored him. "Mrs. Whiting, will you please see if Rose is in her chamber?"

Mrs. Whiting curtsied and disappeared up the grand staircase. No one spoke. No one breathed. Every eye turned toward the stairs. At any moment, Corbin knew that Mrs. Whiting would return with Rose. Either Rose would be solemn and perhaps hurt, if what Lord Stanford had said was true; or she would be oblivious to the drama that had occurred floors below her, and Corbin would know that Lord Stanford had lied.

But what he didn't anticipate was that she wouldn't come at all.

After much longer than Corbin would have thought, a breathless Mrs. Whiting flew down the stairs. "She is not in her chamber, Prince Corbin. She isn't in the library either," she said when he opened his mouth to ask her to check there. "She could be in any of the other wings, rooms, or corridors, but I didn't look there yet."

Lord Stanford nodded, satisfied. "No need, Mrs. Whiting. The princess obviously doesn't want to be found. As I told you, you have broken her heart, Prince Corbin, and she has no wish to see you. It is time for you to leave."

Corbin didn't believe him, he wouldn't believe him. But then, where was Rose? Why wouldn't she come to him? Surely she must know he was being banished. The entire household knew—small as it was. Was she truly hurt and crying somewhere? Could she actually doubt him after everything they had been through?

"Matthew, Baines, kindly escort the blacksmith out of the castle."

Baines stepped forward, but Matthew set his feet and crossed his arms. "No. He's done nothing wrong. I don't think he should leave, and I'm not going to be the one who makes him."

Lord Stanford remained perfectly composed. "You, there. Assist Baines."

A servant Corbin had only seen a few times stepped forward. Rough hands encircled Corbin's arms, but he barely felt them. He knew his stunned and forlorn face gave Lord Stanford great pleasure, but he didn't care. He couldn't comprehend what was happening.

As he was being dragged out of the castle, Corbin looked up in time to see Mrs. Whiting. She must have fought her way through the crowd so that she could meet his eyes before he was gone.

She wasn't crying. She wasn't distraught. A formidable determination blazed in her eyes with a fierceness that snapped Corbin out of his lethargy. He stood up straight and shook the hands off that gripped him.

He turned to face Lord Stanford. "I'll leave, Stanford. But I'll be back."

Lord Stanford only smiled. "We'll be waiting."

CHAPTER 43

The rain had decided it wasn't going to make any of this easier for Corbin. It battered him mercilessly, and the wind blew so violently Corbin had to lean his entire body against it to move forward. He only looked back once after the gates were closed behind him. Standing at the tops of each battlement were two or three guards, and it appeared they had been there for quite a while, perhaps even before Corbin had his conversation with Francine, though he had been too preoccupied to notice. He wondered if Stanford had even brought them up with him from the village on his way back to the castle. As much as Corbin detested Lord Stanford, he couldn't deny the man was an impeccable planner.

The lights from the castle soon faded behind him, the stars and moon shrouded by the heavy storm clouds. The gravel gave way to mud, and his clothes soaked up every bit of rain until the excess dripped from his sleeves and hems.

He had trudged through miles of mud when he reached a familiar forest on the side of the road. Corbin grinned. He knew exactly where he was. Scanning the rain-soaked bushes for a moment, he spotted what he was looking for. He knelt down and touched his fingers to the bare rosebush on the side of the road. All that was left of it were its woody stems and a few brown, crisp leaves—no blooms. Who would have imagined that this plain, lonely rosebush could change everything?

It was even simpler now in the darkness, no brilliant red roses to break the monotony, no splashes of color illuminated by the sun's filtered rays. It stood, almost proudly, in the miserable mud, determined to survive the threat of death in this brutal winter. The leaves hadn't yet grown back, but as Corbin ran his fingers along the stems, he could feel the tender indications of growth, the promise of life.

Corbin stood and he could see pointed roofs beyond the trees at the bottom of the hill. He was closer to his destination now, and his weary footsteps quickened as he passed by the first of the shops and little homes. There were no lights in any of the windows. It might even be closer to morning than night now.

As he walked, he remembered the fierce resolve in Mrs. Whiting's eyes before he was thrown from the castle. It was as if she was trying to tell him something, convey some message beyond encouragement.

Remembering Mrs. Whiting brought a memory to Corbin's mind that he hadn't thought about in weeks—a story she had told him about a young girl and her child. But why he remembered it now, his bleary mind couldn't quite grasp.

Finally, Corbin reached the blacksmith shop at the edge of town. Just as he had that first time he saw it, he was filled with an overwhelming feeling of coming home. He vowed in that moment that if he was some-how able to make it back to the castle, he and Rose would spend much more time in the village, working and contributing. The citizens would no longer cower in fear from their rulers. There would be no more beasts, no more victims. Those in authority would not sit in their high places, benefitting from the toil of those they were supposed to be serving.

But what about Lord Stanford? The chief governor couldn't remain at the castle, and yet, he hadn't committed an act of treason and must be allowed to stay.

Corbin couldn't worry about all of that at the moment. For now, he had to get out of the icy rain. He stopped in front of the blacksmith shop's door and knocked softly. There were no lights nor any sign of life stirring inside. He knocked a little louder with the same result. Carefully, Corbin pushed the unlatched door open and peeked inside.

In the darkness, it looked exactly as it had the day he left. He crossed the room and saw that the bed sat empty, made hastily just as it had been on his first morning there. The items on the side table appeared untouched, covered in a layer of dust that was evident even in the darkness. Bart had told Corbin on that first day that almost no one ever moved to Laurel willingly, and apparently no new blacksmith had come. His tools all hung in exactly the same places he had left them. Spotting the holdfast sitting on the anvil, Corbin ran his fingers over the graceful curve and smiled sadly.

As comfortable and content as he felt in this place, he was now home-sick for another home—his real home.

He walked over to the fireplace and knelt down, hovering his hands over the charred wood. A chill ran up his neck. There was a whisper of heat from flames that had recently died out.

Just then, the door swung open, crashing against the wall. The only light in the room came from the occasional burst of lightning in the distance that silhouetted the huge figure looming in the doorway. He held a bow in his hand with an arrow pulled back on the string. Corbin took a step back and slowly raised his hands.

A deep, throaty laugh reverberated through the darkness, and the man lowered his arrow. "Well, if it isn't the prodigal son!"

"Bart! It's so good to see you!" Corbin stuck out a hand and Bart grasped it so hard Corbin thought he would crush the bones. "Who lit a fire? Where's the new blacksmith?"

"Yer lookin' at him!"

"What?"

"That's right. I took over when no new blacksmith came. I'm not very good at it, but with the right tools—*yer* tools—I get the job done. A very *bad* job, but I get it done. I don't even use most of the tools. Don't know what they are." He laughed, then a shadow crossed over Bart's face. "How'd you escape The Beast?"

Corbin grinned. "Oh, I didn't escape . . . I was banished."

"She banished ya?"

"Actually, no. The chief governor did. Lord Stanford."

Bart scrunched up his face. "I know that name. Pale fellow with pale beady eyes?"

"Sounds right."

"He comes 'round every once in a while. Doesn't talk to anyone, just writes stuff down, then disappears. I didn't know he had power to banish anyone."

"Well, technically he shouldn't, but he's managed to gain much more power than he was ever meant to have."

"Well, what'd ya do to deserve banishment?"

"It's a long story, but would you trust me if I said it wasn't true?"

Bart was nodding before Corbin even finished speaking. "A man as honorable as you? 'Course I will."

"Oh, I don't know about honorable. I'm just . . ."

"No, no. Yer a hero 'round these parts. Ya saved us from The Beast, ya did. Ya stepped right up there and sacrificed yerself and put an end to the whole thing. People are gonna be right glad yer home."

Corbin ducked his head. "That's nice of you to say, Bart, but I really have to get back. Rose thinks, or might think, that what I was accused of might be true. Somehow, I don't believe that, though. Something isn't right and I have to return to the castle as soon as possible."

"You wanna go *back*? Back to *a beast*!"

Corbin laughed despite the hopeless situation and the cold that now burned his fingers and toes. Somehow, Bart calling Rose a beast was comical, as opposed to when Francine called her that out of malice.

"Bart, everything's going to be all right. She's done a lot of good in recent months. She's changed. She's patient and kind and good." Bart raised an eyebrow and Corbin laughed softly. "No, really. Things are much better and happier at the castle, and I think that infuriated Lord Stanford more than anything. He saw that he might lose the power he's built up for himself and he feels threatened."

Bart shook his head. "I never would'a thought it. The Beast isn't a beast anymore. Ya wanna go back to her. The chief governor is actin' like he owns the place. And yer back right where ya started from."

Corbin laughed softly, then the laughter caught in his throat as his eyes widened at Bart's words. His mouth hung open and his heart pounded hard and hot in his chest. When he spoke, it was in a hoarse whisper. "Bart, when I first arrived, I asked you if you knew anyone who lived here by the name of Black."

"Aye, ya did. And I still don't."

"What about," Corbin swallowed, his throat painfully dry, "what about a story . . . years ago . . . of a baby brought into town by a girl?"

"Ah! The maid and her child. Everyone knows that story."

CHAPTER 44

Bart closed the door behind him and pulled up a chair in front of the dark fireplace. Corbin lit a small fire, then stood with his hand gripping the mantle.

"I was only eight when it happened, but the story is as fresh as if it were yesterday." Bart stroked his beard thoughtfully. "I'd been workin' at the docks with me dad, and he sent me up to town to bring in a late shipment of fish to be sold at the market the next day. Anyway, I was walkin' down the street, right there to be exact," Bart pointed toward the window at a spot across the road, "when out of the shadows came this young lass carryin' a bundle in her arms. Don't know if she saw me. Never asked. Anyway, she darted across the road and stopped in front of the blacksmith shop. 'Twas a warm night, not a cloud in the sky. The lass knelt down, held the bundle to her chest, and rocked back and forth. She was whisperin' some words, sounded like a prayer to me—a sad prayer, like a song. She reached into her shawl and pulled out a small basket, like the ones I keep me bread in, and put it on the ground. She kissed the bundle in her arms and laid it down on the basket in front of the door. She knocked on the door and ran away and hid behind the baker's shop. Just right there." Bart pointed to his left. "I was still across the way, a sack of fish slung over me back, and I couldn't move. Moment later, the blacksmith opened the door, saw the bundle, and knelt down. He gasped, and sorta cried. He disappeared into the shop and returned seconds later with the missus. She knelt down and her sobs traveled across the street and straight to my heart, I tell ya. She picked up the bundle, which began to cry. That's when

I knew it was a baby. She walked out into the road, with her bare feet and nightgown, lookin' for whoever had left her the baby."

Bart sniffed and blinked back the tears that looked so foreign in his eyes. "The lass, she took off up the hill and disappeared. The blacksmith and his wife went back in the house. I followed the girl and saw that she took the trail that led up to the castle. I was taught never to interfere with anyone else's affairs and so I let it be. Though I wasn't the only one who had witnessed it. The old baker was already awake, bakin' bread for the next day and had seen it out his window. Some others had witnessed it too, and by the next day, the story of the maid and her child was known throughout the entire village. I never found out who she was, or why she did it, but I do know that she gave the blacksmith and his wife the one and only thing they had ever wanted—a child of their own."

Corbin found his voice after a long moment. "What were they like? The blacksmith and his wife?"

"Best people 'round, they were. He was always makin' little trinkets for us children out of his metal scraps, and she was always givin' us sweets."

Corbin blinked and tried to slow his breathing. "What happened then, after that night?"

"Well, sad as it was, the rumors started rollin' in, as they always do. Who was the mother? What kind of woman leaves her baby in the middle of the night? The Fosters, that was the blacksmith and his wife, couldn't go anywhere without a question and a glare from some busybody. One day, we all woke up and they were gone. I've missed 'em ever since. Good people." Bart sniffed and wiped his nose on his sleeve. "Word was they left the kingdom and changed their names. But I'm glad fer 'em. They always wanted a baby. Oh, and the baby, he had somethin' pinned to the front of him. A paper with somethin' written on it. No one ever did find out what it said, though."

Corbin's throat felt so tight he could barely breathe. "It was his name . . . My name."

Bart's mouth gaped and the tears that were in his eyes slid down his rough face and into his matted beard.

"The baby! Yer the baby!" He stood from his chair, flung his arms around Corbin, and crushed him into a hug. "It's like yer me brother, or somethin'! I need to tell everyone! You've become a legend 'round here! Now yer our prince!" Bart let him go and wiped his tears with his huge hands. He sniffed loudly. "Oh, I can't wait to tell the missus. What a day!"

Corbin smiled and blinked back his own tears, then walked to the front door and opened it. The rain had softened and moonlight peeked through the thinner clouds. Feeling like he was suddenly on hallowed ground, he knelt down in front of the blacksmith shop's doors, touching his fingers to the wooden planks of the front steps. "Can you show me where the trail is?"

"Sure. What . . . now?"

Corbin chuckled and nodded. "I need to get back, and the trail may be the only way."

"Right! Anything for the baby in the basket." Bart limped as quickly as he could across the street to his house. Corbin followed, but waited on the front steps while Bart hollered from the open door.

"Beatrice! I've gotta go show Prince Blacksmith, who is also the baby in the basket, how to find a trail that will lead him back to the castle so he can return to the princess who is no longer a beast 'cause he's been banished!"

Despite the lateness of the hour, a woman's voice called from inside the house. "Does he need a sandwich?"

Bart ducked his head back out of the doorway. "Do you need a sandwich?"

Corbin chuckled. "I would appreciate that. Thank you."

Bart went back inside and returned a moment later with a small bundle in his hands. "Eat it now. Yer gonna need all yer strength and both hands if yer gonna make it."

Corbin ate quickly as he followed Bart out of town, across fields, and through a few scant forests. Finally, they reached the bottom of a forbidding-looking hill.

"Here 'tis. This is where she disappeared. I just can't find the exact spot."

Bart and Corbin circled the area again and again, but the dark, combined with the overgrowth, made it nearly impossible to find any sign of the trail.

Just when Corbin was about to say they'd try again in the morning, Bart called out. "There! There 'tis!" Corbin ran over to him, and they knelt down and saw a faint trail that was almost completely grown over with grass and weeds. They followed the trail with their eyes until it became indistinguishable from brush and branches. "Well now, that won't be pleasant to get through."

Corbin stood and saw that the castle was at least three miles up the trail, but based on where they were standing and the direction of the trail, he knew that it would lead to the little door on the southeast wall. With Bart's help, he had found a way back home. Corbin flung his arms around Bart.

"Thank you!"

Bart laughed thickly and pounded Corbin's back. "Yer welcome, my friend." Corbin heard him sniff. "I never thought I'd get to meet the baby from that night. I never thought I'd learn what happened to him."

Corbin let go and smiled. "Me neither." He stepped toward the fading trail, then stopped. "Bart, in the morning when everyone's awake, can you spread the word about what's happened? They need to know that she's no longer a beast and that Lord Stanford has taken over. They have a right to know. But we'll get it all sorted out."

"Of course. Are you sure you don't want me to come with you?"

Corbin nodded. "There are guards ready to put an arrow through me as soon as they see me. I would hate to put you in danger. But letting the village know what's happening will be a great help." Corbin grasped Bart's hand. "We'll have you and Beatrice over for dinner soon."

"We'll bring the bread."

CHAPTER 45

Corbin couldn't even feel the scrapes anymore, couldn't even see the blood that dripped from his hands and arms. His clothes were filthy, his pants soaked through with mud and torn from rocks and twigs. The rain fell in sheets, but he didn't care. Rose was waiting.

And someone else.

He could see the castle wall looming high above him, silhouetted against the swirling clouds, and he knew he was getting nearer. The trail wound dangerously close to a guard with a sword in his hands—a sword Corbin recognized as one he had sharpened—but thankfully, the guard was sitting against a tree, fast asleep. Mercifully, the clouds cleared after a while, and Corbin had the moon to guide him through the thick foliage.

Finally, as the sky transformed from black to gray to soft, cloudy pink, Corbin reached the stone wall and the cracked wood of the outer door. He had dreaded this moment, knowing that after his laborious climb, he would have to figure out how to break it down. He felt along the hinges, trying to figure out a way he could remove them. Finally, he pushed against the door and then stood there, too stunned to move, as it creaked open.

"Welcome home, my little prince." Mrs. Whiting sat on a bench in the hazy darkness, a tender, weary smile lighting her face. A mangled pile of boards lay at her feet, the nails sticking out wildly. Her hands were wrapped up in her apron on her lap, and Corbin could see crimson seeping through. "I knew you'd find your way back."

Her eyes were merry as usual, but an unmistakable sheen of tears softened them. Corbin stumbled forward and sat next to her on the bench and wrapped his arms around her, holding her close for a moment. Gently, he lifted her hands and kissed them through the fabric.

"Thank you." He pulled back and took a breath, looking at her closely. "Mrs. Whiting, my mother used to have a small basket. She used to keep scraps of fabric in it, or sometimes socks that needed to be mended. One time, I remember her holding it on her lap as she sat in a rocking chair in the corner of our shop in Maycott. I remember it because she was crying and it made me sad. I asked her what was wrong and she smiled at me. She had me climb up onto her lap next to the basket. She told me she wasn't sad. She was very happy. She told me that she had received the greatest gift she'd ever been given in that basket, and sometimes she just liked to sit and remember. When I left Maycott, I left the basket in the shop because I wanted a piece of my mother to stay where I thought my home would always be." Corbin swallowed against the tightness in his throat. Mrs. Whiting listened to his story, her gaze on the ground at her feet, her face too darkened by shadows to read. "I had always known I was born to someone else. My parents always spoke of my mother with gratitude, even reverence. I have always loved my mother."

Corbin could see that Mrs. Whiting's chin began to tremble, and the morning light caught a tear that rolled down her cheek. "I was told that Corbin meant 'raven' for my black hair. But when I told you that on that first day, you seemed a little . . . doubtful. Does 'Corbin' have another meaning that you know of?"

She spoke, though it was barely a whisper, mingling with the morning. "It means 'Gift to God.'"

"And . . ." Corbin paused, tears filling his own eyes, "was I your gift to God?"

Mrs. Whiting closed her eyes and took a steadying breath. "Yes. He gave me you, and I gave you back to Him."

Corbin reached over and wrapped his arms around her once more. He had found his mother, and was finally home. She buried her face in his shoulder and soaked it with her tears.

"When did you know?" Corbin whispered.

"As soon as you walked in the doors, when I looked into your eyes. Their grayness, the shape, the dark eyelashes. They're your father's eyes. You even have that same dimple. You're tall like he was. Handsome. Strong." She placed a hand under Corbin's chin and raised his face to look at her. "Please don't be upset by this. He was a good man, I promise. He was afraid. We all were. He had never been taught how to handle difficult situations. They had always been handled for him. That's where you're different than him, and that's why I knew you would be raised well by the Fosters. They gave you what I couldn't." She wiped the tears from her cheeks. "I'm sorry for my stunned greeting when you arrived."

"I thought you were so disappointed that Princess Rose had chosen such a common man. Your eyes were red when I saw you again and I thought you had been crying."

"Oh, my little prince. I wasn't disappointed. I was astonished. And yes, I was crying, but for joy. You came back to me! It broke my heart to give you up, but though I couldn't explain it, I knew things would work out. I didn't ever imagine that meant I would ever get to see you again. I just knew that you were being raised by the best people I knew—who could give you so much more than I could, and that you would be taken care of. But then you did come back! Please forgive me for being distant. I had to stay detached. I didn't know how you felt about me. I didn't even know how much you knew about where you came from. I didn't want to force you to feel something you didn't. I was just content to have you under the same roof again. I was content to watch you become the man you are today. My joy is complete."

Corbin held her close again, shaking his head slowly back and forth in wonder. He pulled back abruptly. "Wait, you're the mother of the prince. Doesn't that make you a queen, or something? You need a crown and jewels."

"No, Corbin. You are the only jewel I need."

Corbin smiled. "Mother," he said. Mrs. Whiting closed her eyes and smiled, her cheeks wet with tears. "Everyone will know who you are. I'm going to take care of you."

"Corbin, my dear. I have lived my life trying to protect this secret, to protect my honor, and yours. I can't . . ."

"Sacrificing your happiness for mine, living a noble life, serving others every single day, staying to comfort a hurting, mourning young girl when most had decided to leave, and then selflessly standing by knowing that I was your child . . . is there anything more honorable than that?"

Mrs. Whiting sobbed quietly. "But what will they say?"

Corbin reached out and held his mother in his arms. "That you have done a beautiful thing."

CHAPTER 46

Mrs. Whiting kissed his cheek and held his face between her hands for a moment. Then, always practical, she stood from the bench and looked around her warily.

"Guards are all over the castle. Inside and out. One could appear at any moment. They have been ordered to kill you if you make an appearance."

Corbin glanced around at the walls, but could see no guards from where he stood. "Where's Rose?"

Mrs. Whiting shook her head. "I still haven't seen her. I'm worried about her, Corbin. Even in her most violent tempers, she's never stayed away this long. Besides, when she's upset, she usually likes everyone to know about it, or she did, at least. I don't think she's angry at you. I think Lord Stanford is behind this."

"So do I." Corbin glanced down the hill at the Chief Governor's house. "Where is he?"

"He's not in his house. But," she paused, her eyes softening, "Francine is there. He sent her there when she tried to defend you after you left. She was trying to say it wasn't your fault, but he sent her away before anyone could listen. The poor thing. I was upset that she came, but I truly believe she was sent for. Somehow."

"I need to talk to her."

Mrs. Whiting grasped his sleeve. "Be careful."

Corbin forced a smile onto his tense face, kissed her cheek, then ducked behind trees and hedges. He weaved his way to the chief governor's house across the grounds, pausing for guards to pass by every now and then. He reached the door and, without knocking, stepped inside.

Francine sat on a chair by a waning fire, the flames casting dancing shadows on her vacant face. She wore one of Rose's gowns, and jewels sparkled in her braided hair.

The house was impossibly grand. Rich wood paneled the walls. Gold statues and ancient artifacts encrusted in jewels sat on shelves and tables. Elaborate paintings hung from the walls in gold frames. It was as if all the wealth in the kingdom was contained in this one house.

Francine hadn't moved when Corbin opened the door, too absorbed by the flames that swayed before her bleary eyes.

"Francine?" he whispered.

Francine spun around, her hands gripping the arms of the chair. "You're alive! Lord Stanford said they found you and killed you!"

"Not yet. Come with me. We need to get you out of here." She followed him out the door and around the back of the house. Tall trees blocked the house from behind, and no guards could see them there.

He turned to face her and was surprised to see that she didn't look the same as she had the day before, or even when she sat at the fireplace. Her face blazed with fury.

"He used me. Lord Stanford did. He was the one who stopped me when you and The Bea . . . Princess Rose sent me away. He told me that he would see to it that I would get to speak to you alone. He told me you were miserable, that I could make you remember how much you loved me and that you would leave with me. He let me wait for you in the garden, assuring me that you would eventually go out to the shop. And then you did and The Beast left and you were alone, just as he promised. The next thing I knew, he banished you and accused you of treason! I never wanted this to happen."

Francine took a small step forward, but kept a safe distance. "I promise I'm not going to throw myself at you. I do apologize for that. I know I made things difficult for you. But I truly thought that you wanted me. Your letter was so sad. You sounded so lonely."

"Do you have the letter?"

"Yes. I have never parted with it." Francine reached into her sleeve and pulled out the letter, then offered it to him.

He read it silently, unspeakably grateful that he could read, too embarrassed to say the words out loud, though they weren't even his.

Dearest Francine,

These days and weeks and months without you have been a torment. I have thought of nothing but you since the day I left—your eyes, your smiles, your kisses. As you may know, I am married to The Beast of Laurel. This was a grave mistake. I have been foolish and idiotic. I let my broken heart obscure my vision, and I know that it will never be whole without you. Please, come for me.

Yours always,
Corbin

Lord Stanford had definitely written this. Corbin tried to suppress a smile, imagining how much Lord Stanford must have loved calling Corbin foolish and idiotic, without saying it to his face.

"Well, this makes a little more sense. May I have this? It wasn't written by me and it won't help you to keep it."

Francine's eyes welled with tears, her chin trembling slightly, and nodded. He placed the letter in his pocket.

"Francine, do you know where Rose is?"

"You don't know? She . . . she's in the dungeon. I heard Stanford telling that Baines person."

"The dungeon!" Corbin turned away, ready to run to the castle.

"Wait!" Francine gripped his sleeve, but dropped her hand. "The prison keys . . . Lord Stanford took them from your chamber."

Corbin ran a hand through his hair in frustration. That was where he was going to go first.

Francine smiled and reached into her pocket. "But I took them from off his desk when he wasn't looking."

Corbin released a surprised breath and took the keys from her outstretched hand. "Thank you, Francine."

"Don't thank me. This is me making amends." She dropped her gaze to her feet and began to wring her hands. "I don't know what I'm going to do now. Lord Stanford told me I could stay as long as I wish. But I know I can't. I've made a fool of myself. I don't know if I can ever overcome my humiliation. I will relive this over and over in my mind until I die. How could I have been so foolish?"

"You haven't been foolish. You have been tricked by a master of deception. If it makes you feel any better, I once thought of him as a friend. He used to be Princess Rose's most trusted advisor. He preyed on our hopes and our hurts and he did it in such a way that there was no way for us to know. All we can do now is be more aware, more careful, and hopefully, more wise."

"But where will I go?" Francine's desperate voice cracked.

A sympathetic smile softened Corbin's face, his voice gentle. "Go home, Francine. It's the safest place for you. And, this is coming from someone who knows you. Be content. Be happy with having, not always wanting."

"But what if I don't *have* anything?" she wailed, abandoning her forced smile.

Corbin tried not to chuckle at her familiar histrionics. This was, after all, a particularly difficult situation. "Francine, you have more tenacity than anyone I have ever known. You have determination and a good heart. You have the admiration of every girl in Maycott and the hearts of most of the men. You have parents who love you and siblings who adore you. And . . . you have my gratitude and friendship."

"Thank you, Corbin. You have mine."

CHAPTER 47

Corbin told Francine to look for Mrs. Whiting and that she would take care of her. He waited until she was a safe distance away, knowing that the guards were looking for him and if she were anywhere near him, she was in danger. Once he had waited for as long as he could bear, he began to make his way back to the castle. He ducked into the gardens and found protection in the high, neatly manicured laurel bushes. Greens and browns surrounded him on every side and blurred together as he raced through the gardens. He passed the perfectly spaced, growing rosebushes, their stems now covered in tiny, deep green leaves . . . until something white caught Corbin's eye.

A tiny bud, the first in the garden, had just begun to open its snowy petals. Corbin stopped and knelt down, his fingers feeling along the tender branches to the base of the stem, and plucked it. Smiling, he carefully placed the tiny rose in his pocket.

He crept closer to the castle, ducking low to the ground, aware of the guards that were pacing the walls with a little more vigor now that the sun was higher in the sky. The doors were in sight, and flanking either side were two guards with swords. Corbin found a large rock at his feet and, when the guards weren't looking, threw the rock in the opposite direction. It crashed against a nearby wall and a cry of alarm sounded over the grounds. The guards on the wall ran to the spot where the rock had hit the wall, but unfortunately, the guards at the door didn't move.

Just then, the door opened and Lord Stanford appeared in the doorway. Corbin couldn't hear what he said, but the two guards left and ran inside the castle, Lord Stanford following behind.

Taking a quick breath and an anxious look around him, Corbin ran out from behind the hedges and inside the castle. He was ready to duck behind the curtains or a suit of armor, only there was no need. Corbin could hear some sort of commotion near the front of the castle, and it seemed that it had drawn all the attention away from him. There were shouts and what sounded like many hands banging against the front doors. Corbin didn't know what was going on, but he took advantage of the situation and ran undetected through the corridors, down too many flights of stairs to count, until he arrived at the dank, dim stairway to the dungeons.

Without pausing, he circled down the steps, avoiding the rats that fled from his clomping boots until he reached the floor.

A charmingly pleasant voice reached his ears then. "I'd know those common, stomping, beautiful footsteps anywhere." Corbin couldn't see Rose yet, but he smiled and stepped closer to the sound of her voice.

"Rose? Are you all right?"

"Quite. Matthew and I were just talking about how we expected you any minute and here you are."

"Matthew is here too?" Corbin squinted in the darkness, but his eyes hadn't adjusted yet so he could only see the flickering light of the torches on the walls.

"Hello, Prince Corbin!" came Matthew's voice from the dark.

Rose spoke again, her voice even more cheerful as Corbin drew nearer. "Yes, Matthew refused to take orders from Lord Stanford and has been keeping me company."

Corbin was close enough now that he could see Mathew in one cell and Rose in a cell across the room. They both stood with their hands gripping the bars, their eyes expectant and relieved.

Corbin rushed to Rose's cell now that he could see.

"Wait, Corbin. Let Matthew out first. He has been a faithful servant and true friend."

Corbin crossed the room and freed Matthew, grasping his hand in gratitude. "There's a commotion up there, Matthew. Be careful."

"I will. Thank you, Your Highness."

"Thank *you*, Matthew."

As Matthew ran up the stairs, Corbin rushed back to Rose and hastily unlocked her cell. As soon as the door flew open, she was in his arms. One hand held her waist while the other tangled in her hair that fell loose down her back. He kissed her hair, her forehead, her cheeks.

Suddenly, dust inexplicably began to fall from the ceiling and into their eyes and onto their heads. The entire castle seemed to pound with what must have been hundreds of footsteps.

Corbin pulled away reluctantly, then grasped Rose's hand and led her up the winding, dizzying stairs. They climbed the steps two and three at a time until they reached the main floor and blinked against the blinding light of mid-morning.

Shouts of outrage, accompanied by fists punching the air filled the Great Hall and Throne Room. It seemed that the entire village had decided to come to the castle today, and as Corbin surveyed the crowd, he suddenly knew why.

Bartley Fitzjoly stood in front of everyone, towering above the tallest heads, his hand holding Beatrice's. "The Beast is not a beast anymore. The prince told me himself!"

"Of course he would say that!" Lord Stanford cried. He was standing in front of the two thrones, trying to placate the crowd. "He wanted to return to his lofty throne and rule over you. He has thirsted for power since his first day here. Why else would he agree to marry a beast?"

There were some shouts of agreement, but Bart refused to back down. "*And* he said that you have taken all her power and have deceived him, the princess, and the entire kingdom!"

"I have done nothing but serve you! She has refused to rule! I have given my life to this kingdom."

"Yes, and what do you have to show for it? Unbearable taxes and oppressive laws!" Bart shouted back.

This seemed to invigorate the crowd more than anything, and for a moment, real terror widened Lord Stanford's pale eyes.

"Wait!" he cried, his voice high and desperate, and the crowd hushed. "I have documents that the princess herself has signed that proves she has raised your taxes and changed the laws." Lord Stanford held up document after document, signed by Princess Rose. "Here, she raised the taxes on wheat seven percent. Here, she raised the taxes on barley eleven percent! In this document, she . . ."

"Yes, and who wrote these laws?" Corbin, his hand holding Rose's, stepped forward, and the crowd gasped.

Lord Stanford momentarily baffled, quickly regained his composure. "Seize him!" he cried.

"Don't touch him!" Bart shouted.

Corbin never let go of Rose's hand as they walked to the front of the mob of angry citizens.

"It's The Beast!" someone said, their voice shrill.

A ripple of anger spread over the crowd while others tried to hush them.

"But how . . . how did you get out? And how did *you* get back?" Lord Stanford said, his gaze landing accusingly on the nearest guard.

Corbin ignored him and walked forward as the crowd parted. Whether they believed him to be good or bad, it didn't matter at the moment. Curiosity overpowered their opinions.

Corbin and Rose reached the front of the crowd and stood a few feet away from Lord Stanford. Corbin took one of the documents in Lord Stanford's hands, which Lord Stanford grasped at, but missed.

"When I arrived at this castle, I couldn't read or write. But thanks to this woman and her patience and goodness," he squeezed Rose's hand, "I have since learned. Though, anyone could tell you that this document *and* this letter," Corbin reached into his pocket and pulled out Francine's letter, "were written by the same hand."

Lord Stanford chuckled, though sweat trickled down his temple. "Oh, you mean this love letter you sent to your fiancée begging her to come and save you from the clutches of an evil beast?"

Corbin spoke above the hum of scandal and outrage. "I did not write this letter. You did."

The low hum of voices became gasps and appalled mumblings as Lord Stanford raised his hands, attempting to speak.

"It's true!" a clear, defiant voice rang over the crowd, and everyone turned to look at Francine who stood at the back of the gathering. Mrs. Whiting stood next to her, a hand on her shoulder. "Prince Corbin did not invite me here. He loves the princess. Lord Stanford is behind all of this. He wanted me to come so he could disgrace the prince. He wanted to prove that Princess Rose is unworthy to rule, and his plan to take complete control would be complete. But, if you do not allow yourselves to be deceived by him as I was, you will see that your prince and princess will serve this kingdom beautifully . . . together."

Corbin met Francine's eyes with a grateful smile. She smiled back at him, curtsied, then walked quite calmly out the front doors.

Lord Stanford didn't say anything. His pale face was impossibly paler, and he swallowed hard.

"I think we have proven beyond a doubt that Lord Stanford has been deceitful to the point of treason. He has conspired to dethrone and dishonor the rulers of this kingdom. He has oppressed this people for his own gain."

The crowd erupted, realizing then who had truly been oppressing them.

"Put him to death!"

"The penalty for treason is death!"

"Hang him!"

Lord Stanford shook violently and actually collapsed into the throne behind him.

Corbin raised his hands and the cries quieted. "There are many kinds of deaths. I suspect that the worst kind of death to Lord Stanford is the loss of power."

Lord Stanford had rested one elbow on the arm of the throne and was rubbing his head weakly. Rose watched Corbin in silence, wonder in her emerald eyes.

"But, as Lord Stanford has informed us, he has given his life in service to this kingdom, and I think I have a way he may continue to do that, if he wishes. As we all know, Laurel is in desperate need of rehabilitation. The roads are in disrepair and are even dangerous. The buildings are crumbling. The people have been so overtaxed they are unable to provide for their own families. And though he has used treachery, manipulation, and even treason to get where he is, we cannot put all the blame on him. My mother once told me," Corbin found Mrs. Whiting in the crowd who was smiling through her tears, "that things have a way of working themselves out. I do not wish to throw Lord Stanford in prison. I do not wish to banish him. But I think some time learning how to work outside the castle walls will do him much good." Corbin smiled down at Rose who nodded and grinned back at him. "And we, the princess and I, along with Mr. Stanford, will work alongside you to beautify and restore this kingdom. It will be a thriving place once again and people will be lining up to live here. Right, Bart?"

"And we'll finally get a decent blacksmith since the princess stole ours!" Bart bellowed and the crowd laughed and cheered.

Lord Stanford slumped deeper into his seat and kept eyeing the exit. Corbin stepped closer to him and put a steadying hand on his shoulder. "Stanford, Baines will accompany you to the dungeons until we get started on work, so you won't be lonely. We'll appoint Matthew as Chief Governor . . . if he wants the job, that is."

Matthew, his face almost lost in the crowd, looked to his left and right before stepping forward. "Me? Chief Governor? But I don't even know how to read."

"It's not too late to learn. Besides, your loyalty is worth more than letters."

The crowd chuckled and Matthew's cheeks flushed.

"And," Corbin continued, "your first item of business will be to go through the Chief Governor's house, clear out all of the treasures he has accumulated on his many *diplomatic* missions, and put them in the treasury to go toward rehabilitating the kingdom."

Everyone cheered again, and as the applause faded, Bart stood taller, stepping slightly away from the crowd, though his hand still gripped Beatrice's. "And what have you to say, Princess Rose? How will you rule this kingdom, now that you're no longer a beast?"

Rose took a deep breath and gripped Corbin's hand tighter. "I . . . first, I want to apologize to all of you. I have not only been beastly, I have been complacent. I have neglected my duties. I signed those documents without reading them, without caring. I was lost in my own pain, and I allowed it to bring out the worst parts of me, and . . . I am terribly, terribly sorry. I don't know how to make it up to you. I . . ."

Rose's voice faltered, then failed as she met each expectant, yet uncertain eye.

Quickly, Corbin released her hand and knelt in front of her while her eyes widened. Without taking his eyes from hers, he carefully reached into his pocket and held out the perfect white rosebud.

Corbin realized he looked just as filthy, if not more so, than the day he had given Rose that first flower that changed everything. With hands outstretched, his eyes intense and hopeful, Corbin offered her the rose. They both knew he was offering her more than a pretty flower. He was offering her the memory of her past, her place in the present, and the promise of their future together. Tears rolled down her smiling face, and she placed her hands over his, taking the rose from his blackened fingers.

As Corbin stood, Rose turned to face the crowd. When she spoke, her voice rang with sincerity and conviction. "I will rule this kingdom as this rose rules the garden. Like its roots that grow deep and sure in the ground, I will never forget where I come from. Like its petals, I will always look upward and seek for light and truth. Like its thorns that are fierce and sharp, I will defend my people with strength and boldness. Like its leaves, my arms will reach outward to my fellowmen in friendship and goodwill. And, like its stem, I will stand proud in defense of what is right and noble."

No one spoke. Rose looked out into the astonished faces of her people, her face beseeching.

"That's good enough fer me!" Bart said.

CHAPTER 48

By the time the laughter and cheers died down, Mrs. Whiting had made her way to the front of the crowd.

"You are all invited to stay for the coronation of the king and queen of Laurel!" She turned to smile shrewdly at the stunned faces of Rose and Corbin. "It's time," she whispered. She turned back to the crowd. "Is Father Goode here?"

A regal hand lifted into the air, and Father Goode stepped toward the thrones at the front of the room.

"A lovely day for a coronation," he said with a pleased smile. He stood expectantly next to Rose and Corbin.

A hum of excitement floated over the air. Everyone was laughing and smiling, finally feeling that long-forgotten sense of oneness and unity. Hope and optimism for the future was palpable and invigorating. Corbin wrapped his arms around Rose and everyone cheered.

"Stop!" an outraged voice rang out over the enthusiastic pandemonium. "I cannot, *will not* allow this madness to continue!" A thin man with wispy white hair was pushing his way to the front of the crowd. "Have you all lost your *minds*?"

Everyone turned to look at Arthur. This tiny man carried himself with the majesty of a king and those around him cowered. Except for Corbin, who felt the corners of his mouth lift knowingly.

"I will not allow a king and queen of Laurel to be crowned wearing filthy rags. Come with me!" Arthur beckoned for Rose and Corbin to follow and marched forward. He turned back around. "And all of you here. You may all be common, but you can still be clean. If we're rehabilitating this kingdom, we will begin with its citizens. While the prince and princess get cleaned up, you will all go out to the well and wash your hands and faces. And you, baker! You have dough in your beard. It better be gone before the coronation begins."

"Yes, sir." Bart's voice was solemn, though his eyes twinkled.

As Arthur marched them in the direction of their chambers, Corbin turned to Rose. "I guess there's no doubt in anyone's mind about who's really in charge around here."

"No doubt at all." She grinned.

Later, as soon as Corbin's cravat was tied to Arthur's strict standards and Rose was dressed in her ivory gown, they met each other in the corridor. The early afternoon sunlight caught the gold in Rose's brilliant hair and the endearing freckles across her nose. The joy in her eyes made them sparkle like stars, and her cheeks were flushed pink with excitement. The white rosebud had been braided into her hair and tucked behind her ear.

She touched her hand to Corbin's smooth jaw, ran her fingers through his damp hair that fell across his forehead, and smiled. Corbin caught her hand before he let it fall and pressed his lips to it.

"You are so beautiful," he whispered, then he smiled. "I didn't know what beauty was until I met a beast." They laughed softly together and Corbin held her close. "Are you ready?"

She sighed contentedly, her breath tickling his ear. "Yes. I wasn't ready to be a queen until I met a blacksmith."

Corbin looked up when Mrs. Whiting appeared at the other end of the corridor. He grinned and pulled away from Rose, though he grasped her hand.

"It's almost time," Mrs. Whiting said, her eyes dancing.

Corbin nodded, but his smile grew wider. "First. Rose, I'd like to introduce you to someone."

"Is it that huge, one-legged man from the village?" She giggled. "He seems very nice."

Corbin chuckled. "Yes, you'll get to meet Bart. I've already invited him to dinner. But, for now . . ." Corbin took a breath and reached out to take Mrs. Whiting's hand in his free one, "I'd like you to meet . . . my mother."

Rose's eyes widened as they looked from Corbin to Mrs. Whiting and back again. After Corbin told Rose the story, Rose gathered Mrs. Whiting into her arms, tears streaming down both their faces.

As she held Mrs. Whiting close, she looked over at Corbin and whispered, "We have a mother again, Corbin. We have a mother."

The entire kingdom, their hands and faces clean, watched Corbin and Rose be crowned King and Queen of Laurel. They held hands and cried, leaning on each other for support after a long day . . . a long ten years. Excited children sat on their father's shoulders and mothers held content and sleeping babies in their arms. The future was full of hope and it was finally beginning.

The sun was just setting when the people began to move toward the doors. Plans were made to begin work the next day and everyone went home to rest. Matthew had taken Stanford and Baines to spend the night safely in the dungeons until they would be summoned the next day to begin work in the quarry.

Rose and Corbin climbed the stairs and walked hand in hand down the corridor. They paused to look out over the garden and noticed that a few more buds had joined the first. Corbin held her close and felt her tears dampen his shirt. He kissed the top of her head.

"Come with me." She slid her arms from around him, grasped his hand, and led him to her chamber. They sat on the edge of the bed, and she picked up *Paradise Lost* from her bedside table, the iron rose lying beside it. Corbin smiled down at the familiar book, anticipation welling up inside of him. The red, dried rose still marked the place. Rose reached up to take the white rose out of her hair and held both flowers in her hand. She opened the book to the page where the words were marked— words Corbin had never gotten to read, even after he knew how.

Rose smiled and took a shaky breath. "After I met you at the Gift Giving, I found these words. They helped me make sense of what I was feeling for you—a beautiful, common blacksmith with dirty hands and a soot-covered face." She laughed softly and he grinned at her. "For my entire life, people looked at me with either hatred or pity. And I'm to blame. My parents died, and I decided to die too. I let this castle die, allowed it to become a place of decay and loss. Most of the servants left, and those that stayed had no life in them, no vitality. I didn't want to die, but I didn't want to live. I didn't know *how* to live. But, when you gave me that rose and looked at me with . . . hope, with understanding . . . something came alive in me. I was reminded of who I was supposed to be, if only for a moment. And . . ." she paused and met his eyes, "I loved you for it."

"You *loved* me? You had a very strange way of showing it." Corbin laughed and kissed her hand.

Rose laughed weakly, though her face became shadowed with remorse. "I'm so sorry. I didn't understand it and I couldn't explain it and I didn't know how to handle it, so I tried to make it go away, but it only grew. Loving you made me want to improve myself, but I didn't know how. You challenged me and infuriated me. I couldn't continue being the person I was, and I had to rediscover who I was meant to be. And it was harder than I ever imagined." She sighed. "And every time I wanted to give up, I read these words. Every time it made no sense for me to love a common blacksmith, I read these words. Every time you challenged me to become better than I was, I read these words."

She took a breath and held up the book, her chin trembling as it had that night so many weeks ago when everything changed. "'So dear I loved him, that with him all deaths I could endure, without him live no life.'"

Corbin sat motionless for a moment, Rose's image blurring before his eyes as he gathered her into his arms. "May I show you some words I found?" he whispered in her ear.

Rose sat up, her eyes expectant. He took the book from her, but before he opened it, he looked intently into her eyes. "Have your nightmares gone away, Rose?"

She didn't answer right away, but Corbin watched closely as she pondered his question, her eyebrows knitting together.

"I just realized . . . there have been storms, but no nightmares." She took his hand and held it in hers. Then, she placed it on her cheek, and he brushed away the tears that fell from her eyes. "You were here? It was you?"

Smiling, Corbin placed his forehead against hers. "Yes, my little beauty."

She threw her arms around his neck, her gratitude too profound for words.

Corbin wrapped one hand around her waist and held the book open with the other. He spoke softly, his lips at her ear. "'Awake my fairest, my espoused, my latest found, Heaven's last best gift, my every new delight. Awake, the morning shines . . .'"

Placing the book aside, Corbin cradled Rose's face in his hands and looked into her blazing eyes. In that room where Corbin had learned to love a beast, he took beauty in his arms. Finally, with no distractions or misunderstandings, he pressed his lips to hers and kissed her until warm tears rolled down her cheeks and onto his fingers. He held her until the sun fell, and when the darkness came, there was no fear.

Soon, with crowns on their heads, they watched as the flowers blossomed, as their children grew, and as their castle and kingdom came to life. And they lived and learned, and loved and grew, in their garden full of roses.

Discussion Questions

1. Why is it often easier to see the beauty in others than in ourselves? Similarly, why is it sometimes easier to see the beastliness in others than in ourselves?

2. What qualities did Corbin inherit from his birth parents? His adopted parents? Corbin's father had a tendency to escape in difficult situations. How was Corbin different? The same?

3. How was Ella uniquely prepared to befriend and empathize with Rose? Why do people handle the same trial differently? Why was Rose finally ready to accept sympathy?

4. Do you think Rose was the only beast in this story? Who else had flaws and what were they?

5. What do you think of Mrs. Whiting's decision to not tell Corbin what she knew about him and his past?

6. Was Francine justified in showing up at Corbin's house? Are pain and fear ever valid reasons for certain actions?

7. Like Rose, have there been times in your life when you have had to strengthen someone who normally strengthens you?

8. Do you think Corbin was correct in leaving Francine at the beginning? Should he have fought for their relationship and accepted her apology? What prevented Corbin from leaving Rose, even when things were hard?

9. When did you suspect that Lord Stanford wasn't quite as honorable as he wanted everyone to believe? Is it good to do the right thing for the wrong reasons? Was his "service" to his kingdom ever acceptable?

10. What elements of the original/best-known versions of *Beauty and the Beast* did you notice in this retelling?

ACKNOWLEDGMENTS

First, and always, I would like to thank my Heavenly Father, who always sees the beauty in all of us.

Thank you to my amazing Gary for his love, encouragement, and never-ending optimism. Thank you to my five beautiful boys. You bring me unspeakable joy and are the most beautiful things in my life.

Thank you to my wonderful, hardworking, incredible parents. I am forever grateful for you. Thank you to Jenn, Ang, Kif, and Care. There were never such devoted sisters. Thank you to the rest of my amazing family— my two stupendous brothers, my in-laws, nieces, nephews, uncles, aunts, cousins . . . your support means the world to me. Thank you also to my dear friends for your love and support. I am blessed beyond words.

This book bears the fingerprints of many devoted and talented friends—old, new, and both. Thank you to Natalie. Everything you touch becomes beautiful. Thank you to Marilee, my friend behind the fence and over the piano. Thank you to Mandy, my friend across the country yet at my fingertips. And thank you to Heather, who taught me in a very critical time of life that all the best stories end with, "In conclusion . . . it was berry, berry flavor." Thank you Rebecca, Melanie, Ashtyn, Angee, and Amber for your kindness and support!

Thank you to the wonderful Cedar Fort team: Erin, Jessica, Erica, and Hali for seeing potential in that first (terrible) draft and helping bring this story to life. Thank you, Katie Payne, for the perfectly gorgeous cover that I could stare at all day. Thank you, Vikki, for your enthusiasm, passion, and expertise. I am so grateful for all of you!

And I would love to thank all of you who have read this far and joined me on this wonderful journey. You are all beautiful!

ABOUT THE AUTHOR

JESSILYN STEWART PEASLEE was born the fourth of seven children into a family of avid readers, music lovers, movie quoters, and sports fans. Jessilyn graduated from Brigham Young University with a BA in English. Her debut novel, *Ella*, was awarded the Silver Quill by The League of Utah Writers. She loves going on dates with her husband and playing with her five adorable, rambunctious boys. Jessilyn grew up in the beautiful high desert of Southern California and now resides in the shadow of the Rocky Mountains. As you read this, she is probably folding laundry . . . or should be.

SCAN TO VISIT

WWW.JOTSBYJESS.COM